ONCE ENCHANTED

A love story
By Jaclyn M. Hawkes

Spirit
Dance
Books

Other books by Jaclyn M Hawkes

Journey of Honor
The Outer Edge of Heaven
The Most Important Catch
Healing Creek

Other Rockland Ranch Series Books
Peace River
Above Rubies

ONCE ENCHANTED

A love story
By Jaclyn M. Hawkes

Once Enchanted

By Jaclyn M. Hawkes

Copyright © Aug 2013 Jaclyn M. Hawkes

All rights reserved.

Published and distributed by Spirit Dance Books.LLC

Spiritdancebooks.com 1-855-648-5559

Cover design by Roland Ali Pantin

Printed in USA

First Printing August 2013

Library of Congress control number 2013948347

ISBN: 978-0-9851648-5-0

Acknowledgements

Thanks to my team. There is no way I could be successful without you. Thanks to all the readers and editors—even when you're brutally honest. And thanks to Roland for his exquisite artwork. Also, thanks to Mineta for ironing out the formatting kinks with only a mild look of amusement on your face. Thanks to Amanda for not getting testy when I admit I hate marketing. Thanks to my younger children for still doing their chores, even when Mom is buried finishing a book. And most of all, thanks to my husband—for everything, but especially for supporting my need to write. He encouraged me even when at first it seemed a little wacko. But then, he's always been the most uplifting man I know.

This book is dedicated to my husband. Like the hero of this book, he's a tease. He makes me laugh, and he loves to kiss. That is an excellent combination!

Chapter 1

You have got to be kidding! A.J. O'Brien sat in the opulent boardroom in her $1200 St. John suit and began to feel a slow, ugly burn down deep in her gut. Man, she wanted to swear like her mother. She had worked through the entire night to pull everything together for this hyper-critical meeting. And now her boss and several of the other associates were late because their massages and manicures had taken longer than expected? Manicures. Unbelievable!

She looked around the room and couldn't detect anyone else who even remotely appeared to have pulled an all-nighter.

The slow burn that had been coming on for months now ratcheted up a notch into full blown anger under the placid face she struggled to maintain. She didn't even want to admit to herself how many hours she'd spent doing what she'd thought was a team effort. Looking around now, she realized she'd been had. Again.

From the first day with this prestigious law firm of Meyers, Meyers and Victor, she'd been led to believe that if she just worked a little bit harder she'd be rewarded with that nicer office and possibly even be made a partner. This morning she had to get honest with herself and admit that, not only was she not being promoted, but she had also become the go-to for the pressure while they all went to the health club or spa together.

Trent Meyers finally walked in the door, flanked by another couple of neatly manicured men and A.J. wondered what she'd ever thought impressive about him when she'd first come to work here. His aura of self-importance combined with the unmistakable scent of massage oil turned her stomach. It was a good thing she hadn't had time for breakfast, she'd have been positively ill. She felt utter disgust when none of them even tried to hide the fact that she had been the only one pouring her heart and soul into this case, when the whole table turned to look at her as Trent asked, "Okay, where are we? Are we ready to go for this afternoon?"

At six o'clock that evening, when the case had been heard and won, based entirely upon her research, she was more ticked off than ever. Her work had been summarily handed over to one of the other men at the table, who had gone into the courtroom and made a theatrical coup as a brilliant attorney, while she had been handed another mess to get to the bottom of. To make matters worse, everyone else had gone home already, while she'd been practically ordered to stay in her office until Trent had a chance to talk with her at his convenience.

A.J. had been dodging him from day one, and not only was she not going to give in to his inappropriate innuendos, she'd been here long enough to read the writing on the wall. She was never going to be able to climb the corporate ladder here as promised. If her work to this point hadn't produced results, it just wasn't going to happen. Only a few days ago she'd seen the fiscal reports lying on Trent's desk and knew for a fact that in the last six months she'd single handedly produced nearly a quarter of the earnings for the firm that included sixteen full time attorneys.

Trent finally paged her on the intercom and asked her to step into his office. She smoothed her hair back into its twist as she picked up a notepad and her pen and went to meet him.

He was standing outside his door, blatantly checking her out as she came down the hall. She wished she had the guts to put him firmly in his place, but she knew she had to keep him somewhat mollified in order to be able to keep working here until she could find another position.

She hadn't made it five feet inside his door when he sidled up to her much too closely and said, "Ah, A.J., sorry to keep you waiting. Come in. Come in. You look warm in that suit. Can I take your jacket for you?"

"Thank you, no, I'm fine." She smiled blandly as she neatly sidestepped him to pull out a chair and sit down uninvited. She'd found it was much harder for him to be too close to her if she pulled her chair right up to the front of his desk. "What was it you wanted to see me about?"

Obviously disappointed that she had slipped past him again, he went back around his desk with a small frown. "Oh yes, I needed to talk to you about an issue I'm having. You know that I dabble in real estate with a partner. I'm sure you're familiar with Donnelly and Meyers Development."

It was all she could do not to roll her eyes. Donnelly and Meyers Development had been all over the news for weeks now because of a very controversial development they were doing. It had been acquired through a thinly veiled scheme using eminent domain. In her mind, it had been blatantly corrupt, but they'd gotten away with it.

He continued, "We're looking into a project in the Jackson Hole, Wyoming area and have run into some small snags I need you to untangle for us."

He gave a beaming smile that was completely wasted on her and continued, "We're hoping to hire a particular architect and builder who does incredible work, but more importantly, the locals seem to practically worship him. The owner of the piece of ground we're going to develop is somewhat hesitant to sell to us, and we're hoping to get this contractor to talk him into cooperating, without us having to go the blighted area/eminent domain direction."

She wanted to gag. Jackson Hole was one of the fastest appreciating areas in the entire country. If he thought he could have it considered blighted, he was nuts, although she supposed you could do anything if you paid the right person enough. She had no idea what he was after and asked, "What exactly is it you want me to do, Trent?"

"It's simple. We just need you to go out to Jackson, find this guy and use your magnificent gift of persuasion to win him over for us!"

There was something fishy going on here. This sounded like too plum of a job. Why was he all of the sudden giving her an assignment that sounded more like a vacation when he'd never favored her with anything except lewd comments before? "Why me and not one of the guys? This sounds more like a job they would love."

He had the decency to look guilty as he said, "Actually, I've already had two different associates try and they've hit dead ends both times. It seems the Wyoming rurals are extremely protective of their own,

4

and the company is owned by a Wyoming corporation. They don't have to reveal who the owners are there. I can't even find out the guy's name. We were hoping you'd have better luck. Maybe you could wear that short suit I like on you so much."

He gave her a smile again and she colored slightly. She knew exactly what suit he was talking about. Her twin brother Eric had seen it on her once and had told her in no uncertain terms that it was too short and too low cut and that she looked like a call girl in it. A.J. hadn't worn it since then, but it still hung in the back of her closet.

She sighed. "Do I have the option of taking this?"

"Actually, no. We need you, and we need you immediately. We wanted to be ready to break ground within the month and we're way behind schedule. Here's the file." He handed her a thin manila envelope. "This is as far as we've gotten. All we know is that he operates in the Jackson Hole area and the name of the company is On Top of a Stone or something like that. It's all there. Go home, pack a bag, and hop a plane as soon as possible. You can be there by tonight if you hurry."

She looked at him to see if he was serious. He was. He honestly thought he could expect her to hop a plane to some podunk place in Wyoming at a moment's notice, even after sleeping a total of thirteen hours in three days for his hyper-critical court case. She didn't even bother to tell him that the likelihood of her getting on a plane tonight was exactly zero. His request was ridiculous enough without running for an airplane as well. *Wear the short suit! It almost sounded like a call girl. How had she ever gotten to this point?*

She stood up to leave with the folder in her hand

and he added, "Don't come back until you've found him. The people there seem to have him elevated to mythical status, and appear to trust him emphatically. We need this guy on board."

With that, she turned and went out the door without looking back. She shook her head wondering what had ever happened to that vision of being a sharp, young professional. Her dreams had distilled into working like a slave and spending hours a day in snarled traffic to go home to an empty condo, too tired to do anything but work on the next day's case load.

Twenty minutes later, she sat in her Porsche at a standstill on I-5 in a hopeless parking lot as far as she could see. She turned off her ignition to do her part to cut emissions and picked up her phone to call her brother.

Thank goodness for Eric. He'd been her buddy and chief wrinkle smoother from the moment she'd been born just fourteen minutes behind him twenty-seven years ago and she loved him dearly. He was the light house in the rolling ocean of her life and his cool head and calm judgment mellowed her tendency to be a red headed spitfire.

His cheerful voice came across the miles to brighten her up, "Hey, Lexie! What's up? Are there still lots of people in California?" That was his way of trying to get her to move out of the city to where he was insistent it was easier to breathe. He and his wife lived in a log home in the hills above Flagstaff, Arizona, where they'd just had their second baby. His kids were the light in A.J.'s life.

She glanced around at the unending traffic jam and said, "Nope, they've all gone to North Dakota for the weekend. There's not a soul in sight."

He laughed. "You're sitting in traffic again, aren't you?" She told him about her day and listened to him tell about the funny things his kids did and she promised to call him back that night to discuss driving to Wyoming, by way of Arizona, instead of flying. Trent would be miffed, but maybe that's why she seriously considered doing it.

Late the next night, when she opened her car door in his driveway and breathed in the pine-scented air, she decided this road trip was exactly what she needed to get her head on straight and decide where she was going with her life. She'd known sitting at that boardroom table yesterday morning that she had to make some changes. She just didn't know what.

Once Enchanted

Chapter 2

Sean Rockland pulled his truck into his garage and heard the door close behind him as he gathered up his phone and paperwork and a set of house plans to carry them into his house. He always loved to walk into his beautiful home. It gave him a sense of pride and accomplishment to know he had designed and built it himself. But tonight he must have been unusually tired because he felt more lonely than proud. On the way down the lane, he'd seen three different brothers and their wives working together at various activities and in comparison, his lone footsteps echoing off the stone entryway sounded more than a little empty and hollow. He went into his office and put his paper work on his desk and the plans on his drafting table, switching on his computer to boot up as he wandered in to his favorite chair to sit down and take off his boots.

At the keypad just inside the master bedroom he turned on the radio for some noise as he peeled off his clothes in his walk-in closet on the way to the shower. Maybe the pelting hot water would wash away some of his weird mood.

The shower helped, but not enough to make him want to go across the small valley and face all the happily married couples in his family at his parents' house for dinner. He pulled on his favorite worn jeans and went out in his bare feet to fire up the barbecue on the deck to grill himself a steak. While it heated, he went back into his office to check his email, wondering to himself if there was even anyone he wanted to hear from.

There was no one he could think of and he glanced through them without reading any, then went back into the kitchen to finish dinner. He took it down into his home theater to eat as he watched a movie, opting for one of the Bourne movies. Hopefully the action would cure his doldrums and keep him from feeling old at twenty-six for wanting to stay home alone. Maybe he should have taken his younger brother Treyne up on planning to spend this weekend rodeoing. He needed to do something to perk himself up.

He loved his business and he was thrilled with the growth he had experienced since getting his degree in architecture two and a half years ago. He had all the design work he could ask for and a waiting list, but he also enjoyed the building end of it and had his general contractor's license as well. He'd incorporated as House Upon a Rock Inc. and professionally, he was happy as a clam.

But his personal life was dismal.

In town the next day, at his good friend Brandon's auto repair shop, Sean had his truck inspected while he waited to hear from the driver who was bringing him a load of materials. They were to be taken up into a gated community and he had to be there to let the truck in, but so far, the load was several hours behind schedule. Supposedly, the guy would be arriving within the hour, but they'd been saying that all afternoon.

Sean had learned to be patient about things like

this in his years building here in the mountains, and spent the time working on his laptop doing the paperwork end of his business that he hated. At length, he finished even that and was enjoying just hanging out with Brandon while Brandon worked on a car. They had been buddies since the third grade and other than Sean's brothers, Brandon was his closest friend.

Brandon took a phone call and Sean could hear him talking to his wife. From his one side of the conversation Sean figured out she had dinner ready and wanted to know if Brandon was going to be home in time to eat with her and their son. Sean was glad he was the only one there and that his truck was done.

Hanging up, Brandon said, "Hey, you wanna come have dinner? Meatloaf. It's marvelous!" Sean shook his head and Brandon added, "Well, I can just hang out here for awhile then. Where is the load now?"

Shaking his head again, Sean said, "Head home to dinner and your wife. It's nuts enough to have one of us hanging around forever. He's probably lost somewhere at this point. I'll wait another half hour and then I'm heading home."

Picking up a jacket off the back of a chair, Brandon opened the door and said, "Just lock the door behind you then. Take it easy." Brandon was walking out when his phone rang again and this time from his half of the conversation Sean could tell he wasn't very happy to get the call. Hanging up, Brandon sighed and said, "Well, dinner with the family *was* a good idea."

Disappointed for his friend, Sean asked, "What's up?"

"Some woman hit a deer out on 89." Brandon went

to pull the keys to his wrecker off the hook behind his desk as he replied, "Looks like it'll be cold meatloaf later on tonight. I was looking forward to it too. Ange makes a great meatloaf."

Sean put his hand out for the keys. "Go on home and get your dinner. I'll pick up the deer slayer. My load won't be here for awhile anyway and if he gets here before I do, he can wait for me for a change."

"Really?"

Sean nodded and snapped his fingers and Brandon said, "Thanks, man!" Brandon gave him a huge smile, the keys and then a high five. "Call me if you have any trouble."

"It's probably just Eunice Freeman and the Mad Buick again anyway. Say hi to Angie." Sean climbed up into the huge wrecker that sported a large "Bubba's 24 Hour Towing" logo and headed down the road to pick up their little old lady neighbor who had gained a reputation for thrashing the deer population of southwestern Wyoming. At least Brandon had a pretty wife and family to go home to.

When Sean pulled up to find it wasn't Eunice, but a beautiful red head in a positively sweet Porsche with California plates, he was pleasantly surprised—until he walked around her car to realize she hadn't hit a deer at all. She'd hit, Cactus Jack, the bull elk he'd been scouting all spring. They'd nicknamed him because of the profusion of points that covered his massive antlers. Looking at the poor beast that had been so majestic and was now laying there in the road with two broken legs and frightened eyes, was heart breaking.

As Sean went back toward the wrecker to dig

under the seat for the rifle Brandon kept there for just this situation, he couldn't help but notice what gorgeous legs this woman had as she stood up from sitting in the open door of her sports car. Her dress was too short in his estimation, but my it was a beautiful view! As he got closer, he couldn't help but notice the dress was just a hint too low cut up top as well.

Pulling his thoughts back to the elk, he was focused on what he was about to do and nearly dropped the gun when she practically screamed, "What are you doing? You can't shoot it! That's horrible! We'll take it to a veterinarian! Stop that!" She strode toward him in her rather revealing suit, to try to grab his arm. "It's an innocent deer. Leave it alone!"

He just raised his arm and kept on walking back toward the injured animal and said, "Lady, in the first place it's not a deer, it's an elk. And in the second place, he needs to be put out of his misery. Even if there was a way to get him to a vet, there's not a thing they could do for him. His legs are shattered. If this guy was a ten million dollar race horse, you couldn't put those legs back together. The only humane thing to do is put him down."

He looked back at her as he tried to make her understand what he was telling her, and softened his voice as he said, "It has to be done. I'm sorry. You're not going to want to watch this." She went back toward the wrecker and held her hands over her ears as he went up to the front of her car and regretfully put the animal down.

He was cussing to himself as he walked back to return the gun to its place of concealment. He could see her watching him as he reached into the storage to pull a cable out. She was looking at him like he'd just done something diabolical and he felt as if he ought to keep defending himself. What did she expect him to do? Wrap it in a blanket and call an ambulance? How in the world did she think they could get a full-grown wounded bull elk to a vet? He felt almost guilty under the stare of those big green eyes.

Pulling the wrecker around, he hooked the cable around a sturdy corner fence post of the field beside the road and then hooked it to the elk and slowly dragged him well off the road and into the deep bar pit beside it. Then he put the cable away and began to load her car onto the truck as he'd helped Brandon do before. She was still watching him wordlessly as he lay down near her front bumper to hook the chain to her Porsche. He didn't know which was worse, the shouting or her big, sad, quiet eyes.

As he started to walk back to the truck she leaned into the seat of her car to retrieve something and her dress hiked even higher. He swallowed hard and averted his eyes, feeling himself flush. *Holy smokes!*

He cleared his throat. "Is there anything else you need out of your car? It's a lot easier to get now than once it's on the truck."

She popped her trunk and went around the car, but he hurried to beat her to it, half-hoping, half worried she'd lean into it too. *She did have a pair of legs!* When she came to stand next to him at the trunk to point at her luggage, the top of her dress flustered him even further. He pulled the luggage out to place it in the truck almost laughing at himself.

It had been forever since a woman got to him like this. He winched the car on, secured it, cleaned up the broken glass and wreckage on the road, then came around to help her up into the passenger side of the wrecker, thinking, *this ought to be interesting.*

He tried not to enjoy the whole process too much, but finally just gave up and watched in unabashed appreciation as she tried to maneuver the short, tight skirt and heels up into the high cab. She tried several different ways without success as his smile grew wider and wider until finally, she turned to look at him.

"Do you have a step or anything I can use?"

He folded his arms across his chest with a grin. "Nope."

She gave him a look out of those green eyes as she tried again. Finally, he just picked her up by her waist and set her in the cab of the truck and she turned to him with an irritated, "Thank you."

Going around to his side of the truck, he climbed in without even trying to hide the grin as she said, "You could have pretended not to enjoy that quite so much, you know!"

He just smiled and said, "If you got it, flaunt it."

She made an angry sound. "I'm disappointed. I didn't have you pegged for that kind of a guy."

He laughed right out loud. "You're wearing *that,* and insinuating that I'm some kind of a questionable guy for enjoying the view? Oh, come on! I'm completely innocent here!"

"It's a business suit. I'm a professional. I don't usually have to climb into stomper trucks in it."

"Oh, it's a business suit all right. The only question is just what kind of business you're in."

Green sparks started to fly! "How dare you!"

He just laughed again. "Honey, in this situation, I am *not* the daring one."

She folded her arms across her chest fuming and

he said, "Oh lighten up. It can't be that big of a deal or you wouldn't have worn it anyway. Chill out." They drove for a few minutes in silence and then he turned on the radio low. Finally, he asked, "So honestly, all jokes about your very attractive legs and uh racy clothing aside, what the heck are you doing in that dress and that car on this road on a Thursday evening in late May? This can't be your typical pleasure cruise."

Still angry, she snapped, "Not by a long shot! I'm an attorney in L.A. I've been sent out here by my unbelievably chauvinistic boss to find some stupid hick construction worker they can't seem to live without! The deer was just the icing on the cake."

"Elk. We've been watching him all spring. You went and killed him in a most unglorified and disappointing manner." He was just teasing her and he was sure she knew it, but she couldn't let it go.

"*I* didn't kill it! I'm the one who sat there and petted him for a half hour to keep him from being afraid while I waited for you. You're the bloodthirsty one here. That was horrible!"

He turned to stare at her. "Petted? You petted a bull elk? You petted a wounded bull elk?"

She nodded matter-of-factly. "Yes, why?"

"You're nuts! You could have been killed!"

She mimicked his easy western drawl, "Oh lighten up. It can't be that big of a deal." She was mocking him and he laughed again.

At that, she growled, "I'm glad you're being entertained by this whole situation, because I don't think any of it is very funny!"

"Actually, Sorrelly, you are the most entertainment I've had all week. You could have charged admission to that getting into the cab deal and I'd have paid it!

16

And you're very funny when you're mad. You actually are very entertaining. And I needed that. It's been a very unentertaining day."

"My name is A.J., thank you. Not Sorrelly."

He laughed again and extended his hand across the cab of the truck. "Well, A.J., Sean Rockland. It's entertaining to meet you." She refused to shake his hand, staring out the window, and this time he laughed heartily and turned up the radio and sang along for several minutes. It was a twangy country song about a guy who was more concerned with fishing than keeping his wife. It was a silly song and he sang it with gusto and hoped she was struggling to stay mad and not laugh with him.

Finally, he turned the music down and asked, "Why A.J.? Do you honestly not have a real name?"

"Of course I have a real name. My law professors just thought I should change it to my initials because they thought it was too pretty to be professional."

He nodded. "Oh, well sure. Can't be unprofessional just to be pretty. That would be, well, unprofessional. And your husband is okay with that?"

"I'm not married, and even if I was, he wouldn't be the one to decide what I go by."

"No, I suppose not. That's the law professor's place." He rolled his eyes. "And this too pretty name would be?"

She answered almost sullenly, "Alexis. Alexis Joy O'Brien."

"So Alexis Joy O'Brien, who is this stupid, hick construction worker you've come to find? If he's from around here, I might know him."

She sighed. "That's the problem. We don't know his name. He's pulled some slippery legal shenanigans and incorporated blindly so he doesn't have to reveal who the owners of his business are."

"Sounds to me like he's trying to avoid slippery legal shenanigans if he's trying to avoid a bunch of California attorneys."

She grudgingly agreed, "You may have a point there."

"What's the business name? Maybe I'll recognize it."

She reached into the portfolio beside her on the seat. "It's something about a stone. Here it is. No, It's House Upon a Rock Inc." Sean started to chuckle, and then laugh. He would have bent double and belly laughed if he hadn't been driving and known it would make her even madder.

Finally, she said, "What?"

He sobered slightly. "You're probably right. With a name like that, he probably is just a stupid, hick construction worker." He went back to chuckling again.

Disgustedly, she said, "If he gets into business with my boss, he's more than just stupid. He'd have to be crooked too. I think they're planning to develop some poor farmer's land against his will."

That took him back for a moment. "Can they do that?"

"Theoretically no, but like I said, doing business with my boss means you have to be stupid or crooked."

He was silent for a few minutes and then asked quietly, "So what does that make you?"

She met his eyes briefly and then looked away and mused seemingly more to herself than answering, "That's exactly what I've been asking myself for awhile now."

Chapter 3

When Sean the tow truck driver asked that question, it made her more sad than angry and defensive. What had she become as she'd pursued her professional goals? What would she become if nothing changed?

They rode in silence for a time and then his phone rang. He answered it to listen for a few minutes and then said rather curtly, "Matt, I waited four hours for that truck today. I'll expect it first thing Monday then and I'm back charging you my time. Next time just call and let me know! That's true. The reception can be iffy in those canyons, but four hours? Okay, keep in touch. See ya." She couldn't understand anything he'd just talked about.

He ended that call and then pushed another number. "Hey, Bruce. It's Sean. Good, how 'bout yourself? Hey, I have some bad news. I've just been out on highway 89 and a woman hit Cactus Jack. I know. I guess that's just the way it goes sometimes. Anyway, I shot him. He had two broken legs. And I pulled him down into the bar pit right at mile marker 32 on the north side of the road. Yeah, wiped out the front of a sweet Porsche. Yeah, I think she's okay." He looked sideways at A.J. with a grin. "A little cantankerous, but okay. I don't know how he didn't land in her lap. Anyway, I just thought I'd let you know what happened to him. Take it easy. Yeah, let's go Wednesday afternoon. I'll get some wooly buggers before then. See ya."

He hung up and she looked over at him. "Wooly buggers?"

He put his phone up to his ear again. "Fly fishing flies. He's with the fish and game, but we fish together too." Then he turned away and spoke into the phone, "Hey, Brandon. I'm almost to town with this car. It wasn't Eunice. It's a drop dead gorgeous red head in a mini skirt and a Porsche. Do you want to come look at it?" He glanced over at her and grinned and said, "No Brandon, the car. I don't know. I'll call you right back if I need you."

Ending the call, he turned to her, smiling. "Okay, Red. What's the plan here? You're obviously not driving that baby anywhere 'til it can be fixed. What do you want to do?"

"What do you mean, what do I want to do? I want to get my car fixed and continue on to Jackson. Why?"

He rolled his eyes. "I figured that much, but what do you want me to do with you?" At his question, he got a wicked grin again.

She decided to ignore his humor. "Is there a place I can rent a car nearby and get a hotel?"

Matter-of-factly, he said, "Nearest hotel is fifty six miles into Star Valley, nearest car rental is ninety four back into Park City."

"Ninety four miles?" She was horrified. "Fifty six? What in the world do people do here in this situation?"

He smiled at her obvious disbelief. "Honestly, if they don't appear too likely to be an ax murderer, some local—usually my mom—will take pity on them and put them up while their vehicle gets repaired, or at least overnight. If they look too questionable we let their triple A haul them to the city."

Now she was really taken aback. "You actually

take strangers home with you overnight?"

"Well, you have to remember this isn't exactly the main thoroughfare, and usually whoever has trouble either lives here or is somebody's cousin. We don't very often get L.A. attorneys in mini skirts and Porsches."

She didn't even rise to the bait. "Even if I passed your ax murderer test, how do I know you're not one yourself?"

He grinned. "That's a good question, but one you probably should've asked a half hour ago when I had you all to myself with a gun in my hand." He gave her a shrug. "Typically, I'm judged to be pretty harmless. And my mother is the greatest woman on the planet and nobody, but nobody questions that!"

She was watching him, wondering if all this was for real, and she knew he could see that in her eyes. He pulled the wrecker into a place called Bubba's Towing and Auto Repair, hit a remote to open the shop door and pulled inside. Getting out, he came around to her side to fold his arms across his chest again as if he was waiting to watch her climb down. She was just enough of a rebel that she flashed him a look, hopped down, and then reached back up into the truck to retrieve her purse and portfolio. With that, she turned around, smiled and asked innocently, "How do stranded motorists pay for their accommodations?"

At first he seemed too flustered to even understand the question, then said, "Uh, well, I think they have to feed cows, haul hay, that sort of thing."

She waved a hand at him. "Piece of cake. Take me home to momma!"

He seemed to hesitate for a second and then said, "Uh, not to be rude, but have you got anything a little

Once Enchanted

less, uh, striking to wear in these bags? If you do, you might want to change here. That whole first impression thing, you know. I have five brothers and I'd hate for my mother to wonder what kind of business you were in. She might make you sleep in the barn or something." He was trying to joke with her, but she could tell he was serious about having her change.

For a second she was almost mad again until she remembered what Eric had said. And if she was honest, she'd felt like an idiot dragging it out of the back of her closet to begin with. She picked up her suit bag, went into the nearby restroom and came out two minutes later in a much more conservative tailored charcoal gray suit with matching heels, a white blouse and gray pearls. There was no question about this one's modesty.

"Better?" She twirled for him.

He gave her that adorable grin again. "That depends." He picked up her bags and carried them out the door to place them in the back seat of a truck, and then came around to open her door. He pulled out a step from under the pipe running board so that she could step in easily, and handed her in with a flourish and a smile, saying, "It's not nearly so entertaining, dang it! But it's a lot quicker. And the women don't get nearly so feisty during the drive." Then he closed her door and walked around to the driver's side laughing.

Chapter 4

When A.J. had looked up to suddenly see the huge animal in front of her she'd tried her absolute level best not to hit it. Braking hard, she'd tried to swerve and as she hit, she was surprised her airbag didn't deploy. She'd put her head right down on the steering wheel, feeling like she wanted to cry.

Now, five hours later, her life had become completely foreign to her. She was in rural Wyoming at a humongous ranch, miles inside a locked gate, with the most unusual family she'd ever met. There were enough tall, blonde men who looked remarkably like Sean, that she was hopelessly mixed up, and they said there was actually one more who was out of town somewhere. At least she could remember which one Slade was. He was the only dark one. They said he was adopted, but he had a different last name, so even he was a little confusing. There was one sister, Joey and three sister-in-laws that she'd met as well as Sean's parents, Rob and Naomi.

Then there was little Mimi Star. She was the only child in the family and at almost two; the whole ranch appeared to revolve around her. When Sean had led A.J. through the front door of the house, Mimi had come running as fast as her short, pink overall clad legs would carry her. She'd squealed his name as she launched herself into his arms to be twirled around and then tossed into the air. She laughed uncontrollably as he tickled her and then snuggled her

Once Enchanted

close as he carried her into the kitchen, looking as delighted to be with her as she was with him.

A.J. had been frankly amazed to watch this large, adult man go from almost a little brusque with A.J., to the openly adoring uncle in seconds. It was as if he let his guard down and was completely himself with the toddler. It was enlightening to see. Trying to equate the tickling uncle with the man who had summarily put the elk out of its misery was a bit mind-boggling.

When Mimi saw A.J., at first she was hesitant as Sean said, "Alexis Joy, this is Mimi Star, and Mimi, this is Alexis Joy. She crashed into an elk this evening and is going to stay with Grandma tonight."

Mimi's little face scrunched up as she asked, "Did you kiwd it? My momma and me kiwd a elk too, one day. It scareded me."

A.J. wasn't sure how to answer that and she looked at Sean who was watching her with a smile on his face and then said, "No Mimi, she didn't kiwd it. She just hurt it. It was her car that got kiwd."

Mimi became serious. "I'm glad it was your caw and not you what got kiwd. You're vewy pwitty." She leaned from his arms to give A.J. a hug too. A.J.'s reaction to the tiny arms around her neck floored her. For a second there she thought she was going to cry. She must have been more upset about the wreck than she realized.

Sean must have been serious about occasionally bringing home an unfortunate traveler, because the only thing his mother did when he checked to see if it would be okay if A.J. stayed overnight was ask if she had been injured.

The whole family gathered around a massive table for dinner and the addition of another didn't seem to even register. A.J. had never been to a dinner quite like this one. The whole family laughed and joked and put away more food than she had ever seen outside of a restaurant setting.

They all ate, cleaned it up, and then went outside to sit on the expansive porch in rocking chairs to watch a couple of the brothers have a cutthroat game of horseshoes at the side of the sprawling lawn.

A.J. looked around at the ranch in wonder. It was like a little village. There were houses in various spots around the small valley separated by fields and pastures. Around them all was a road fenced in with white rails. She could see horses and cows and a number of barns and sheds. The fact that it was a working ranch was unmistakable when a little before dark a tractor pulled out onto the road, pulling some kind of farm equipment behind it.

While they were sitting there, Mimi came up and climbed onto Sean's lap as he sat in the chair next to A.J. and turned to look at her with big blue eyes and asked, "Do you gots any yiddo tids I can pway wif?"

A.J. colored and Sean laughed at her and then told the toddler. "No Mimi, Alexis doesn't have any yiddo tids. She's a professional, that's why she can't have a pwitty name to go along with her pwitty face. Professionals don't get to have tids. They just have to go to work and sit in their cars in traffic. They miss out on all the fun stuff."

Mimi put a finger in her mouth, considered this for a second, and then said around it, "I'm sawy." A.J. gave Sean the look.

He just shrugged as if to say, "What? Deny it."

Finally, at dusk, Sean got up to go home. He told everyone goodbye and got a boisterous hug and kiss from Mimi and headed to his truck. As he walked away, he said over his shoulder, "Good luck with Lexie, Mom. You should know, she can be ornery and cantankerous, and she admitted to being involved in slippery legal shenanigans. Oh, and she has definite issues with getting in and out of vehicles." A.J. could still hear him chuckling as he climbed in and drove away.

Now, standing in a private bathroom brushing her teeth, she looked at herself in the mirror and had to ask herself honestly if what he'd said about being a professional was true. If someone would've said something like that to her a year ago, she would have taken their head off, but tonight, in light of the last several months of her life, he'd pretty much summed up her existence in five unpleasant sentences.

She pulled on a pair of cotton boxers and a t-shirt, turned out the light and flounced onto the bed in a grumpy huff. *Stupid, tow truck driver! He was right, but he didn't need to be so brutally honest about it.*

She had to get a handle on her life and get back to her plan to truly be a sharp, young professional, with the interesting, lucrative life that she had thought would come with it. Punching her pillow into shape, she determined to try to make up for the lack of rest that she still hadn't caught up on and tried to go right to sleep, but she just kept seeing the way his shoulders had stretched the seams of his shirt as he'd laid under her car to hook it up this evening.

🐎

It felt like she'd only been asleep for seconds when suddenly she heard his voice at the same time the blind at the window went flying up. She attempted to open her eyes, wondering what in the world was going on, when she heard him cheerfully announce, "Time to start earning your keep! Wake up, merry sunshine! It's that time of the morning when we greet the day with love in our hearts!" She groaned and turned away from him to bury her head with the pillow.

The next thing she knew, all of the sheets and blankets landed on the floor beside the bed with her in them as he cheerfully added, "I said Wake Up, Alexis Joy! You have fifteen minutes until we need to leave to go start fixing fence in the north pasture, so shake a leg!" She wrestled herself out of the wad of bedding to raise her head, pull her tangled curls out of her face and look at him in disbelief.

"What are you doing? Have you lost your mind? It's not even light yet. What time is it?" She shoved her long hair out of the way to try to see the face of her watch in the dim light from the window. When she looked back up at him, something in his face stopped her from tearing into him.

He stepped closer to her and put his hands into her hair, "Wow! That is hair! Holy smokes!" His voice held almost a note of reverence as he grabbed a handful of her riotous red curls. "Why in the world did you pull all of this up tight when it's this gorgeous?"

He paused, studying her face as she wondered what to answer and then he said, "This is another one of those too pretty to be professional things, too, isn't it?" When she didn't deny it, he gave her hair a tug. "Did it ever occur to you that there's no such thing as being too pretty? This whole try not to be pretty thing is the dumbest theory I've ever heard in my life! I had you pegged for smarter than this!"

With that, he unceremoniously picked her up, bedding and all, and tossed her back onto the bed. In the process, he knocked her purse that was sitting on the nightstand off and it fell to the floor. As it fell, it came open to reveal a variety of items, one of which was her small hand gun. He looked at the gun and then at her without revealing his thoughts, although his eyes narrowed for just a second.

Turning back for the door, he said, "Get dressed. We need to be out of here in the next few minutes. I hope you have something other than just business suits, 'cause where we're going they'd be trashed in minutes. Do you prefer pancakes or hash browns?"

She looked up at him from her pile of bedding and self consciously pulled the sheet over to cover one long tanned leg that'd come uncovered when he'd tossed her back on the bed. She was still too sleepy to be able to figure out if he was in earnest, and she hadn't a clue how to handle his assessment of her hair. Finally, she took him literally. Maybe he was serious about having to haul hay and stuff to pay for staying here for the night. He was looking at her as if he was waiting for her to object. He probably thought she couldn't fix fence and be professional too.

The rebel spirit in her heart reared its head and she replied, "Pancakes." and promptly climbed out of the tangled blankets to hop off the bed and walk into the bathroom where she firmly shut the door.

Ten minutes later she appeared at the dining table dressed in khaki zip-offs and hiking boots, and a button down flannel over a white tank top. She caught him checking her out and asked, "Will this do?"

He was alone in his mother's kitchen flipping pancakes and bacon on a griddle. "Very nice. Except for the hair, you look great!"

She began to set the table with the dishes he'd set out as she asked, "What's wrong with my hair?"

"Well." He came around behind her, pancake

Jaclyn M. Hawkes

turner in hand, and before she realized what he was doing, he began to pull the pins out that held it secure in its twist. She turned and tried to grab his hands as he insisted, "It's far too professional for fence fixing. It'd better come down." He made another grab for her hair and as she lunged to get away, her hair came cascading down anyway.

He put his hands into the curls again. "Wow, it's even prettier after it's combed! This is much better than professional." He tugged on it gently for a second until they both realized the pancakes were burning, and he let it go to turn back to the stove. About two seconds later, the smoke alarm in the kitchen went off. Rob and Naomi appeared in their robes, followed by two more of the family from the stairs.

Naomi looked at the clock with tired eyes. "What on earth are you doing, Sean? Are we on fire or are you just preoccupied with something else?" Sean's younger brother laughed and turned around to head back down the stairs with Joey right behind him, as Naomi continued, "Why are you up before it's even light? Alexis, what has he roped you into doing this morning?"

He replied, "We're headed to the north pasture to fix fence. We just have to get an early start so Ruger can turn cows in, in the morning."

Naomi looked skeptical, but she didn't comment other than to say, "Sean David Rockland, don't you be pulling that old tenderfoot stuff on this girl. I daresay you'll have met your match if you do!" With that, she and Rob turned back around and went back to bed.

A.J. asked sweetly, "Just what exactly is that old tenderfoot stuff?"

Meekly he replied, "I think she just meant that I

29

should take it easy on a wimpy city slicker like you. It would be a pity if you broke a nail or something. It would throw a complete kink in your quest for the stupid, hick construction worker." He laughed as he piled pancakes and bacon on her plate and brought orange juice and milk to the table.

When he sat down beside her, he automatically bowed his head to pray and she followed suit. He said a short prayer over the food and then sat with her while she began to eat. The food was good. Other than burning the pancakes while they had the tug of war over her hair, he was a great cook! She just wished he'd brought her some coffee. She wasn't even sure she could start her day without it.

When she realized he wasn't having anything, she asked, "Aren't you going to eat too? You haven't poisoned this have you?"

"I ate earlier at my house. I had some things to do this morning that I didn't get done last night."

She glanced at her watch. "You ate earlier than five thirty? Tell me, what does a tow truck driver have to do that is that pressing at that hour of the morning?"

He laughed. "Oh, just stuff."

"What does your wife think when you're doing stuff at that hour of the morning?"

"I'm not married. If I was, I wouldn't get out of bed at all at that hour of the morning, especially to haul the beautiful elk murderess up."

She shook her head and laughed. "No, I suppose not."

When she was through eating, they went through to a mudroom and he handed her a pair of leather gloves and a lined denim jacket. At first, she wasn't going to take them because of his quip about breaking

30

a nail, but then he said, "Lighten up, I'll be wearing some too. John Wayne himself doesn't work with barbed wire without them. It would eat you. Trust me on this one." She looked at him, thinking. She did trust him. She wasn't sure why, but she did, and for an attorney, that was saying something.

They went outside and went to a four wheeled ATV equipped with a cargo box on the back parked below the deck. Turning to her, he asked, "Have you ever ridden a four wheeler?" She shook her head no and he asked, "Would you like to drive?" She was surprised by this. Most of the men she knew would have climbed on and driven away without even considering asking. She almost said yes just because he'd asked, but then decided to wait until she'd at least ridden one first.

Instead, she said, "You drive first so I can get used to riding, and I'll try it in awhile." He climbed on, she got on behind him and they drove off in the gray of early morning, as the sky to the east began to lighten.

She tried not to touch him at first, but occasionally, when they went over a bump, she had to grab him to hang on. Once as they went over a series of pipes laid into the road she held on and he put his hand over hers too to hang onto her. Finally, she just left her hands at his waist to keep herself more secure.

Riding behind him in the predawn chill as the light seeped over the countryside was incredibly refreshing. The morning was brisk and the wind in her face made her feel more alive than she'd felt in months. There was mist rising off the meadows and the streams, and twice he stopped to watch deer beside the road. Once it was a stately buck and another time it was a female and two smaller deer that were sleek and beautiful.

They stopped on a wooded ridge top and watched

31

the sunrise without getting off the ATV. It began with a hint of pink, then glowed as if the entire heavens were on fire, and then faded to purple and mauve and finally just pale lemon tinged the clouds. Looking around at the forest primeval she said, "The trooping fairies would love this."

Glancing at her over his shoulder, he asked, "Who are the trooping fairies?"

"The little, winged, woodland fairies from the old Irish legends. They're the mystical dream people who enchant humans and protect them from misfortune. They spend their nights playing music and dancing around fires deep in the woods, and being intimate. Sometimes they fall in love with beautiful or handsome mortals, shoot them with fairy darts and steal them away. Sometimes the humans just hear their music and pine away and die for the love of it."

She paused to breathe in the morning breeze and continued, "They say when you see the wind lift the leaves or the glittering pattern of frost on a window, that the fairies are about. My grandmother used to tell us all about them and the mermaids and rusalkas. When I was little, I used to love to pretend I was a trooping fairy. I always wished they could have been real."

Looking confused, he asked, "I know the mermaids are half human, half fish and would sing and enchant the sailors away into the ocean and to their deaths, but what's a rusalka?"

"They're like the mermaids. They're a water nymph that comes out at night and dances and enchants human men. They lead them away to the river bottom to be with them forever. Neither one of them wanted to lead the men to their deaths. They were just too alluring and the men couldn't help themselves. Some say the men didn't die; they are just living in the mystical places with their true loves. They would have loved this place."

Once Enchanted

Chapter 5

At length they arrived at the north pasture and he showed her how to stretch the wire tight and either replace clips that had come loose from the metal posts or pound big staples into the wooden posts to hold the lengths taut. They worked side by side for a couple of hours, one of them stretching the wire and the other one securing it, small talking back and forth when she finally asked, "What would you have done this morning if I'd been sleeping in my sweet nothings?"

He looked up at her and laughed. "I don't know. I just assumed you'd deem that unprofessional."

As he bent over the post he was working on she watched the muscles bulge under his shirt. He had sun bleached blonde hair and his hands were brown and calloused. She couldn't seem to put him and the image she had of a tow truck driver into the same mold. He was clean-shaven and in glorious physical shape and smelled slightly like aftershave. She'd never have believed that was what he did for a living if she hadn't seen him tow her own car. He must only have to work in the evenings, because it was nearly eight o'clock and he didn't seem in a hurry to leave.

It started to warm up and she went over and sat on the four-wheeler and removed the borrowed jacket, zipped off the lower legs of her pants and took off her flannel shirt. As she walked over to resume helping him, he watched her approach him and then shook his head as he bent back over the fence and said, "You might as well give this whole professional thing up. Your body's too pretty too. In the long run somebody's going to find out what you're hiding under those initials and suits and hairpins, and the jig is going to be up."

He just kept on working while she tried to figure out how to take what he'd just said. After a minute, she asked, "There was a compliment in there somewhere, wasn't there?"

He looked back up to glance over her again and gave her a small smile. "Yeah, there definitely was."

They got back on the four-wheeler to go to the next section and she asked him as they drove, "What have you got against professional women? It can't be a bitter against your mother thing, you obviously adore her, so what's up? Did you have a professional girl friend who dumped you or what's the deal?" They hit a bump and her arms tightened around his waist while he thought about his answer.

He stopped the machine and stayed sitting as he said to her over his shoulder, "I don't really have anything against professional women. I just feel sorry for you, that's all." He stepped off the bike and turned to help her down, then picked up the tools and headed back over to the new section of fence.

Considering what he'd said, she went to work beside him and finally insisted, "Okay, explain that last one. You can't just say something like that and then leave it hanging out there."

He pounded another couple of staples in and then stood up to look at her. "Well, look at the life the modern day working woman in general has been dealt. I put it that way because I don't think it was the goal of the females of the species to have it turn out this way. It seems to me that women, to a certain extent, have been the ones to shoulder a lot of social trends that haven't necessarily been that rewarding.

"Forever women have wanted equal rights, but what they got isn't equal at all. What they got was the opportunity to share in the stress and responsibility of being the breadwinner, while for the most part; they still carry the lion's share of the burden for being the homemaker too.

"And if they decide to have a family on top of that, they get to try to fit in another huge responsibility that the dads can help with, but honestly, she often still does most of the parenting. No one can take her place as a mother, so then she tries to juggle that and the guilt that comes along with sometimes not being able to keep up the whole Wonder Woman thing."

He continued, "Even if she's single and just working, it seems to me that whether it's supposed to be all equal in the workplace in theory, it never really is. There are still a lot of men out there who don't treat females the same as their male co-workers, and probably even a lot of women who do the same thing. And even when women are treated the same and paid the same, they still often tend to put their kinder, gentler tendencies aside to be competitive in a dog-eat-dog corporate world. Your name and hair are just small examples of that."

He shrugged. "Gentle isn't necessarily a positive in the business world of today. Many of the women who become truly successful in corporate America tend to be tough and hardened. The thing that I think is the saddest of all in this is that those women often seem frustrated and miserable to learn that what looked glamorous and powerful, is actually exhausting and not nearly as rewarding as they thought it would be."

He shrugged again. "When you figure in things like child care and commute time and convenience food to compensate for not enough time at home, to me it just doesn't seem worth it. Even if a woman made hundreds of thousands of dollars per year, if she's working seventy hour weeks and her kids are raising themselves, while her husband sees his secretary ten times more than he sees her, to me it looks like a raw deal. Maybe it would make some sense if a woman didn't have a choice, but . . . "

Wiping his forehead with his sleeve, he went on, "If I was female, I'd rather choose what I felt was the most important thing and do it well and be happy and feel needed and loved and successful and leave the whole idea of taking on the world because society does it that way, to the birds. There are actually women who are happy and fulfilled without the stress of wearing all the hats. Their families mean more to them than the mighty dollar and they dress up for their own husbands instead of their boss. I'm sure you'll think that ridiculously old fashioned, but from what I've seen, they have a better quality of life. At least that's how it seems to me."

He went back to working on the fence and her first gut reaction was to tear into him and tell him exactly what she thought of his theory on modern women, as the feminist in her bristled. But he wasn't being argumentative about it. She could tell he really did honestly feel that way and it was a perspective she'd never had spelled out so succinctly before. She definitely could identify with parts of his theory, but it didn't paint a very intelligent picture of the life she led.

She kept her voice completely neutral as she said, "Well, I guess there's no question about whether you have an opinion on the subject anyway." She leaned in beside him to stretch the wire. "You've put a lot of thought into that opinion. Where did you come up with all that modern wisdom? Do you come in contact with a lot of professional women driving a tow truck?"

With a laugh he replied, "Actually, you're the first." He bent down to pull a loose strand of wire out of a tangle of grass. "Hey, at least I was honest. What do you think about the whole professional woman thing after being one? If you were home in LA, where would you be right now? What would you be doing?"

It took her awhile as she thought about that. Right now she would have been driving for over an hour, after getting up in the dark and rushing to gather up the papers she would have taken home to work on.

She was quiet a long time, while she pondered some of the issues he'd touched on. She knew she was becoming more hardened, but she wouldn't have admitted that to him for anything. And the children thing. He'd hit it right on. Her few professional friends who had kids struggled to find time to fill their needs and always seemed to be feeling guilty about missing one thing or another. Eric was forever going on about how kids today are disposable because their parents are too busy to bother making sure they turned out okay.

She considered Sean's thoughts on marriage. She'd always hoped to be married and she'd been floored on her last birthday to wake up and realize she was twenty-seven. Lately, she just tried to put it out of her mind, telling herself she'd work on her personal life just as soon as she reached her professional goals.

The wakeup call from the other morning's meeting made her realize that something had to change or she was never going to ever reach those goals, and she'd wake up and find herself seventy and old and alone. But the whole idea of not being a working woman was too far out there to even consider. In the first place, she had to make a living, and in the second, the only women who didn't work that she knew of, were on old reruns of TV shows from decades ago that played occasionally on cable.

"No comment?" She realized she'd never answered him when he stood up to pause in straightening a wire to look right at her. "Have I made you completely speechless? Or are you really, really, really ticked off?"

She took the end of the wire to put it in the stretcher and pull it taut as she said, "I honestly don't know. Both I guess. I'd like to tell you to take your ideas and take a flying leap, but some of them are incredibly thought provoking. I guess the biggest thing I want to know is, in all this theorizing, what are the options to you? You sound like you think what I do is ridiculously stupid, but just how do you propose I make a living if I don't work in corporate America?"

"Being taken advantage of and being stupid are not necessarily the same thing."

"They are if you insinuate that I'm letting myself be taken advantage of."

He shook his head. "I don't think most women intended to let men and society give them more than their share of the load. I don't even think the men realize they're doing it most of the time. It's just that when we had women take over part of the money responsibilities, we forgot to take over our fair share of the housework and child care."

She stood up and put her hands on her hips. "So tell me the options, hot shot. How do I make a living without being a professional? And don't tell me to let Mr. O'Brien take responsibility for my bills, like you intimated, because there isn't one."

"Whose choice was that?"

She opened her mouth to retort and then shut it again, and he picked up the tools and went back to the four-wheeler with her behind him. He must have been able to feel her anger, because he helped her onto the bike and said in an apologetic tone, "I'm sorry I offended you. And no, I don't have all the answers. I just know that the life most families lead these days is not what I want my life to be eventually."

"Oh, so you want some little, uneducated, redneck girl who will stay home and have your babies, and never need a life of her own? Is that what you're saying?"

He looked at her and shook his head sadly. "You've missed my entire point. I want my wife, if I ever find her, to be totally fulfilled. That's what I'm saying. I don't want her to have to be a slave to a career just because society decrees it. If she wants to, that's fine, although I don't know that I could ever be truly supportive of a seventy hour work week. I'm just not convinced that being a professional is more fulfilling than being a homemaker. In my short twenty six years, in the lives of the women I've seen, it hasn't been."

"Maybe you just haven't seen enough fulfilled professional women."

"I'm sure you're right." He sighed and climbed back on the bike and started it. "You tell me. You're the professional. Is your life fulfilling? Do you have that life of your own you're talking about? And is that all you need, or are there holes?"

He put out a hand almost defensively. "Look, I'm not trying to be critical. I'm sorry I come across that way, but isn't trying not to be pretty just a little bit twisted?" He reached up, pulled some of the pins from her hair again, and then gunned the four-wheeler so she had to grab his waist to keep from flying off as her hair cascaded down her back.

They fixed fence for another hour and she got over being mad, although she was thoughtful the whole time. She never did answer him about whether her job was fulfilling. It was too galling to admit he was right, and she couldn't lie to him, so she just didn't say anything and they talked about other things. She was over her mad, but her head was starting to ache terribly. She never had headaches and wondered why she would have one now when she was away from the stress of work.

Finally, he declared they were done and packed up the tools and they headed back to the ranch houses. When they got there he said, "I have to go to work, but you can hang out here with my mom until Brandon calls about your car. Call me and let me know what your plans end up and I'll take you where ever you need to go when I get back. Thanks for your help this morning. You did a great job and never even complained. I'm impressed."

"Heading back to the tow truck?" She was a little disappointed to see him go.

He smiled his heart-stopping smile. "Actually, no. I should be honest with you and tell you I don't always drive a tow truck."

"What else do you do then?"

His smile became a little mysterious. "Oh, stuff. Lots of things."

"Like?"

"Just stuff. You know fix fence, steal hairpins, lots of things. Have a great afternoon." She watched him stride away and climb into his truck.

Once Enchanted

Chapter 6

Naomi was there with lunch ready and said the shop had called about her car. "He said it would be at least tomorrow depending on if he can get the parts he needs." She sat down and invited A.J. to eat with her. "Everyone else is gone somewhere, so it's just us. Would you like a chef's salad? I usually have a light lunch."

A.J. accepted and joined her at the table. Naomi prayed and they talked as they ate. Naomi asked her, "Did you enjoy yourself this morning, or was he too rough on you?"

"He was fine." A.J. smiled. "I think at first he didn't believe I could do it, but it wasn't too bad. The scenery was incredible and we saw some deer and watched the sunrise. Other than the fact that he doesn't approve of working women, it was a great morning."

Naomi looked confused. "Sean told you he doesn't approve of working women? That surprises me. I've never known him to mind when the women around here work."

"The women here work?" A.J. was nonplussed. "I would have thought they were all just housewives from the way he sounded." Then she back peddled, "Not *just* housewives. You know what I mean."

"We are housewives. Well, everyone except Joey.

She's not married. We're housewives, but we all have
our own respective careers too. Just none of us is full
time and we're all self-employed. Isabel has a
Thoroughbred horse farm, although it's in California
and she lives here. And she and Slade do investments.
I'm sure you recognized Kit as the rock singer Kit Star,
but she's also a sculptor. Marti is a veterinarian and
raises racehorses, and I'm an attorney when I decide to
take a case. I usually have to be coerced or somebody
has to really tick me off, but I still occasionally practice.
Mostly I'm just completely happy working on the
ranch beside Rob and being a wife and mother."

"You're an attorney?" A.J. stared at her, stunned!

Naomi laughed. "No, I'm really a mom who
occasionally practices law. It's much more fulfilling
that way. Why?"

"And the other women I met last night, horses and
Kit Star, and a veterinarian? You're kidding me! I had
no idea. But you're so far from most anything here,
how do you function?"

Waving a hand, Naomi replied, "Other than actual
court, I can do almost everything on line or by phone
or fax. Isabel left her farm under her brother's care
when she came here to be with Slade, and Marti just
drives her truck like any rural vet.

"Kit does have to fly to L.A. a couple of times a
month, but she and Rossen take Mimi and go together.
He's self-employed too, so it's not too much of a
problem. And Sean is planning on building an airstrip
here, so someday they'll be able to fly directly from
here and not have to go to Salt Lake or Jackson. It's a
priority to Rossen that Kit has the freedom to do the
things that are important to her, so he wholeheartedly
supports her. I've always thought Sean felt that way

too, so it's weird that he told you he doesn't approve of women working."

A.J. clarified, "He didn't exactly say he didn't approve. He just said he felt sorry for us."

"Hmm." Naomi mused, "He doesn't like the big city. Maybe that's what made him say that. I don't know."

She changed the subject. "Can you stay here with us overnight again while you wait for your car, or is there someplace you have to be?"

With a grimace, A.J. answered, "I should be in Jackson Hole already, trying to find this architect, but I'm so disgusted with my boss right now that I don't care when I get there. Would it be an imposition if I stayed another night? I'd be happy to fix fence again to earn my keep."

"Oh, honey you don't have to earn your keep." Naomi laughed. "We'd love to have you. You're no problem at all and you're a better woman than I am to volunteer to go out at O dark thirty to mend fence. At least you got the fringe benefits of the sunrise and the deer."

A.J. wondered about her thinking she'd volunteered. Once she was out there, she'd enjoyed herself, even with the whole professional discussion, but she certainly hadn't volunteered! Her mind wandered for a moment to when he'd talked about her hair as he'd tossed her out of bed.

It had been far too long since any man had said he liked her hair. She'd just about decided to finally cut the length of wild curls off because she always wore it pulled back severely, but she'd never been able to bring herself to do it. The riotous tangle was the real her, even if she had to make it less pretty, as Sean had said, for the sake of professionalism.

Naomi broke into her thoughts, "Is there anything you can do from here to find whatever it is you're looking for? We have computers and faxes and the whole nine yards in all of our home offices and you're welcome to make yourself at home. Or if you need to you can take one of our vehicles."

A.J. nodded. "Actually, I would love to take you up on borrowing your office. I've done a basic search on the internet, but I could do a more in depth one and maybe make some phone calls. What I really need to do is call my brother. My phone doesn't work here and he's probably having fits because I haven't called to let him know I arrived safely."

They finished eating and cleaned up and Naomi showed her into her and Rob's home office. "I need to come in a little later and do some paperwork, but you're welcome to use this desk and computer and there are three phone lines, just push the button. I'll be right here in the house somewhere. If you need anything just call."

A.J. was floored. "You don't even know me. How would you trust me alone in your office?"

The older woman looked her in the eye. "Aren't you trustworthy?"

"Of course, but I'm a complete stranger to you!"

Patting her on the shoulder, Naomi said, "Sean thinks you're safe enough to have here, and he's very good at discerning things like that. I'd trust his judgment with my life. In addition, everything electronic is pass coded and you'd have to cross the whole ranch and then make it out the locked gates if you did decide to pull something. And Brandon still has your Porsche." She smiled. "So I guess I'm willing to take my chances with you."

A.J. had been working for almost half an hour when Sean walked in. She was surprised to see him, assuming he'd gone into town. In his hand, he carried a frosty can of Coke and said, "I brought you some caffeine to tone down that headache. My mom probably doesn't have any in the house."

She was confused. "How did you know I had a headache?" It was true, but she hadn't said anything. "I never get headaches, but this one is a kicker. It hit about ten o'clock and my head is pounding."

"It's the caffeine. You're a coffee drinker aren't you?"

She nodded. "I can hardly start my day without it." She gave him a self-deprecating smile. "It's what helps me put in those ridiculously long hours you were accusing me of."

"Yeah, well if you're used to having it everyday and try to go without cold turkey it can be pretty ugly."

"Apparently you've been in my shoes before."

"Not me personally actually, but some of my . . . Just some people I know have been there. The Coke doesn't have as much caffeine as coffee, but it'll take the edge off."

She accepted the soda gratefully. "If this really works, you'll be my hero. I never go without coffee in the morning. I was dying and didn't even see a machine in the kitchen."

"There's not one. Nobody here drinks coffee. Actually, I'm about the only one here who even drinks Coke. I'm the rebel of the family! I drink Coke and I'm the only one who's ever tried smoking. 'Course I was four years old, and when Rossen caught me he didn't even tell mom, he just trounced the tar out of me. I've

49

never dared to try anything since then." He smiled his devastating smile on the way back out the door.

She drank the soda and went back to her computer work, wondering how he knew she had a headache. While she worked, she phoned Eric, forwarding the charges to her phone, and told him what was going on in her life. He told her she sounded happy and as she hung up the phone, she realized she was. The frustration about work she'd been feeling for what seemed like forever had faded in the dawn of this clear Wyoming day.

Chapter 7

She worked through the afternoon, both on the computer and on the phone. She found nothing on the internet and even using a couple of people finder searches she didn't come up with anything. She resorted to a service that frankly didn't appear on the up and up, offering information that shouldn't necessarily have been public, but they all only dead-ended with the blind corporation.

She finally graduated to the local phone book and called every construction company and architectural firm listed. There were only a handful, but no one would give her the information she was looking for. She was astounded that even this guy's competition was completely closed mouthed about him.

How can you inspire loyalty even among your competitors? She began to be a little intrigued. Whoever this guy was, he was certainly well liked for this many people to have his back. Packing up her portfolio case, she decided to call it a day. She could hear members of the family starting to come back in from their day's work and went to see what she could help with in the kitchen.

She helped Naomi chop vegetables for a stir-fry and had to laugh again when they ended up with piles of ingredients ready to be put into the huge wok. "Do you always have this many people at meals?"

Naomi was setting out dishes and utensils. "We all

live so close that most days I have the whole family here at some point or another. Either that or we're at one of the kids' houses together. The more in-laws we get, the more fun it is. One of these days, we're going to have to get another table! Lately, Sean sometimes doesn't show up, but he's the only one really, unless the younger ones are away at school. Sean tends to work a lot during meals as of late. I think it's just an excuse, but we let it go. He'll be back when he's ready."

A.J. set the table and then sat at the bar watching Naomi toss things into the hot pan. At length, A.J. asked, "How does an attorney end up on a ranch in Wyoming with how many kids? And handle a wok the size of Texas?"

"I have six who are my own and who knows how many others? There's always been a handful of the kids' friends who seemed happier here than where ever it is that they call home. Slade has been like my own forever, and several years ago when his entire family was killed by a drunk driver, we tried to include him completely. He's always been close, but it wasn't until he found Isabel a year or two ago that he finally, truly became at peace and settled in. I daresay there will be others before we're through, and now we're finally starting on the grand kid chapter. It's been more fun than I ever dreamed it would be!"

Almost to herself A.J. said, "Your family is extraordinary. I've never been around people who are this happy together and there is an uncanny sense of peace here. Even when everyone is talking and laughing, or when we were on that noisy four wheeler, driving through the morning breeze, there is this sense of . . . " She hesitated. "I don't even know what to call it. Insulation maybe. The rest of the world with its frantic rat race seems like it's worlds away. I'll probably be hopelessly ruined for going back to LA."

"I'm sure you'll be just fine." Naomi smiled through the steam from the wok. "You wouldn't be there in the first place if that wasn't where you truly wanted to be. I couldn't do it anymore. I grew up in Seattle, but I never enjoyed it there and was more than happy to move away when I went off to college. However, there are those who can't seem to function without all the people and urban sprawl, and bright lights as far as the eye can see. I'll bet you're one of those who even love the whole tangled freeways. I have a little sister like that. Being out here drives her crazy. She says it's so quiet she can't even sleep."

A.J. thought about this. Where was it that she really wanted to be? It had to be the big city. She'd worked for years to achieve just the life she was living, hadn't she? She watched Naomi tossing her food in the wok and thought about the differences in their two lifestyles. A.J. had the status and the prestige, but she wondered if maybe Naomi didn't have the better lifestyle.

A.J. had never even considered being self employed, or working out of a home office. Money would probably be slow at the start up, but then expenses would be minimal too. Being her own boss was incredibly intriguing. Not only would she not have to answer to some self-important snob, but also she would be the only one who would decide what cases she would take and no one else would get credit and fame for her hard work. The idea was thought provoking.

She asked the question that had come into her

mind when Naomi had mentioned she was an attorney. "Several years ago there was an attorney named Naomi Rockland who came into L.A. from out of town and won a case against my boss that was pretty damaging to him. I wasn't there at the time, but it's still whispered about. Something about overturning a development project that had been obtained through eminent domain. You wouldn't happen to be that same Naomi Rockland would you?"

Naomi looked a bit hesitant to answer. "Who's your boss?"

"Trent Meyers. He's one of the Meyers of Meyers, Meyers and Victor. He's the Meyers of Donelly and Meyers Development. I think the suit was against the development company and Trent was also the attorney handling the litigation, so he got beat twice. It's not something you'd want to question him about, I'm sure."

Naomi tossed a bowl of bean sprouts into the wok as she answered, "Yes, I won a case against Trent Meyers several years ago. He tried to have some prime real estate in L.A. County declared blighted and took it to build a highway project on. He got away with most of it, but he only wanted to pay the original owners pennies on the dollar for their homes and businesses. I was approached to fight for them. We went after the development company and got more than ten times the original offer for the land. Even that wasn't fair market value, but it was enough to get Donelly and Meyers to back off. The project still went through and the people all lost their homes, but at least they didn't lose everything."

She pulled the wok off the stove and like magic

people began to appear for dinner. Sean didn't show up and A.J. was disappointed about that for some reason. When he showed up ten minutes later, she had to ask herself why she felt so happy. His hair was damp and he must have just showered before he came in. He sat across from her at the gigantic table and she couldn't help but notice how good looking he was. Even in simple jeans and a button down, he was incredibly handsome.

It was too bad he was only a tow truck driver. If he'd been a little more ambitious, she might've been tempted to get to know him better. He caught her watching him and smiled at her as she dropped her eyes to focus on her plate.

Throughout the meal, she took in everything going on around her. Sean's parents were obviously very much in love and presided over their family with a partnership that was unbelievable. They openly adored each other and worked together in a way that was almost incomprehensible to A.J. When she tried to compare them to her own parents, there was no comparison.

Her own parents had divorced when she and Eric were just little and their mother had then spent the rest of their childhood and youth struggling non-stop for any kind of victory over their father. She was a high strung, overly dramatic, self centered, beauty queen has been, with a hot temper, who would stop at nothing to try to take advantage of her ex-husband. He was a laid-back, city raised cowboy who didn't really care what their mother did as long as she didn't bother him too much. The fact that all of her conniving didn't get to him drove her mother crazy, and A.J. and Eric had been unhappily caught in the middle. If they hadn't had their Aunt Julie running interference for them, A.J. didn't know what they would have done.

She and Eric stuck together through it all and Aunt Julie would come and rescue them when things got unbearable. Somehow they'd survived to leave home forever and go off to college. Looking back, and now watching Rob and Naomi together, A.J. wondered how she and Eric had made it, and if it was possible to have the kind of marriage she was just now watching, when you were raised by lunatics.

If she'd grown up around the mutual respect and concerned equal partnership she was witnessing here, she may very well have chosen marriage instead of her career. What they had here was wonderfully appealing, and she had to question whether they were really this good of friends, or were just putting on a show for her. This larger than life, happily ever after family didn't even seem real.

After dinner, the whole bunch pitched in to clean it all up and then they all went outside again. They were talking about a jackpot team roping, whatever that was, that the Rockland Ranch was hosting tonight and A.J. sat on the porch in a rocker with Naomi while she watched everyone else disperse toward the other houses and the biggest barn. Presently, one by one, they reappeared leading saddled horses and went into the big outdoor arena, as trucks and trailers began to pull down the gravel road.

Naomi got up and said, "Come on. We should go over and sit near the arena; this'll be fun to watch. We do this from time to time and it's very entertaining. Of course, my sons always win and that's why it's so fun, but you won't want to miss it."

They headed over and met Kit and Mimi on the

way. Isabel was already there riding a horse and leading another one around, inside the arena. As they sat in a couple of rows of seating to the side, the arena cleared and a set of sprinklers set into the perimeter fence came on for just a few minutes and dampened the arena floor. Slade and Sean's oldest brother Rossen came and took the horses from Isabel and the roping started.

A.J. had no idea what was going on and she must have looked it, because Joey came up and sat beside her and started to explain what they were all doing, and why, "A jackpot is where somebody hosts it and gets the word out, and then ropers from all over come, and everyone puts their entry money into the pot. Then they rope, and who ever wins takes home the jackpot. You watch. My brothers always win at least two out of the top three. Sometimes they win all three.

"Usually Rossen and Slade take first although Sean and Treyne have been giving them some competition lately. Rossen and Slade roped full time for a few years and, in fact, were the world champions a couple of years ago. Now they've settled down and gotten old and married and the younger brothers are crowding them. Dad and Ruger never take it all too seriously, but even they can hold their own."

It was fascinating and they watched for a couple of hours together. There were steers loaded into a chute and the pairs of team ropers would take their horses into a space on either side that Joey called the box. Someone would release the steer, then the cowboys would chase it down, one of them would rope its head, and then the other one would rope its back feet. Or at least that was the idea. The Rockland brothers would catch their steer consistently, but sometimes the other teams would catch only one or the other or miss the steer completely.

A.J. had ridden horses occasionally, but these guys' riding was amazing. It was like watching some kind of larger than life ballet, and even though she watched as closely as she could every time, she still couldn't figure out how in the world the heeler could catch the running steer's back legs.

Sean rode like he'd been born on his horse and it seemed to know what he wanted it to do almost magically. He and Treyne came in second on the first set of steers, but when they ran them back through a second time, they edged the world champion cowboys out by a tenth of a second. As they came back around to stand at the end of the arena with the rest of the cowboys, Rossen moved his horse over to give the two of them an exuberant high five. The depth of the friendship of these brothers was heartwarming to see.

She watched until her eyes hurt and she caught herself yawning. She still hadn't made up for her sleepless nights, and her abrupt awakening and early morning fence fixing trip were coming full circle. Finally, she stood up to leave and Sean caught her eye from his spot near the fence in the arena. His intense blue eyes smiled at her and she almost felt like a teenager again when her heart quickened.

Excusing herself, she wandered back across to Naomi's house to head to bed. She stood at the top of the lawn for one last, long look around as the sun began to set. The whole valley had taken on a brilliant yellow cast as the last rays of the day went almost side ways from the western horizon. The lemon colored light on the rich emerald green made the whole valley glow like a priceless gem. Craggy snow capped

58

mountains surrounded the valley, and were covered with nearly black pines that made the grasslands below seem even brighter. It was as if the whole ranges were standing guard of this mountain valley to protect the calm and tranquility within.

Before her trip here, she had thought she wanted excitement and fast-paced challenges, but she could feel the peace of this place seeping into her bones. It was almost healing to her soul. She'd only been here a day, but it felt like L.A. was half a world away. She looked back toward the arena and she could see Sean looking toward her. She wished he wasn't just a tow truck driver.

Once Enchanted

Chapter 8

As Sean drove home after spending the afternoon visiting his various project sites, he smiled to himself when he thought about the abrupt about face from his doldrums of two days ago. His enthusiasm for life had bumped so drastically that he had to stop and give himself a lecture about how this girl wasn't a member of the church. And she would be leaving to return to L.A. just as soon as she figured out that he had been less than forthright with her about what he did for a living, and who he was.

He could just imagine the sparks that were going to fly from those green eyes when she finally figured it out. Until then he was going to enjoy the whole deal. That afternoon he'd talked to everyone who worked for him and sent out a blanket email that he didn't want anyone to tell her who he was. He'd even called the county and the chamber of commerce. He knew she'd find out eventually, but he didn't want it to be any sooner than it had to be.

He started to pull into the drive in front of his parent's house knowing they were probably ready to start dinner, but then he decided to run on home and have a shower first. He didn't dig too deeply into why he didn't want to show up dusty when he'd never been concerned about that before.

The whole afternoon he kept catching himself daydreaming about how she had looked after slipping off her flannel shirt and zip offs when he'd glanced up from fixing fence. She'd been beautiful in her business suits, but they didn't hold a candle to how gorgeous she was in her shorts and tank top. Her hair was still up then, but it had already started to come loose and there were striking red tendrils hanging around her face looking as rebellious as the spitfire spirit he had glimpsed on a number of occasions now.

If he wasn't thinking about that, he was thinking about the long tan leg that'd slipped out of her blankets that morning when he dumped her back on her bed. He fought to focus on work, and was surprised at how fast this woman had gotten under his skin.

As he walked into dinner, having her there with his family felt as natural as if she had been there for months instead of just one day. He caught her eye as he sat across from her, surprised again at how unbelievably pretty she was.

That evening roping, he felt a whole new excitement as he rode and when he and Treyne beat Rossen and Slade's time it hadn't even seemed that wild to have just beaten the world champion duo. Everything in his life seemed to be brighter and sharper since that tow truck trip. He knew she was watching him and when she got up to leave his eyes had found hers without even trying. A few minutes later, when he'd looked up the hill to see her standing there, her hair had looked like a living flame in the last brilliant rays of the setting sun.

That night, finally alone in his own home, she owned his thoughts enough that he began to give himself another lecture about how foolish it would be to fall in love with a nonmember who wanted a career instead of a family. But it didn't keep him from deciding to go roust her out of bed again in the morning to take her on another outing.

Once Enchanted

Chapter 9

For some reason, Sean waking her up in the dim light of predawn felt perfectly normal this second time. She didn't know if she had been expecting him, or just hoping, but her grumbling was much more for show than because she wanted to stay in bed. She pretended to fight him as he hefted the entire bedding to the floor again, but she was up and dressed, with her hair somewhat under control and twisted back in a clip, before he'd even gotten the eggs scrambled. This time he ate with her and then got her some gloves and the jacket again before he took her to the big barn where he brought horses out to saddle up.

Before he went to get them, he asked, "How much have you ridden horses?"

She smiled apologetically. "Enough to say I can do it, and enough to know that there's no way I can keep up with the kind of riding I saw you doing last night."

"But you've been on a horse before?"

"My aunt, who was really more mother to me, rented a couple of sweet, old plugs that we'd ride around an arena from time to time. Sorry, that's about the extent of it."

He turned to walk into the barn. "That'll do."

Leading out a striking sorrel mare with three tall stockings and a flaxen mane, he said, "This is Mamie. She's as sweet and mellow as they come. You'll love her."

They were well out onto the trail with saddlebags packed behind their saddles before he thought to ask her if she'd come, or she thought to ask where they were going.

This morning was the beauty of yesterday times two. It was all rolled into the peace of a stillness broken only by the occasional creak of saddle leather or chink of an iron horse shoe on stone. The tranquility was like a drug and neither one of them appeared to want to break the spell with mindless small talk. This trip they saw deer several times because they were being so much more quiet, and as the sky lightened in the east, they walked over a small rise to glimpse a whole herd of elk.

She'd never really understood the difference before, but here in their own habitat, the difference was marked. It was a thrill to sit quietly on her horse beside him and watch these animals for a few minutes before they realized they weren't alone and ghosted off into the trees. There were fifteen or twenty of them. Cows and a handful of spotted calves and she couldn't believe they could disappear like that so silently. The morning stillness was such that when they were gone she could almost believe they'd never been there at all.

When the sun rose in its glory of color, they paused once again to take it all in. She couldn't even remember the last time she had seen the sun rise or set, but here it had become an elemental part of the opening and closing of her day. She took a deep breath and released it with a sigh to break the silence for the first time, "I don't know how I'm ever going to face I-5 again. You may have single-handedly ruined my life, Sean Rockland."

He only gave her a smile that almost seemed sad and started his horse up again.

Jaclyn M. Hawkes

They'd been riding for about an hour when he took a dim trail through the trees near a stream that emerged near a small pond. Tucked into the woods on the other side of the clearing was a small cabin that looked like it had grown there although the ends of the logs were stark white and looked brand new. They rode across the stream and around the pond, then up to a hitch rack in front of the quaint wooden structure.

He stepped down from his horse and came around to help her down and it wasn't until then that she realized she was going to be sore. She was stiff and awkward as she got down and stood there for a second next to Mamie to let the blood flow back into her legs before she dared walk. He pulled the saddles and hung them on the hitch rack, led the horses to the stream to drink and then took them to a little corral hidden back in the trees that she hadn't even seen.

The quiet of the clearing felt almost reverent and she hesitated to mar it's stillness as she softly asked, "What's on the agenda for today, boss?"

"Come on. I'll show you." He led off around the little cabin to walk up next to it and show her the mortar between the logs. "This is my latest project. I've always wanted to build a cabin just like my great, great, great, great grandparents did when they came here in the late eighteen forties. I've done a few things using modern technology, like a solid foundation and a roof that will hopefully never leak, but for the most part this is just as they would have built it. It has no running water or electricity. It will be heated with the fireplace and lit with oil lamps. It's one room with a loft and even the door is hand made.

"I've cut all the logs myself, hauled them over with horses, and lifted them with an old-fashioned block and tackle. I even hauled all the cement up here on horses. It's given me a completely new appreciation for what my ancestors went through. It's almost finished. All I have left to do as far as the actual building is to finish chinking the inside. It will be the same as this mortar here on the outside. Are you up to helping me?"

"Are you kidding me? I'm a chinker from way back."

"Really?" He looked at her for a minute in disbelief.

With a laugh she replied, "Of course not, but I'm a fast learner!"

He mixed a batch of cement using an old rubber grain barrel and water from the stream and showed her how to push the cement into the cracks and into the nails he'd pounded there and then bent back. Then he showed her how to smooth it. When she first tried it, she said, "I'm afraid my talents run more to the intellectual side. If you let me help, this might be even more rustic than you bargained for."

"It's all good." There was something in his voice that made her turn to look up into his face. What she saw there made her raise her eyebrows at him before she turned back around to go back to work. Drily, she said, "You weren't even looking at my chinking when you said that."

A few minutes later, he came up behind her, took the clip out of her hair and tossed it out the door and into the pond. Then he turned around and went back to work without even giving her an explanation.

She called him a questionable word before she asked, "At what point are you going to stop pestering my hair?"

"That will probably be about the same time you climb in that pretty little Porsche and drive on out of here. Until then, there's not really any point in being all professional is there?"

She put out her bottom lip and tried to blow the rebellious strands out of her eyes. "You're going to have to help me wash the cement out of my hair then."

"No problem." He chuckled. "I'll just throw you into the pond. It's actually not too bad. There's a hot spring that drains into it so the temperature stays warm and moss and stuff won't grow on the bottom."

They worked along in silence until she said, "By the way, your mother told me you don't usually make people fix fence and chink things to earn their keep. She thinks I volunteered to fix fence yesterday out of my own good will."

He didn't skip a beat as he answered, "Think what you would have missed if I hadn't volunteered you." She laughed at him and spilled some of the concrete off her trowel.

"Don't make me laugh. Now look what you made me do!" He came over to look down at the lump of gray mud on his rough-hewn wood floor.

"That's it. You're getting a dock in pay, and I have half a mind to call the EPA. There must be some kind of a law against this sort of thing. I'll have to consult a lawyer."

Three hours later, her back was tired and the chinking was done, with only a few of the little globs of mortar dotting the floor. He told her to just leave them and when they dried he would scrape them off and haul them back out. Going to his saddlebags, he produced sandwiches, fruit and a Coke to combat the headache that had appeared on the crack of ten again.

She sank down beside him on the porch step to drink it.

As they ate, she asked him, "Why are you building this? Other than to have an appreciation of your ancestors, I mean?"

He leaned back on his elbows on the step above them, and stretched his long denim clad legs out in front of him. "I don't know. I've just always wanted to. There have been a few times in my life when I dreamed of coming here and building this, where there were no people and traffic and sirens and jackhammers. Is that silly? Haven't you ever just wanted to leave the stress of the modern-day frenzy behind? I know the pioneers struggled with basic things like food and warmth and shelter, but sometimes that seems like nothing compared to all the stuff that pulls on us today. I know I have to live in the real world, but every once in awhile, when I have time, I come out here and work on this for a day and then all the other stuff goes back into perspective. I remember what the goal is and can focus on the vital stuff instead of just the urgent."

She took another bite or two of her sandwich before she asked, "What's the goal?"

He answered without looking up. "Just to pass the test of this life and return to our Father in Heaven with honor."

She was quiet for a long time before she softly said, "I think I lose track of the goal a lot."

After a second, he sat back up and leaned against her shoulder as he ate. It was a sweet, companionable silence that stretched between them, unbroken until she commented, "The fairies would love it here, too. Even the mermaids and rusalkas would, with the stream and pond."

At length he got up, cleaned up the mortar, and saddled the horses. He carefully shut the door of the little cabin and stood looking around from the porch before coming to hold her horse so she could get on. Hesitantly, she said, "I'm not sure I can even get my leg up there. I'm afraid I've stiffened up while we've been here."

He showed her how to give him her foot and on three, boosted her onto Mamie, then he stepped into his saddle and they headed back down the trail. They arrived back home in the early afternoon and he left her at his mom's to check on her car as he went off to work. She watched him stride to his truck wishing the cabin had been just a little further away.

Once Enchanted

Chapter 10

In his mom's office, she called Brandon about her car, only to be informed that the specialized parts it required hadn't arrived and it would be at least Monday afternoon before her car would be ready. She sighed as she hung up the phone and Naomi asked what the matter was.

A.J. told her and then said, "I guess I'd better just break down and go to Park City and get a rental car and go into Jackson Hole and get on with it. My time here has been like living on a western resort, but I can't ask you to put me up or put up with me any longer. You've been so much more than kind just to take me in, in the first place."

Naomi came over and studied her. "Are you unhappy here?"

"No, of course not." A.J. shook her head. "I've enjoyed myself immensely, but I'm sure I've worn out my welcome and I need to get to Jackson, and get with the program of finding this guy."

"You haven't worn out your welcome at all. You've been a pleasure to have around and have certainly done more than your fair share of work around here. What if instead of going clear back to Park City to rent a car, I lend you my Jeep for the day and then you can come back here tonight or if you're not comfortable with that, you could get a room in Jackson and bring my car back in a day or two when you've located this

Once Enchanted
man you're looking for."

"Won't you need your car?"

Naomi waved a hand. "The only place I'll be going the next day or so is to church, and we can take Rob's truck or ride with any of these others. You're welcome to come to church with us by the way. It's tomorrow at nine o'clock in the morning, but we'll need to leave here by about eight thirty five or so." She went to the key rack on the cupboard. "Here, take my car and even take my phone so you'll have one that has reception and go on into Jackson this afternoon. If you can't find what you're looking for, come back here and I'll start digging with you and we'll get to the bottom of this. In the mean time, remember that you are more than welcome around here, so come back here tonight if you'd like to and come to church with us tomorrow."

Later, as A.J. drove down the wild Snake River canyon, with the steep and rugged mountain rising abruptly on the one side and the other plunging into the river gorge, she sang softly along to the radio. Breathing deeply of the pine-scented air that wafted in the open window, she was grateful she wasn't a timid driver.

Her drive time she spent planning how best to go about her afternoon, frankly disgusted that finding one stupid contractor was proving to be this difficult. She was hoping that asking questions in person would prove to be more successful than her efforts thus far. When she reached the small tourist town, she went first to the Chamber of Commerce, but found a sign on the door saying they wouldn't be back until Monday.

Going back out into the town, she stopped into a shop and asked the sales clerk where she would be likely to find any of the area contractors. She was

74

directed to a nearby bar where the locals sometimes hung out and then the clerk added, "If you can't find any there, try just driving out toward Wilson and checking any of the new subdivisions where they're building those monster homes. I'm sure you'll find more than you bargained for there."

She found the bar and hesitated just a moment before she stepped into the dim and smoky interior. Man, she hated this kind of thing. How had she ever let Trent have this much control of her life? Letting her eyes grow accustomed to the dark after the bright sunshine of outside, she studied the handful of customers before deciding on a likely looking man. He was hunched over a long necked bottle, watching a boxing match on the TV over the bar. "Excuse me. I wonder if you could help me. I'm trying to find a certain contractor, only I'm afraid I only know his company name. You wouldn't by any chance be a local are you?"

He turned toward her and gave her a thorough checking out before he drawled, "I am. Sure I can help you. What's the name of his company?"

She felt a little like washing her hands as she answered, "House Upon a Rock Inc. I believe he's an architect as well as a builder. Would you happen to know who the owner is?" She held her breath waiting for his answer, hoping she was going to get the one little break she needed.

He leaned back on one elbow against the bar and said lazily, "Old Sean, huh? Who wants to know?"

She wasn't sure if it was a legitimate question or if this guy was just trying to find out more about her, so she answered, "I'm actually asking for my boss. He's seen some of this old Sean's work and wants to hire him but, we can't seem to find out his name."

He glanced at her up and down again as he commented, "Give me your card and I'll pass it along when I see him. If he wants to find you, he will. Are you going to be in town long?"

She hesitated before deciding against leaving her business card. The glossy card of an L.A. attorney probably wasn't the best idea under the circumstances, so she decided to just write something down. Then she wondered what to leave with him because so far she hadn't had any phone reception since shortly after having her car towed.

Finally, she said, "I'm having trouble getting phone reception in all these mountains. I'll just leave the number to the people I've been staying with. It's the Rockland family down south of here. I don't know if you know them." She scribbled the number on a Post It from her purse and as she handed it to him, he glanced at it with a puzzling smile.

He shook his head, still with that strange grin and said, "I'll pass this on, and I'm sure he'll call. What did you say your name was?"

"A.J. A.J. O'Brien. Thanks for your help."

With a last subtle glance, he said, "No problem, A.J. O'Brien. Good luck." He turned back to his match, still shaking his head, chuckling.

She looked down at herself wondering what he thought was so funny before checking over the other patrons of the bar and deciding she didn't want to find this guy bad enough to approach any of the other unsavory looking customers. Outside she climbed back into Naomi's Jeep and consulted her map to figure out where she needed to go to head toward Wilson.

It was a pleasant drive and the scenery was

incredible.   As she approached the obviously
prosperous area the sales clerk had mentioned, she was
amazed at the scope of the new building. Not only
were these the "monster" homes she'd mentioned, but
there were lots and lots of them. She looked around
floored. Who would have thought she would find this
kind of mountain home grandeur in Wyoming of all
places? She'd heard that Jackson Hole had become a
hot spot for real estate, but what she was seeing was
unreal! This looked like the last boom in Aspen
Colorado, except here instead of the massive homes
being perched on the mountain hillsides they were
scattered across the rolling river valley, surrounded by
the awesome Teton Range.

Hesitantly, she pulled into the driveway of one of
the homes currently under construction, thinking to
herself the contractors around here must have found a
cherry market. It was no wonder her boss wanted to
develop here, or that he was finding it tough to pick up
this builder.

She approached different job sites for the
remainder of the afternoon, convinced each time she
got out of the Jeep that her search was just about to be
over, but either the men she approached truly didn't
know who she was looking for or they wouldn't tell
her. A good portion of the time they weren't the
slightest bit concerned with who she was in search of,
they just wanted to visit with her. She gave out
Naomi's phone number a couple more times, hoping
she wouldn't be offended about that. As the shadows
began to lengthen and she was finding more and more
homes had been abandoned for the day, she called it
quits and turned the car back toward the town.

She'd actually pulled into a hotel to register when

she started the Jeep back up again and pointed its hood south toward the Rocklands. That was where she really wanted to be. She wanted to see Sean again and felt Naomi had been sincere in her invitation. Moreover, the invitation to church had been intriguing. Her Aunt Julie had tried to encourage her and Eric to attend church whenever they were with her. Julie had been a Methodist, and when A.J. and Eric had been very young, they'd loved going with her. The feelings they felt at church and in Julie's home had been what had helped them get through their childhood with their mother. Then, when they'd gotten older, some of the novelty of church wore off. As teenagers, A.J. and Eric had probably sapped any form of spirituality from the whole experience, they'd hassled Julie so much about going.

However, in college the two of them had started attending again, even without Julie's encouragement and now she knew Eric and his wife attended the local Methodist church with their children every week. And although A.J. wasn't strictly devout, she went most of the time. She'd come to deeply value the spiritual lift she received there. At times, she had some reservations about how all the doctrines tied together with each other, but she knew that living the way the Bible taught had kept her sane in the jungle of LA.

She didn't think the Rocklands were Methodist; at least she hadn't gotten that impression. But she'd come to know even in a couple of days that they were Christ like, clean living, and had a charitable streak a mile wide. Whatever they were, she knew she would like their style of Christianity, and she knew she could use a weekly dose of the Spirit in her life right now. Her time spent with Sean had especially been encouraging.

78

He'd teased her a time or two, like when he'd stood to watch her get into the tow truck, but he was always the perfect gentleman, and she'd come to trust him in two days in a way that she still didn't trust any of the men she worked with, even after two years.

Thinking about him again, she sighed, still wishing he'd chosen to become something more respectable than a tow truck driver.

Once Enchanted

Chapter 11

She pulled into the Rockland's valley and stopped the Jeep at the top of the rise just to look. She knew she'd already missed dinner and had even missed the sunset, so there was no reason to hurry. Gazing out over the peaceful valley in the dusk, she wondered again if it really was possible for the people who lived and worked here to carry on a traditional business from such a remote place.

Apparently they did make a living here while maintaining this incredible quality of life. She hadn't seen any signs that money was tight. She had to smile at herself. In college, the thought of living without parties and dances and movies and shopping within minutes of her door would have felt like a fate worse than death. However, now she lived smack in the middle of Tinsel town and hardly even went out to dinner because she was too busy with her career and too tired afterward. From that perspective, peace and tranquility were of much greater value than an exciting nightlife.

That almost sounded questionable for someone single, who boasted a high profile career. The guys at work would have been skeptical and insinuated that she needed more entertainment or that she was getting old.

Actually, the opposite was true. She'd felt younger

here than she'd felt in years. It was as if the old Lexie was slowly reappearing. She grinned. Maybe it was because she tended to have her wild hair down a lot more than normal, due to Sean's constant pestering. She reached up to pull the pins that had held it in it's conservative twist all afternoon to shake it out and let it fall down her back, hearing his voice in her head say there was no reason to be professional right now.

Looking across the valley below her, she wondered which house was his. She'd seen him pull away from his parent's, but had never figured out where it was that he went home to. There were five houses scattered around the view before her, one of which was just being built. There was one that was a simple cottage, but all of them appeared to be lovely homes. A couple of them even along the lines of luxury homes, and she could imagine him in any of them, but she couldn't for the life of her, picture someone affording any one of them on the pay of a tow truck driver.

There in the deepening dusk, she realized there were headlights coming up behind her, so she started Naomi's Jeep up and pulled more to the side of the road to give them room to pass. As the vehicle pulled up beside her, she recognized Sean's white truck. He stopped and rolled down his window. "I thought you were my mom. Is something wrong?"

She could tell he was tired and wondered what he was doing coming home this late. The last couple of days he'd been home much earlier. "No, nothing's wrong. I'm just looking at your beautiful valley. Have you been out rescuing more stranded motorists?"

"No, not this time." He chuckled and shook his head. "More like dealing with mindless idiots this time. Stranded motorists are much more entertaining.

Where have you been?"

"Just off to Jackson Hole on a wild goose chase." She sighed. "Whoever this guy is, he certainly inspires loyalty. I think some of the people who gave me the run around today were even his competition, and still no one will tell me who he is."

"Really? It's just because they've never seen you fix fence. If you'd wear the shorts and leave your hair down they wouldn't be able to resist you!"

She smiled tiredly. "I did find a couple of guys who were willing to pass my number along to him. I guess that's a start. Maybe I'll be in luck and he'll actually call me back."

"I'd guess if he wanted your boss to find him he'd have already been in touch. Don't worry about it. I'll bet he's just a stupid, hick construction worker anyway and you'll be disappointed when he finally shows up."

"Ah, my boss." She groaned. "He's probably having a fit wondering what's going on. I have no reception here and it's been so nice that I haven't even called in. I'll probably never hear the end of it."

"My phone is a satellite phone. It usually has reception if you can see the sky. I need it when I'm in the mountains so much." He moved across the seat to hand her his phone. "Call him right now and leave a message on the office machine. Mention that's it's . . . " He looked at his watch. "Nine thirty on Saturday night and that you've been slaving night and day and that he owes you extra special treatment when you get home. Maybe that will buy you points."

Taking the phone, she started to key in the numbers. "I could never tell him that or he'll think I'm finally going to break down and be a little too friendly with him after two years of his prodding. Better just to let him know I'm working late and leave it at that." She left her message and handed him back his phone. "Thanks. It was nice to be able to leave a message and not have to talk to him in person."

He laughed. "Sounds like you adore the guy."

She felt a bit guilty. "Sorry, he's not really all that bad I guess. I was just naive enough to believe everything he told me when he hired me. How's that for stupid? I trusted an attorney." She paused for a second and then apologized again. "Sorry, I didn't mean to insult your mom."

"It's all right; she's not really an attorney. She's a mom who just happens to practice law from time to time." A.J. didn't even want to discuss this. She was still trying to figure him out and she was too tired tonight to have another argument about women.

He must have been able to see it in her eyes and put his truck in gear. "Did you eat in town?"

She shook her head. "I wasn't terribly hungry at the time. I forgot you're a long way from fast food out here."

"Come on. Follow me in and we'll find something. I didn't eat either."

He drove on down the lane and she followed. She was surprised when he drove past Naomi and Rob's and kept on up the gravel road. He drove up to the nicest house, the garage door opened and he drove his truck in. She pulled Naomi's Jeep into the drive outside and shut off the engine, looking at the mansion that rose up in front of her.

Something funky was going on here. Something wasn't right. This was not the house of a tow truck driver and she was completely lost. She got out and walked slowly past the waterfall that cascaded off the
84

Jaclyn M. Hawkes

mountain of boulders beside the pavement, the water glinting from the carriage lights as it tumbled down its path. She followed him inside; dying to ask what was going on, but hesitant to act as if anything was amiss.

They went through a mudroom that was all but luxurious and into a gourmet kitchen that was luxurious and then some. He walked across and into a room off the front entry and deposited a pile of papers and a long white roll and then firmly shut that door and came back into the kitchen to start digging through his fridge. "I don't cook all that much here so we'll just have to see what I have. We could have salmon, or hoagies or something with chicken. Does anything sound good?"

She didn't answer him and he turned as she was looking all around his house. "Uh, Lex, you were deciding what you'd like to eat." She still didn't answer and he went on, "Ah salmon. Excellent choice, madam. It was fresh caught in Alaska by me personally just a few weeks ago."

She put her hands on her hips. "All right, what's going on?"

"What? I really did catch it myself. What's the problem?" He was digging through the cupboards, pulling out spices and ingredients, and then pulled lettuce and tomato out of the fridge. "Hey, are you helping me or what? Quit standing there with your mouth open and come over here." He was laughing at her as he cooked.

"I am not helping you one bit until you tell me how a tow truck driver lives in a house like this!" Her hands were still on her hips and she could feel the skepticism coming from her eyes.

He put the salmon out on a tray and began to

season it. "You got a problem with a tow truck driver having a nice place to live?" Leaving the salmon on the counter, he went to walk out a French door off the kitchen and she stepped in front of him and put both hands on his chest.

"Hold it right there, mister!" He looked down at her hands, and now there were frissions of blue electricity coming from his eyes. She was suddenly a little nervous. For a moment, she almost forgot what she was asking. Then, gathering her senses, she said, "What's going on? Why were you towing my car the other night?"

He slowly licked his lips as he looked down into her face. "Because you'd just wiped out my trophy elk. Remember?"

He went to move around her and she got in front of him and backed him right up to the granite counter. "Nice try. You know exactly what I mean! Are you, or are you not, a tow truck driver?"

Swallowing hard, he said, "I came and picked up your car, didn't I?"

She moved even closer. "Sean David Rockland, yes or no?"

He was looking at her mouth as he asked, "Does it matter?"

She knew he was completely flustered and for some reason it made her feel incredibly powerful. "Probably not, but I'd like to know why you're making a total fool of me."

He ran a hand through his hair. "I'm not trying to make a fool out of you. I never told you I was a tow truck driver, and it doesn't matter to me. I met the most entertaining girl I've found in forever with that tow truck and I happen to like that truck a lot now."

He ended with a teasing smile.

"Sean, how often do you drive that tow truck?"

"Uh, not very."

"Why were you driving it two nights ago?"

"Because Brandon, my very good friend who owns the towing company, was headed to dinner with his wife and family when you called. I volunteered to go pick you up so he could be with his family. We thought you were Eunice Freeman, our seventy something year old neighbor who's known as the deer slayer in the Mad Buick. Now, are you satisfied?"

"Just about. What is it that you do? For a living I mean?"

"Honestly, most of my living, I make with my investments."

"And the rest of your living? What is it you do full-time?" She was watching him watch her lips and could feel herself becoming flustered too.

At length, he shook his head and said, "D' you know what? I'm not going to tell you what I do. It'll tick you off. I know it's going to happen sooner or later, but I'm not in any hurry to have you mad at me again. So you might as well give it a rest and let me get our dinner."

She backed off just a bit, confused. "Why would it tick me off?"

He reached up to touch a tendril of hair that had fallen over her brow. "It will. Just trust me on this one. I should have told you that first night, but you were being so feisty that I was being a rebel and now it's kind of a case of self-preservation. Let's just let it go, okay? You know I'm not a tow truck driver. We'll simply say that I'm educated and gainfully employed, huh?"

She looked up at him puzzled, wondering if she

should keep pushing or, in fact, trust him as he
suggested. For some reason her hesitation made the
sparks in the back of his eyes glow brighter. He put a
strong arm around her, and pulled her against him and
she watched the blue sparks, mesmerized, as he slowly
brought his lips down to hers. His other arm came
around her and she wasn't sure if she couldn't breathe
because he was holding her so tight or just because she
couldn't breathe.

For a minute or two there, all thought processes
ceased. All she could do was feel his kiss. His mouth
was warm and firm and its touch was incredibly sweet.

She grasped his shirt in her hand and began to kiss
him back and it was heavenly to stand there in his
kitchen in his arms. Everything that was feminine and
pretty and soft about her came rushing and she reveled
in his touch as his hand came up to tangle in her hair.
As he pulled it gently, his kiss became more
demanding and she was lost in it, enjoying his sweet
passion and basking in his embrace. It had been
forever since she had been kissed and she'd never been
kissed like this!

The gentle heat that filled her body warmed her
soul, and she pressed closer to share it as she lost track
of time. At her reaction, he held her even tighter and
then finally, much to her regret, he reluctantly pulled
his mouth away. He kept her held close, with his face
against her hair and after a moment, murmured, "I
should never have done that."

She looked up at him and gently put her fingers to
his lips. "Don't. It was nice."

He pulled on the back of her hair again and as she
leaned her head back, he lowered his mouth to her
neck and began to kiss her in the soft hollow under her

ear and then whispered, "Nice? It was nicer than just nice, but it was probably stupid and will haunt me when you're back in LA." His mouth traveled up her neck and then claimed her mouth once again. Demanding for just a second or two, and then gentle for another. He groaned as he raised his head. "Help me out here, Lexie. You go stand over there and make a salad and I'll go outside and turn on the grill."

He said the words, but he didn't push her away and she stayed there in his arms feeling like she was finally home. He was right, this was probably stupid, but she was enjoying it anyway.

Finally, he gave her a gentle shove and running a hand through his hair, he went out to fire up his grill. He didn't come straight back in and she went out to find him standing at the railing looking out over the valley in the night, the mild evening breeze in his face. The shapes and hills were softer in the dark, and there were a few lights glowing yellow from the other houses and barns.

The moon starting to come up over the ridge to the east threw the crags and ragged pines on the skyline into sharp relief. Wispy clouds around the moonrise gave the night an almost mysterious feel, as she came up to stand beside him, wondering what he was thinking. It would have been the perfect night for the fairies to dance.

He didn't say anything and she didn't ask and they stood there like that until they could smell the grill beside them and he said, "I guess I'd better see about the salmon."

He walked back into the house, but she stayed for a moment still enjoying the view. It was amazing that people lived like this. It was as far as you could get from a night in LA.

He came back out with the salmon and she said, "It doesn't sound like this at home. It doesn't smell like this, or feel like this, and it certainly doesn't look like this. Before this trip I would've thought I'd be afraid out here at night, but even though it's pretty wild here, I feel ten times more secure than back home in my condo."

He put the fish on to grill and came back to stand behind her and said almost reverently, "It's home. I spent a couple of years away from here and I used to dream about evenings like this. I couldn't wait to come back and swore I'd never leave again."

"Roots like that must be incredibly comforting. When my brother and I were finally old enough to go off to college, we swore we'd never *go back* to where we grew up. Other than the obligatory visit on Mother's Day or something, we never have. It's not really a place either of us wants to be."

"Does that make you sad?"

She turned to look up at him. "I don't know. At times, I guess. Should it?"

He shrugged. "My family are my best friends. Sometimes living just this far across this little valley even seems far removed from all the fun. I'm sure I gave my parents fits as a teenager, but now even my parents are friends."

"You do understand that your family is very different than most, don't you?   My mother isn't interested in being friends, and my dad would be only if it didn't require any effort. My brother is by far my best friend, and I love to spend time at his home now, but our home growing up was more of a war zone. My parents didn't necessarily have an amicable divorce."

"I'm sorry." He paused and then asked, "If you

were home where would you be right now?"

She knew she sounded a little guilty as she admitted, "Probably at my condo, alone, working on next week's case load."

He didn't say anything. At length, his stomach growled and they laughed and went inside to finish getting dinner. He turned some music on low as they stood side by side making a salad and garlic bread, and he got out lemon sorbet to soften for dessert.

After eating, they were cleaning up when an old Air Supply song came on. He went across the room and dimmed the lights, then came back to her and took her in his arms to dance there in the kitchen. At first, she couldn't figure out what he was doing and then when she realized, she hoped the song never ended. It would have never occurred to her to slow dance in the kitchen, but she decided right off it was one of life's great pleasures.

Another sweet, mellow ballad came on and they continued to dance through it. As the song played, she could feel herself dancing closer and closer until finally, they weren't dancing at all and he was kissing her again, their bodies close and his mouth teasing her senses until she lost all track of time.

At length, he pulled away and bent to kiss her neck again and sighed as he said, "You taste really good, but we'd better get you home to my parents'. I think my mom thought you were staying in Jackson tonight so they're not even expecting you. I'll call them." He put his hands into her hair and almost tugged on it for a second before he bent to kiss her one last, incredibly sweet time, then took her hand to walk her out to the Jeep.

As they got there and he opened the door, she

Once Enchanted

looked back up at him. They simply smiled at each
other for a second. Somehow, she felt like reality
would set in with the light of day tomorrow. All forms
of fairy tales would be gone and this magical spell
would be broken. She wasn't sure she wanted it to be.
She climbed into the Jeep and backed out of the
driveway as he stood there and watched her go.

She still didn't know what he did for a living, but
after tonight, even if he had been a tow truck driver,
she wouldn't have cared.

Chapter 12

The next morning when A.J. woke up, she heard people in the house moving around and realized Sean hadn't come to haul her off on an adventure. She was disappointed and a little worried, wondering if he'd decided against it after kissing her last night. She lay there and thought about him and found herself smiling. She hadn't pegged him as a softy, but she had never done anything as romantic as dancing in the kitchen. It had been incredible. She touched her lips when she remembered his heavenly kisses. Who would have thought that such a big, strong, tease would be the one to turn her heart to mush after the lemon sorbet?

Her tender thoughts were interrupted when Naomi knocked on her door and then poked her head in and said, "A.J., I'm sorry to wake you, but I wanted to make sure you knew you were welcome to go to church with us this morning. We're going to eat in a minute and then we need to leave by about eight thirty five or so."

A.J. jumped out of bed, flew into the shower, just slightly blew her hair dry and then ran in wearing a warm up suit to eat with her hair in long, damp curls that hung all the way down her back. It was the first time she'd purposely encouraged them since she'd been here and Naomi walked all the way around her checking them out, and then said, "When I get to the

Once Enchanted

other side, I'm going to have a talk with the good Lord about why some people get hair like that and the rest of us just get hair. That has got to be the most beautiful mane I've ever seen in my life!"

Sean was just walking in right then, dressed in an exquisite black suit that would have fit in with the best-dressed men in her firm, and between Naomi's comments, and him looking good enough to eat, A.J. was slightly breathless. He pulled out her chair to seat her and then his mother's. When he sat across from her and their eyes met, he gave her a mysterious little smile that somehow helped her to know he wasn't regretting their closeness of the last evening at all.

Sean's younger brother Treyne came flying in and as he sat down, he said enthusiastically, "Dang, Alexis! You look great! Are you coming?" At her nod, he turned to Sean and said, "You should take advantage of her coming with us to keep the stink bugs away!"

Sean laughed and Rob asked Joey to pray and they all bowed their heads while A.J. wondered what in the world Treyne had been saying. When the prayer was over, A.J. looked over at Treyne and asked, "What exactly did you mean by that stink bug thing?"

Naomi interrupted, "It's not a very complimentary way to talk about perfectly nice young ladies, Treyne."

Sean laughed again while Treyne defended himself, "Perfectly nice! You call Allison Thompson perfectly nice? Or Ivie Ellen McGrath? Mother, come on! More like predatory. Poor Sean is going to have to change wards." He got a mischievous grin. "Either that or show up with a drop dead gorgeous red head! Stink bugs hate that kind of thing!"

A.J. laughed as Sean looked embarrassed and

94

Naomi tried again to encourage Treyne to be kinder. Joey caught her eye and gave her a thumbs up and interjected, "You guys aren't even going to have a chance to use Alexis for your stink bug control. Every single guy in church is going to be trying to lure her away from you! You'll just be standing back in line!"

Rob broke in, "You're going to scare her into not even going." He turned to A.J. with a smile. "Ignore them. They're just a trifle shell shocked at having such a beautiful visitor at our breakfast table."

As they ate, Slade and Isabel came in and sat down to join them, and then Ruger and Marti. Isabel said, "Wow. Alexis. Where have you been hiding that hair? It's incredible!" Then she added, "Rossen and Kit aren't coming to eat this morning. Mimi had a rough night and they're running behind and will just be ready in time to leave."

A.J. finished eating, then put her dishes in the dishwasher, and went back into her room to put on her suit. She emerged ten minutes later in a cream-colored linen suit dress, with matching heels and understated pearls. She was carrying her Bible and a small notepad and when she walked back in she knew she looked good just from Sean's eyes. It was her power suit and sometimes, when she had a particularly challenging case, she wore it to make her feel more confident.

Rob's softly spoken, "You look very pretty, Alexis." went a long way toward taking away her mild nerves about going to a strange church with these people who had so kindly taken her in.

They all piled into four different vehicles and she was surprised that even some of the hired ranch hands went with them. She ended up in Sean's truck with him and Slade and Isabel, and Ruger and Marti. As

95

they drove the twenty minutes, she listened to the five of them talking back and forth. After finding out that Isabel and Marti had their own businesses, she was watching them all interact. All three of the men listened to Isabel and Marti when they made a comment with absolute respect and sometimes even sought out their opinion on things.

She'd been around them all a few times in the last couple of days, but she had never made it a point to notice whether the men took the women here seriously, as she was now. For some reason she needed to be reassured that not only was Sean okay with them, but she was interested to see if the women had any of the hardness Sean had referred to when talking about females in corporate America.

Both women seemed to be the friendly, open, intelligent women she'd thought them from the first, and Sean didn't appear to have even a hint of attitude about them. Their husbands openly adored them and A.J. continued to notice an unusual blend of respect mixed with a sense of chivalry that was completely refreshing. Nobody here had the slightest thing to prove, and the little things like opening doors or helping the women out of the truck were as natural as breathing to them all.

A.J.'s sense of being a feminist was all mixed up. These women had it all, but somehow she'd been led to believe that being a happily married wife was in some sense breaking the sisterhood. Kit was the only one with a baby, but she was probably the most successful woman of them all in terms of how the world would judge. She was one of the most up and coming talents on the pop music scene and yet she appeared to be completely happy puttering around the ranch. If A.J.

hadn't been familiar with her music, she would never have believed she was a famous singer.

Moreover, her husband Rossen, who A.J. knew was an engineer because his office was next door to Rob and Naomi's in their house, was almost a storybook father. He handled Mimi Star as if he'd grown up dealing with a tiny female person. He actually appeared to parent her more than Kit. By the time they drove into the rapidly filling parking lot of a large church, A.J. had a lot to think about.

They were inside the building and walking down the hallway when Treyne's head poked around the corner in front of them and hissed, "Stink bug alert!" His head disappeared again and A.J. laughed right out loud at the grimace on Sean's face over this ludicrous announcement.

She reached down and took Sean's hand and gave it a squeeze as she laughed again and said, "Not to fear, I'll save you."

Sean glanced down at her and at their clasped hands and then abruptly pulled her into a nearby doorway. He swung her around so her back was to the wall next to the door and leaned in close to ask, "What are you doing?"

In a discreet whisper she asked, "What? You can kiss me like that last night when we're alone, but then not even hold my hand today when we're in public?" She was smiling as she said it and he had to know she was teasing.

Shaking his head, he said, "You don't have to do this. I'd love to hold your hand, but I don't want you to feel like I'm using you as pest control." He smiled a little sheepishly as he said it.

"Won't it work though?"

He laughed. "Probably like a charm."

She dropped her eyes and started to play with his fingers. "Is that all you need from me? Holding my hand?" She knew she had a wicked grin and he eyed her, with a questioning look.

With a low chuckle, he said, "Probably for now, since we *are* in the church. Why? What else were you wondering about?" He moved closer to her as he asked.

Her voice was absolutely innocent as she meekly answered, "Oh, I don't know. We could start out discussing what you do for a living. That worked pretty well for us last night."

Backing her up against the wall, he put his hands on either side of her head and leaned in. "It did, didn't it?"

He was just about to kiss her when two boys about thirteen years old walked in. They were almost speechless they were so surprised. They both blushed and one gave a swallow that everyone could hear as the other one said, "Brother Rockland, what are you doing?" He sounded flat out horrified.

Sean chuckled as he took A.J.'s hand and moved toward the door. "Actually, I was just about to kiss this girl, but since you two busted us, I guess I'd better just take her to her class. I'll be right back."

He hustled her out the door, laughing as he went. "I'm sure that will make for a lively conversation this morning. I'm their teacher and the lesson is on the blessings of chastity. I guess you and I will be the perfect segue into what's appropriate and what isn't." He was still chuckling as they came around the corner into a lobby with a few people standing around visiting. He leaned into her and mouthed, "Stinkbugs,

Jaclyn M. Hawkes

three o'clock." It was all A.J. could do to keep from cracking up as she discreetly looked over to see two college-aged girls looking at her with barely controlled disgust. She gave them her friendliest smile and hello as she and Sean breezed past.

As they continued on down the other hall she said, "I had no idea church was going to be this entertaining."

He took her to a room filled with only women. "My mom and the other girls are right there. I'll be back to join you in about fifty minutes." He looked down into her face again with a mischievous smile and whispered, "The stinkbug mothers are sitting right in front of them. This is going to be even better than we thought! I may have to bring you back out from California on a regular basis!" With that, he gave her a hug and spun and walked away as she turned to face the matriarchal insects. They were obviously not very happy to see her.

Naomi must have seen the scowls, because she stood up to hug A.J. as well and offered the seat next to her. A.J. had already decided their church was fun before it had even started. She didn't have a clue what the doctrine was or even what the planned meetings were, but she'd gained a great respect for the Rockland clan, and so far, the others she'd seen all looked like wonderful people, give or take a jealous stinkbug or two.

As she sat there looking around, she noticed a beautifully lettered sign hanging at the front of the room that seemed to be a credo of some sort. The title read, "The Relief Society of the Church of Jesus Christ of Latter-Day Saints, and below that it said, "We are beloved spirit daughters of God, and our lives have

meaning, purpose and direction.   As a worldwide
sisterhood, we are united in our devotion to Jesus
Christ, our Savior and Exemplar. We are women of
faith, virtue, vision, and charity who:

- Increase our testimonies of Jesus Christ through
  prayer and scripture study.
- Seek spiritual strength by following the
  promptings of the Holy Ghost.
- Dedicate ourselves to strengthening marriages,
  families, and homes.
- Find nobility in motherhood and joy in
  womanhood.
- Delight in service and good works.
- Love life and learning.
- Stand for truth and righteousness.
- Sustain the priesthood as the authority of God
  on earth.
- Rejoice in the blessings of the temple,
  understand our divine destiny, and strive for
  exaltation.

   She was deep in thought, thinking about what she
was reading, seriously considering writing it in her
notes, when the class began. A couple of these things
didn't make much sense to her, but for the most part
they sounded outstanding and she marveled that
women in this day and age had the guts to declare in
writing that they stood for such principles as these.
Much of the world seemed to make light of values this
wholesome and basic. She made a mental note to ask
Naomi about the things she didn't understand as she
focused on what was going on in the class.

   They sang a hymn, said an opening prayer, and

then made some announcements. The woman who appeared to be in charge asked if there were any visitors and Naomi stood and introduced A.J. as a friend of the family who was visiting from California. A.J. was floored by that. She'd expected her to give them the explanation about her car incident, but Naomi hadn't mentioned it. When Naomi sat back down beside her to take her hand and give it a squeeze, she did indeed feel like a friend. This whole situation was unreal.

They sang again and then another woman stood up to give the actual lesson. It was a dissertation on a speech given some time before, by someone else entitled "Mothers who know." The teacher put some bullet points on the board in the front of the room stating the seven points of what 'mothers who know', do.

Even though A.J. wasn't a mother and if she was honest with herself, it wasn't looking like she ever would be if she didn't change something, she took notes. She always did, whether she was in a church class or a meeting. She'd gotten in the habit in college when she'd found she retained far more of what was being presented if she jotted down just enough to jog her memory when she glanced back over them.

The very first point was, 'mothers who know' bear children. A.J. was a bit confused from the get go. How could they help but bear children if they were mothers?

The teacher continued on through the bullet points of women honoring sacred ordinances and covenants, and being nurturers, and when she came to a bullet point about 'mothers who know' are leaders, A.J. perked up. She was having trouble associating mothering with leading, but being a leader was something she could identify with. She'd been in leadership positions from the time she was in Jr. High.

The teacher went on to say that these leading women were in equal partnerships with their husbands and they lead a great and eternal organization, and that they were to manage that responsibility well. She emphasized the fact that wise leaders were selective and didn't try to do it all, but conserved their limited resources of time and energy to focus on what mattered most. This lesson was becoming more and more intriguing. That was great counsel for anyone.

Next, the teacher touched on mothers as teachers, and the fact that they are never off duty, and how powerful their influence was. Somehow, A.J. had never looked at mothering that way.

The instructor was moving on to how 'mothers who know' do less. She explained that that meant they chose to be careful not to do things that would take them away from their priorities, or to allow less unwholesome influences into their homes, and instead do more things to strengthen their homes and families spiritually and temporally. The lesson ended with the topic of these women standing strong and immoveable. She went on to reiterate that women must not give up in difficult and discouraging times, that those around them were looking to them to remain grounded and steadfast.

The teacher ended with, "May we go away from this morning's meeting with a positive attitude, looking forward with joy and confidence and the resolve to reach a little higher." When the teacher finished and sat down, A.J. felt as if she had just sat through a motivational speaker encouraging her and the women around her to believe they were capable of most anything. It was a class she would have paid good money for, even on a professional level.

They had a closing song and a prayer and then they opened the back doors, and the men came in to sit among the various women. A.J. barely had time to wonder what had happened to all the children and youth before Sean came to sit beside her, followed by his brothers and dad. She looked at his face as he sat down and then whispered, "How did it go?" He was pretty gutty to tackle the subject of chastity with a class full of teenage boys.

His smile was easy and honest when he whispered back, "Very well actually. Believe it or not, boys have questions about things like kissing, and sometimes it's easier to talk about them with someone you just about busted doing it, than a parent. I've become pretty good friends with them and their usually comfortable with me, so it was quite a candid conversation. The boys were far more comfortable than the other leader." He chuckled at this last comment. "How did your class go?"

"It was great." The meeting was beginning, so their conversation was interrupted and she tried to focus on the speaker. She turned her head to the front just in time to notice the two stink bug girls checking her out again from a couple of rows away. Sean saw them too and smiled down at her. As she reached to hold his hand and squeezed it, he whispered, "I owe you."

A.J. smiled to herself as she began to try to listen, wondering how he would repay her.

They had another prayer and this time three men taught the class. The basis for their lesson was a document they passed copies of around, called "A Proclamation to the World". A.J. was torn between reading the copy that had been handed to her, and listening to the teacher, and watching the two nearby girls furtively watching Sean. He seemed oblivious to the girls and soon A.J. ignored them too. The lesson was too compelling to bother with them.

The proclamation was an official statement of Sean's church's beliefs concerning the family unit. It was much like the credo hanging in front of the women's class in that it was a no holds barred statement issued about unwavering values.

It stated that among other things, marriage was ordained of God and that the family was the fundamental unit of society and vital to Gods plan for his children. It further stated that men and women each had their own definite responsibilities in this life, and that they were to work as a team of equal partners, and that if they blew these responsibilities off, they would be held accountable to God. One of the points was that couples were supposed to have children and that physical intimacy was only to be employed between lawfully married couples. It said the children thereby created were entitled to be born within the bonds of matrimony and to be raised by a mother and father who were completely faithful to each other.

Wow! There was a novel idea in this day and age! Yet as she considered this, she knew it was exactly right. Wouldn't the world be a better place for the small people if they all were born into homes where that was the case?

As the second man took a turn and the lesson went on, she became engrossed. Never before in any church service had she ever sat in on a lesson where the doctrine was so firmly set as to have no question of its interpretation. The principles this paper proclaimed were to the point, and there was no equivocation involved. Even as the teacher went on and comments were made or questions asked, it was only to enlarge upon topics that were already crystal clear.

Families were to be based on the principles of faith, prayer, repentance, forgiveness, respect, love, compassion, work and wholesome recreational activities. At this point, she was just about in open amazement at how clearly and concisely this document went about discussing what sounded like the ideal situation for the human race. Who had come up with this? It was like the U.S. Constitution for humankind! It was incredibly well thought out and written!

The third teacher stood up to take over and moved on to state that by divine design men are to preside over their families with love and righteousness, and are to provide for the necessities of life and protection of their families. And that women are primarily responsible for the nurture of their children.

A.J. was suddenly a bit uncomfortable with the direction this lesson was going and could almost feel Sean begin to squirm beside her even though he didn't even look up at her. She had to consciously focus to hear the rest of the lesson, deciding to take the issues she had out later when she had a minute to examine them more closely.

The teacher followed up the portion she considered rather chauvinistic and sexist with the statement that husbands and wives were to help each other as equal partners, and that some circumstances would necessitate adaptation. This mild disclaimer helped mollify her somewhat.

The lesson wound down with an almost biblical warning that disintegration of the family would be calamitous all around, and with a call to responsible citizens and governments to help strengthen families everywhere. Just before the final prayer, they mentioned that anyone who didn't have their own copy could have one of the ones they'd passed out, and she decided to keep hers to think about later. She folded it and put it in her Bible and stood up when Sean did, to file out the door with the others.

He didn't say anything as they left the classroom, but his earlier teasing mood seemed to have dissipated completely and she wondered what had happened to wipe his smile away. She tried to think back and figure out what would be bothering him and decided she didn't know him well enough to even know which of those principles would trouble him. The whole nurturing woman and bread winning man thing sounded to her like just what he'd been preaching the other morning as they fixed fence. She wished as they went into the main sanctuary of the church that they'd had a moment or two to talk about what they'd just been taught. He didn't hold her hand once as they went in to be seated near the others, but he did put his hand on the small of her back as they paused to settle into the pew.

When they were seated she heard him let out a slow sigh and she looked up at him, a little troubled at his obvious lack of smile. She caught his eye and he looked back at her almost as if he was trying to read her thoughts as much as she was trying to read his. She didn't know what was wrong, or if she'd caused it, but she'd learned long ago that head games were a bad idea, so she made a mental note to come right out and ask him when she had the chance and for now, reached for his hand. As she took it, she looked at him again. The other girls were nowhere near, so he had to know this was for her not them. He met her gaze and when she leaned her head gently against his shoulder, she could almost feel him take a breath and relax.

Chapter 13

When Sean finished teaching the deacon quorum, he was in a great mood. His class had gone remarkably well considering that sexual purity could have been a rather uncomfortable topic. Not only had his class gone well, but being with Lexie had a definite upward pull on his attitude, even without having the chance to touch her, and holding her hand and almost kissing her brought on a ridiculous mild euphoria.

He had to smile to himself as he went back into the Relief Society room for gospel doctrine class. She looked good sitting there with the other women in his family. He was surprised again at how beautiful she was. She'd been incredible the first time he had seen her in the racy suit and with her hair all pinned back, but that was nothing to the way she looked today in her classy suit and her hair down in all it's glory! He sat down next to her hoping to be able to hold her hand again, uncaring that his brothers were going to have a heyday at his expense over it.

Her "Great!", when he asked how her class went, was comforting. He'd been somewhat worried that someone would get into some deep discussion this first day that would offend the latent feminist in her, so her positive answer had eased his mind. That was until he got a glimpse of her notes. The lesson had been on Julie B. Beck's conference talk about the mothers of the stripling warriors, and it had been mildly controversial even among active women in the church. Sister Beck wasn't one to mince words and that talk had ruffled a few of the more liberal women's feathers. Seeing her notes now, he had to wonder that she thought the lesson was great. It certainly hadn't been a talk championing professional women.

As he sat there and began to understand that the Sunday school lesson being given by the bishopric was to be on the family proclamation, his stress level ratcheted up a notch or two. For some reason he wanted her to like church today with a hope that was all out of proportion to the length of time he'd known her.

Even though the bishop and his counselors were teaching a wonderful lesson, he kept catching himself focusing more on Lexie and her take on it all than trying to get his own measure of good out of it. He knew she was listening intently, and her note taking was singularly impressive, but he knew what the proclamation contained and in his small portion of wisdom, he wished the lesson today was on anything but nurturing mothers.

He struggled to feel the Spirit, and when he could tell that she got a little uncomfortable with the men presiding and breadwinning part, he felt the leak in his earlier euphoria deflate with a rush.

Knowing there wasn't much he could do at the moment to soften the forthright doctrine, he prayed for her, and for guidance in what to say in the conversations he felt sure would come up sometime. He was too stressed over wondering whether she was offended, to even think to enjoy the whole stinkbug pest control thing on the way to Sacrament meeting.

But when she looked up at him with those honest green eyes and took his hand in an obvious gesture of goodwill, it went a long way toward warming his heart. She knew exactly what he was feeling somehow, and was making the effort to comfort him, even though she probably didn't know why he was uptight.

He was sure she had been less than enthusiastic about a couple of parts of that last lesson, but she was drawing a distinct line between her friendship with him and whether she embraced his beliefs without question. He wanted her to understand and believe the doctrine, but he also valued their budding friendship. A moment later when she almost snuggled over against his arm he relaxed and decided to just enjoy the journey, leaving all the aspects he had no control over up to the one with far greater influence than he could ever have.

That was a great theory, but after a youth speaker on temple marriage, and a recent return missionary talking about the importance of priesthood in the home, when Sean understood that the high councilman would be speaking on David O. McKay's quote, "No Other Success Can Compensate For Failure In The Home", he looked right at her and sighed. You couldn't have hand picked a slate of topics for the day that would have been any more pointed. She gave him an almost sympathetic smile and squeezed his hand again. He wasn't sure if that meant she wasn't offended or that she wasn't buying into any of this enough to care. Either way, he wished they could have just had a good old-fashioned talk about honesty or Christ.

On the way home, it ended up being just her and him driving in his truck, and as they approached it, he was almost a little depressed until he saw her try to get in without the step pulled down. Her struggle to get her heels and dress into the high cab made him laugh out loud again. He put a hand on her shoulder to gently pull her back as he reached under the running board for the step and said, "It really isn't as entertaining, but I guess it's necessary from time to time to be accommodating."

Straightening her linen suit and buckling up, she asked, "Is it honestly necessary to have a truck this tall, or is this a self image thing?"

He pulled out of the parking lot. "Please tell me that was a rhetorical question. Is my self image really in question because I have a big truck?"

She studied him across the cab for a moment. "No, I guess you must need the truck. What exactly do you need this tall of a truck for, may I ask?"

He chuckled. "Uh... To drive over tall stuff? Wouldn't that be the only logical reason? Nice try though."

You can't tell me what you do yet? Is it really that bad? You don't seem like the kind of guy to do questionable work. I've been trying all morning to figure out what could be so terrible."

With a tired smile he said, "I didn't say what I do is bad. I just said it's going to make you mad. There's a difference. What I do is actually very cool, but you're not gonna like it."

She focused on his face and gave a slight frown that seemed to mirror his own worries, but then only said teasingly, "You're pretty sure of me. How do you even know what I like and don't like?"

With a sigh he said, "This one's kind of a no brainer, I'm afraid."

Changing the subject, she asked, "Where did your smile go in church? What made you so unhappy in the last meeting?"

He decided to be honest. "I was hoping today would be one of those golden rule, Jesus is the Christ and we should be honest kind of meeting days, but I'm afraid you got a triple wammy on subjects I wasn't sure you'd agree with. I just don't want you to be offended." He smiled at her and looked back at the road. "I can't imagine the whole 'husband should preside over the home' bit went over all that well with you, did it? It's not exactly the feminist's point of view these days."

"You're right. It's not, but then none of the 'have babies and be a nurturing mother, and happy wife' stuff is. Heck, being Christ like isn't even a feminist view. I guess you just have to decide whether you believe the Bible to have truly come from God or not, and then worry more about what He thinks than what the feminists think."

He stared at her so long that she pointed out the windshield like she was worried he would drive off the road and he said, "That is *not* what I expected you to say. Then you don't necessarily buy into the whole feminist thing in its entirety?"

She shook her head. "Please tell me that was a rhetorical question." He could hear the smile in her voice. "There are several places in the Bible that talk about how God wants men to be the head of the house. I actually liked today's version of that best because there was a very succinct addendum about equal partners and presiding in righteousness. Women wouldn't have near the power struggle plugging into what the men in their lives recommended if they were

111

always sure he was plugged into what God recommended first, like Paul taught. Not many people want to have all of the control; they just want to be respected when it's their turn."

"But what about being a feminist?"

"I prefer to analyze the data and then make an intelligent decision based on fact and my own good judgment. I hope the day never comes that I let someone else decide what I'm going to think or believe simply because we're the same gender and they create the most fuss. That's a bit frightening isn't it? Can you imagine being expected to think along with the most loud and obnoxious men?"

"Why were you giving me so much grief about professional women the other day then? Isn't that along the same lines?"

She was hesitant to answer him, but finally said, "In all honesty I've spent a great deal of time mulling over your take on society and women in the last couple of days, and I've come to the conclusion that . . . I need to do a lot more thinking. I was probably just miffed the other day by your comments about my suit. Mostly I was ticked off because I knew you were exactly right and that I should never have dragged that thing out of the back of my closet." She gave a self-deprecating laugh. "Eric calls that my call girl suit."

"Who is this Eric who he would dare to say something like that to you?" He wasn't sure he liked the sound of someone that casually close to her.

When she answered, her voice was happier than he'd ever heard it. "Eric would be my twin brother. He's the human solely responsible for preserving my sanity for the last twenty-seven years. He puts up with me and that's saying something!"

He turned to stare at her again. "Do you mean there's a male red headed spitfire somewhere?"

"Oh heavens no! He's dark with coal black hair and he's as mellow as the summer sun. How do you think he puts up with me?" She continued, "He's about half earth groupie and lives in a cabin up in the hills in Arizona, with his wife and kids. He's a photographer with that whole artist who has no need for analysis thing down. My drive to figure things out and fix them makes him crazy!" Her voice softened. "Sometimes I wish I could be as laid back as he is. He has nothing to prove, while I feel like I have to prove everything. It's terribly exhausting sometimes."

He wondered if she was saying that to him or to herself and asked, "If you wish you didn't feel that way, can't you just decide not to go there? Can't you just make a conscious decision to let some things go?"

"Now you sound just like him. He thinks I can, but so far, I've always felt like I had to prove I was capable and valuable. That I could do whatever it takes just to prove I'm all right. When I put it into words it sounds so unstable."

He reached across and took her hand. "Incredibly competent yes, unstable no. Do you feel like you have to prove things when you're around Eric?"

She loved the feel of Sean's calloused hand holding hers. "No, that's the only time I can relax and simply hang out. He loves me no matter what, and I'm all okay when I'm with him."

"Why is he in Arizona and you're in LA?"

She shook her head. "I wonder that a lot. We grew up just north of LA, but after college, he and his wife went in search of peace. They found it in Flagstaff. He seldom ever goes back to the city. But I needed to be there to pursue my career."

Once Enchanted

He thought about that for a few moments and then asked her what her parents were like. When she tried to explain her mother, she seemed to have a hard time describing her and almost sounded bitter, and he knew she still had a long way to go before she could stop feeling like she had been cheated in that department. It sounded like she' must have been about three when she started feeling as if she was the one raising her mother. He wondered aloud, "Maybe she's the reason you feel like you have to prove your worth. Because she never did."

She considered that for a few minutes in silence and he changed the subject again. "What kind of church do you attend back home?"

She looked over at him as if trying to figure out where that came from. "Methodist, why?"

With a shrug, he said, "I was just wondering how closely what you were hearing today matched with what you hear there."

Again, she considered that for several seconds before she answered, "The Methodists are a pretty conservative bunch, but today there was almost a feeling of exactness that I've never felt in any other church. Usually what you get is the interpretation of whoever happens to be preaching at the time, but today it seemed like there were definite ways every concept was to be taken. That would be great if you could know that that particular definite way was indeed God's interpretation of the principle."

After a moment, he commented, "I think you're absolutely right. But how would you ever know that? That it was God's interpretation?"

Still thoughtful, she finally said, "Well, you'd either have to ask Him directly, or ask someone who could

114

speak for him. I'm afraid my asking directly tends to be less than satisfying. I'm sure He answers my prayers, but sometimes I scramble the answer trying to listen.

"But then I never know what to believe when I ask different preachers who supposedly can speak for him. You'd think that His answers really would be the same yesterday, today, and forever." After another minute, she mused, "It's a shame there aren't still prophets around today. They would be very helpful in things like this. I wonder why God used to talk to his children here on earth, but not anymore."

Sean almost wanted to just keep letting her ask and answer her own questions. Her analytical way of considering what an intelligent God would do was causing her to ask the right ones. She probably would have figured all of life out eventually, but he told her anyway. "There actually is a prophet on the earth today who speaks for God. He only lives a few hours from here. You're right. God wouldn't quit talking to his children."

This time it was her turn to turn and stare at him. At first, she seemed to think he was joking, but when he glanced over at her, he tried to make sure she knew he was sincere. He hoped she knew from the time spent with him that he was at least half way intelligent, and he thought she'd learned to trust him.

She didn't answer him right away. Apparently this was one that she had to take out and examine for awhile before she could decide how she felt about it. At length she asked, "How do you know he's a prophet?"

Without hesitating, he said, "I asked God directly. You were right about that concept too."

She frowned, confused, and asked, "Is this a personal thing? Or is it part of the church we went to today with your family?" Her mind was still asking the right questions.

"He's the head of the church we went to today. The head of Christ's church here upon the earth. He's the prophet for everyone in the whole world, but not everyone believes in him."

After considering this, she said, "All the prophets throughout history have had that same issue, unfortunately."

Chapter 14

Good heavens! Literally! A prophet. And Sean didn't seem like a wacky religious radical. Actually, the furthest thing from it. A.J. almost felt like she'd been knocked over the head with a new paradigm, but it made sense.

They rode almost the whole rest of the way in silence, each busy with their own thoughts, but the quiet was comfortable. As the miles fell behind, it seemed they both felt there was a new found depth to their friendship.

After coming through the locked gate, they came upon the other cars from the family stopped. There was a whole herd of cows both loose on the road and grazing in the unfenced field beside it.

Sean stopped and got out to help his dad and brothers drive the cows out of the field and up onto the road. When he came back to the truck to continue home, he said, "That rich alfalfa will kill them if they eat too much of it, so Dad and Treyne are going to stay and keep them on the road, while the rest of us run up and change out of our suits. They're actually the neighbor's cows. I'm not even sure where they got out of."

As they continued on up the road, she was amazed that these guys could go from ranch hand, to elegant suit, and sometimes even do both at the same time with such ease and style. Had she met him in a board room in what he was wearing right now, she never would have believed he was as at home on a horse with a rope in his hand as he was dressed to the teeth. And that didn't even deal with his casual offer to go tow her car for his friend Brandon, or what a marvelous cook he was. She watched him as he drove, more intrigued than ever.

He dropped her at his mom's and gravel went flying as he sped away to his home to change and go back to herd cows. She went in and changed her own clothes, deep in thought about their recent conversation. He had spoken of the prophet in such a matter-of-fact way that it wasn't until now that she realized she'd accepted his explanation of a relatively earth shaking concept without much struggle. Somehow, she'd known, even as he said it, that he truly believed it, and that he was correct. His sincerity, and an almost tangible spirit there in the truck, had left her with no doubt.

Now she had no idea what to do with this little bomb he'd just dropped. She wished Eric was here so she could talk to him in private about the things she'd been taught today.

She came out to the great room where she found Isabel with her hair pulled up into a wild knot on the top of her head, busily cooking up a storm in the kitchen by herself and A.J. asked her what she could do to help. Isabel gladly said, "Can you peel and chop the potatoes? I'm sorry, there appear to be thousands. Feeding this whole family still amazes me. I grew up around jockeys who all weigh like a hundred and seventeen pounds. Sometimes I watch how much food we eat when we're together here and it blows my mind!"

A.J. was good with the relatively simple potatoes.

She was much more comfortable with an office than a kitchen, but wanted to pitch in, so the vegetable peeler was actually very reassuring. She peeled and watched Isabel bustle around as if she was a chef, seasoning simmering dishes and mixing and pureeing. Isabel, on the other hand, obviously thrived in this environment, and finally A.J. asked, "So you grew up in California and came here with Slade?"

Isabel tasted the sauce she was making and said, "I was raised just to the east of the L.A. area out in the country. Well, when I lived there I thought it was the country, but living here brings a whole knew definition to rural!"

"But you still have a business there don't you? Didn't Naomi say you had a farm there or something?"

Isabel stopped bustling for just a moment, thinking. "It seems so far away now. My brother and I have Wind Dance Farms there. You may have heard of it. We actually had the Kentucky Derby winner last year. He and his father run it completely now that I'm married. When I was younger, I assumed that I'd grow old and die there, but after being here with Slade, it doesn't even feel like home. I miss the people sometimes, but I'm happier here by far."

A.J. was stunned! That was one of the biggest and most famous Thoroughbred farms in the country! They were always in the news for some new world-class race winner!

Almost reverently, she said, "Wow, when Naomi said you had a horse farm in California, she really meant it! How long have the two of you been married?" A.J. had noticed that although Isabel and Slade were exact opposites physically, she was smaller and blonde and he was tall and dark, they were close and very much in love. Slade treated her with a deference that was positively inspiring.

Isabel smiled a serene smile. "A little over two years. It's been the best time of my life. I joined the church just before that and, between having the gospel and being with Slade, I'm happier than I ever dreamed possible." She bent to take a huge roast out of the oven.

"You mean you haven't always been a member of their church?"

Isabel shook her head. "Only for a year or two. I wish I'd always had the church in my life. If I'd been raised in the gospel, my childhood would have been much more pleasant, but perhaps knowing what life is like without it has made it all the more precious to me. Kit is so glad she found the church she's almost a fanatic about sharing it. She had a horrible childhood and grew up in a foster home, and the gospel is her greatest treasure."

The surprise must have shown on her face. Isabel smiled as she continued, "Don't be surprised. Naomi and Marti and Slade all joined the church as adults. Rob was the beginning of it all for this family. Maybe that's why it's so important to us, because most of us had to muddle along as best we could without it for so long. We've felt the difference that knowing who we are and why we're here has made. It's a wonderful thing." A.J. put the cut potatoes into a pot of water while her mind struggled to picture the people Isabel had just mentioned as outsiders at church just as she'd been today.

After a thoughtful moment, she said, "Sean told me today there was a prophet. I'd been wondering why God would leave us without one to try to figure out which interpretation of the Bible was the correct one.

120

Do you believe this man is really a prophet of God like Noah or Moses?

Isabel turned to look at her squarely. "Yes, I absolutely do, but you don't need to take my word for it. You can ask for yourself. He'll help you to know for sure." Looking at her watch, Isabel said, "I wonder how long they'll be with the cows. I hate to let all this food get cold. I guess I'll just let it all sit in a warm oven until we see the whites of their eyes."

A.J. asked, "Who?"

Isabel looked at her as if she'd lost it. "I beg your pardon?"

"Who should I ask? About whether this man really is a prophet or not?"

"Oh. God, of course. For a minute there, I thought you were asking who'd gone with the cows. I wondered if holding Sean's hand had rattled your brain!" She gave A.J. a smile as she teased her, "Those stink bugs weren't very happy to see you today, were they?" Her musical laughter peeled out, and A.J. couldn't help but laugh with her.

They were laughing together as Marti and Kit came in holding Mimi's hands between them. As she automatically began to help with the dinner, Marti asked, "What are you two in here giggling about?"

A.J. blushed and Isabel winked at her and said, "We were just laughing about how Sean's stink bugs weren't very happy to see Alexis here at church holding his hand."

Naomi bustled in, saying, "I heard that Isabel! Cooper has corrupted the whole family. He was the one who started calling them stink bugs."

When A.J. looked up at Naomi wondering who

121

Cooper was, she must have been able to read her mind, because Naomi went to her kitchen desk, picked up a framed photograph, brought it over and said, "These are my boys. You know Rob and Rossen, and Slade, and, of course, Sean." She nudged A.J. with her elbow. "He's the one the deacons caught you almost kissing this morning!"

Marti looked up and said, "Wow, Sean kissed you? Really?"

A.J. blushed and looked around and they all laughed as Naomi went on, "And here's Ruger and Treyne. And then this last shorter one is my youngest, Cooper. He's on a mission right now in Paraguay; he'll be back in just a couple of months. He'll probably have grown three or four inches by then like they all did on their missions, so he'll be about the same height as the rest of them when he gets home. Isn't he handsome?"

He was, just like the rest of them. They were the most strikingly good-looking bunch of men A.J. had ever seen. The whole bunch of them looked like something out of a magazine. A very masculine magazine! A.J. said, "He is very handsome. All of your boys are. Except for Slade, they look just like your husband. I'll bet he was a lady killer in college."

Naomi got this dreamy look in her eyes, and the others all smiled as she fairly sighed, "He was the most beautiful man I'd ever seen! I know men aren't supposed to be beautiful, but he was. He still is." She smiled as she pitched in to help. "I'm very lucky to have him! There were a number of other girls who were rather determined that I wasn't going to get him! I had to use all of my feminine wiles!"

Her eyes twinkled. "You'd better not get me

started on how cute Rob was in college. The guys will be back and I'll have forgotten all about dinner."

They all went back to their various tasks and Kit put Mimi in a high chair beside her with some little toys. Finally, A.J. had to ask, "How did you all know that Sean and I almost got caught kissing this morning?"

Amidst several different laughs, Kit said, "The boys were talking about it in the foyer and Gladys Maggleby heard them. Once she gets a tidbit, it's all down hill from there."

Naomi chuckled as she said, "Look at it this way. Hopefully those two young ladies will think you and Sean are practically betrothed and maybe he'll have some peace again at church around here."

Putting a hand on A.J.'s arm, Kit reassured her, "You don't need to worry. Sean has an impeccable reputation. No one will think a thing about it except to be surprised that he has finally found someone he's interested in kissing. Your reputation could never be harmed by a man as wonderful as Sean."

"Speaking of church." Naomi cut in, "How did you deal with that full palate of dissertations on the ideal Mormon woman and family? We don't usually get that big of a load all in one day, but today we sure did."

Almost speechless with surprise, A.J. turned to them all and asked, "Mormon? You're all Mormons? But, I thought Mormons were an anti Christian cult that dealt with stifled and downtrodden polygamist women? You're kidding me! That was a Mormon church I went to with you this morning?" She looked from one to the other of them as they all looked back at her.

Finally, Isabel said with a completely straight face,

123

"It's true. We're all hopelessly downtrodden."

"And stifled." That was Marti.

Kit added, "I'm the most stifled and downtrodden of all."

Isabel turned to her, "Hey, you can't be the most downtrodden! I'm sure I am!" They began to go back and forth. "I am. No I am." This went on for a couple of seconds until they began to hit at each other's hand like paddles.

Marti interrupted them, "Wait! We're supposed to be polygamists too. Who's going to be whose wife?"

Isabel jumped in, "I get Slade! And I'll also take…"

She pretended to be deep in thought as A.J. burst out laughing and finally said, "All right, all right! I get the point. I'm sorry for being an uneducated lout. I deserved that!" She looked around her at these obviously happy and adored wives and mothers and wondered where she'd gotten so turned around.

They were laughing uproariously when the men all came in. Some of them had laughed themselves to tears and the guys looked at them as if they'd lost it. They'd almost gained some semblance of sobriety when Rossen said, "Oh, great!" with a stupid French accent. "The loose cows have finally pushed them over the edge!" The whole room cracked up again and it took them almost twenty more minutes to get the dinner that was ready onto the table. Through it all, Mimi sat in her chair watching as if it was some hilarious movie, giggling at these crazy adults with two fingers in her mouth. It was after three o'clock before they were even through with Sunday dinner.

Afterward, everyone pitched in to clean it all up and put everything away. A.J. thought back to her and Sean's discussion about how women had gotten the

124

short end of the stick as far as being breadwinners and still having to do most of the housework. That certainly wasn't the case here. The men always pitched in after the meals to help straighten up. She was taking it all in very thoughtfully when she realized Sean was watching her. Sometimes she wondered if he could read her mind.

Once Enchanted

Chapter 15

When the kitchen was restored to its proper order, everyone went his or her separate ways to a certain extent. She and Sean found themselves in rockers on the deck, along with Rossen, Kit and Mimi, and Slade and Isabel. She could see Rob and Naomi walking hand in hand on a path across the valley nearing the pond. Treyne and Ruger were having a game of horseshoes down on the lawn while Marti had gone out on an emergency call.

They'd all been sitting there for a moment just quietly watching the game when Mimi climbed down from her mother's lap and up onto Sean's. She snuggled over, laid her head on his chest, and with two fingers in her mouth went right to sleep. It was all A.J. could do not to stare at them. He was an incredibly attractive man, and snuggled there with the little girl who so obviously adored him, his appeal was almost hypnotic.

Slade and Isabel were in a hanging porch swing, and at first they were rocking a little but they soon began to snuggle too and just when it was about to get a tad embarrassing, they got up and announced they were going home. Kit and Rossen weren't far behind them and they peeled Mimi off Sean's chest and set off across the way.

Sean pulled his rocker over close to A.J.'s and took her hand. It was so easy and natural to be here with him like this. She leaned toward him in her own chair and leaned her head against his. The lazy peace she felt at sitting here on the porch of people who had been complete strangers would have amazed her except she was too comfortable to even think about it. She gave his hand a gentle squeeze as she felt herself drifting off to sleep.

When she woke up more than an hour later, she found him sound asleep beside her, his head still leaned against hers and her hand still cradled in his strong brown calloused one. She caressed the back of it with her thumb.

She thought about her office back in L.A. and tried to figure out what exactly it was that she wanted in life. She'd pulled out of there several days ago knowing she had to make some changes and hoping this road trip would help her find her way to a clear decision. Her thoughts at that point were to put out some resumes to other law firms in the greater Los Angeles area and simply switch firms. Now, she looked across to see Rob and Naomi slowly making their way back toward their home and her mind struggled over the idea of making much bigger changes than that.

So many new experiences here had changed her whole outlook on her life. She wasn't sure she could go back to the life she was living before. She wasn't sure she could even go back to the same goals she had before. When she realized she was actually thinking that, she almost stood up to pace. She would have except she didn't want to wake up Sean and have him move away from her. She felt his breath gently in her hair and she could smell his aftershave.

128

She tried to concentrate on her decisions and not him, and it took all the will power she had. There were so many things to try to figure out. Probably the first thing she needed to do was decide for sure in her own mind what she wanted—really wanted, out of this life. She thought back to his comment about remembering what the goal was. What was the goal for her? After seeing life lived on the Rockland's terms, she wondered if she would ever be satisfied with being just a professional ever again.

She had to smile to herself when she caught herself thinking the phrase "just a professional". For about forever, being a professional was what she'd thought she wanted more than anything.

His stirring beside her interrupted her mental note taking. He leaned around the edge of their chair backs to kiss her gently on the mouth and ask sleepily, "What are you so deeply thinking about behind those green eyes?" He looked into them before kissing her one more time.

His mouth had completely wiped out her train of thought and he smiled at her when he could see the look of confusion on her face for just a moment or two. Finally, she said, "Honestly, I was wondering if being here this week hasn't changed my whole life's perspective, but I would never admit that to you for fear of losing my feminist image."

This time it was him caressing the back of her hand with his thumb. He leaned around even more to look her full in the face and studied her. He didn't say anything, just looked at her, and she marveled that he didn't try to influence her thoughts. Finally, he asked, "Is that a good thing?" He was watching her intently while he waited for her answer.

Her brow wrinkled slightly as she tried to gather her thoughts. "I truly don't know. In the first place, it's hard to think with you so close, and in the second, it's hard to even face wondering if I've spent so much time and effort barking up the wrong tree. I wish there was a fortune teller who could tell me what the right course of action is for me. I know something has to give back home. I knew that before I ever left L.A. I'm pouring my heart and soul into somebody else's success and even though I'm carrying a great deal of the load there, instead of gaining their respect and getting ahead, they all think I'm just their sucker that they can take advantage of. I have to make some changes and I know that, it's just a pain to make the decision and take that first step."

He still looked at her without saying anything, and at length, she asked, "Now what are you thinking behind those blue eyes?"

Leaning back in his chair again, he said, "That you're beautiful. And so smart that I'm sure whatever you come up with will be exactly what your Father in Heaven has in mind for you." He squeezed her hand as he closed his eyes again.

Now how was a person supposed to deal with input like that? She'd never have admitted it to him, but she'd been hoping for some wise counsel. At first, she was slightly disappointed, until she realized he'd just given her a huge commendation while at the same time, a couple of subtle hints to try to help her make her decisions with an eternal perspective while still embracing her femininity.

Somehow, he'd known innately that it would never work to order her around, but that she needed to know he thought she was capable and trusted her judgment. It took every bit of the rebellious spirit right out of her.

They sat there in comfortable silence while she continued to try to think about her future, and he occasionally stroked the back of her hand. Naomi and Rob came up onto the porch on their way into the house. They smiled at her in passing, but didn't say anything, probably thinking Sean was still asleep.

A.J. still had trouble comprehending that Naomi was an attorney. She was the consummate mother and had obviously done a wonderful job. Her children all seemed to be good, honorable, hardworking people.

Naomi worked around the ranch. A.J. knew she was always doing something, whether it was the cooking, tending to her large garden, working beside Rob with the animals, or in their office. But A.J. also knew that Naomi was doing what she wanted to be doing, and not following orders while somebody else called all the shots. Rob always treated her with the utmost respect, and the fact that they worked together as parents was never left to doubt. She'd said she still practiced when she felt truly compelled to, but it wasn't her focus that she poured all of her passion into. There was no doubt that Naomi's family was her life's work and that she wanted it that way.

A.J. had come to feel like Naomi was a true friend in these last few days and she valued her wisdom and experience. She decided to pick her brain the next time she got the opportunity.

Beside her, Sean stretched in his chair and asked, "What are you going to do this evening? Do you have anything in mind?"

She looked over at him. "Are you up to the same walk your parents just took?"

Giving her an easy smile, he said, "I don't know. That's a lot to ask isn't it?"

"I know, but you know me. I just want it all."

He got to his feet and stretched again, then reached down for her and pulled her to her feet beside him. "Do you need something to eat first or are you okay without?" He put his hand on the small of her back as he asked.

"I'm okay for now. How about you?"

"I want to at least take something with. And you'll want a sweatshirt or jacket before too long. You grab something warmer and I'll run home and grab a hoody and some snacks and meet you back here in ten minutes." He gave her hair a tug before heading off the deck and to his truck. She watched him get in and drive away before she turned to go in search of her jacket.

Ten minutes later, hand in hand, they set off on the same trail Rob and Naomi had come back in on. It wound its way past the pond and then up toward the ridges that guarded the little valley. Their pace was a definite meander and she marveled at the scenery and the wildflowers growing along the trail. The path led through meadows and then woodlands, seemingly at its own pleasure. Part of the time, it followed a small stream that cascaded down through the little valley in a series of miniature waterfalls and deep amber pools. The evening sun cast long shadows that speckled the water gold and brown, and then silver and deep green, while each little fall murmured and riffled as they walked by.

Eventually, they topped the ridgeline and paused to take in the view of the world all around. She could see mountain ranges in every direction, the ones in the distance still snow capped at their peaks, and down in the next little valley a river glistened in the late afternoon sun. The breeze that blew into her face smelled of sage and pine and the creek. It was cool and fresh and felt like she was drinking in clear, cold water. It was almost too cool when they weren't walking and he wrapped his arms around her as she leaned back against him.

Leaning on him was the most secure feeling she'd ever experienced. There was no other way to put it. From the moment he'd stepped down from that stupid tow truck she'd known he was a man who had everything under control. She hadn't seen him get the slightest bit uptight, even when she knew she'd been a pill at times. The only time she'd seen him the tiniest bit flustered was when they had been kissing, and that was a good sign, wasn't it?

Turning in his arms to look up at him, there was something in his expression that was almost a little sad. She wondered why she felt so good with him, but he didn't look very happy. It was going to be awful when she had to drive away from here tomorrow. He must have been reading her thoughts again, because he wrapped his arms around her once more and said, "I'm going to miss you when you're car is fixed. I keep wanting to call Brandon and tell him there's no hurry. How selfish is that?" She pulled back enough to look up into his face and he gave her a halfhearted smile, took her hand again and turned to continue down the trail.

The way she felt about him and little comments like that confused her even further. They walked in silence again while she tried to figure out her life and what he was thinking at the same time. He was usually a pretty easy read. She'd never been around a guy who was confident enough to not play any kind of

Once Enchanted

head games at all. He was always honest with her,
even when he knew she possibly wasn't going to be
thrilled with what he was going to say. At least she
always thought so.

Sometimes she'd been ticked off, but she was never
in doubt about where he stood. Even when he was
telling her he liked her, he was pretty matter-of-fact
about it. However, the only time he had ever talked
about seeing her, once she left Wyoming, had been
when he'd been joking about the stinkbug thing. She
had no idea what to think about that.

They'd been on the trail for well over an hour when
they topped another rise as the sun was going down.
There was a huge fallen tree beside the trail and she
pulled him over to sit on it. This time there were no
clouds, and the sunset wasn't the spectacular glory of
color that the other sunrises and sets had been. The
brilliant yellow light was simply there, and then, all too
quickly the sun slipped below the horizon and it was
gone. It felt almost symbolic as she'd been thinking
about going back home to L.A. She wondered if her
time spent here that had felt like that sunny warmth
would simply slip away like the daylight.

They started back as the air noticeably chilled
within just a few minutes. The dusk falling around the
hills was still beautiful, even though her thoughts had
definitely dampened her mood, and she marveled at
how this wild, Wyoming countryside could be so
enchanting in any setting.

They weren't far along the trail when they stopped
to slip their jackets on. Tonight felt so much cooler
than the other nights had and she wondered if her
somber thoughts had somehow affected her body too.
Finally, she commented on the chill and he reassured

134

her, "There's no cloud cover tonight to hold the heat in. It'll probably be ten degrees, or more, colder than it's been since you've been here. We'll walk faster and warm up. That way we won't be walking so far in the dark."

He picked up the pace and when she started to breathe more heavily, she was a bit embarrassed until he said, "The air's a lot thinner here than down at sea level. Even after being here a few days, you probably can't breathe like you're used to."

Stopping for a breather, when she started to zip up her jacket, he pulled her into his arms again and she lingered there, against his heart listening to the strong, steady beat. This walk was probably not the best idea. She was more mixed up about her life than ever. Being this close to him completely loused up her concentration, and she was sure his strong arms skewed her perspective as well. A moment later, when she looked up at him and he lowered his head to kiss her, all concentration and perspective went completely out the window. She wasn't thinking of anything except his mouth, and how being held close made her feel.

This time their kiss was slow and mellow. It was almost as if they both wanted to slow down and savor the moment, making it last the way they both wished their time together could. The gentle pressure of his warm, firm mouth on hers brought her a peace that was heavenly even as it filled her whole body with sweet, sensual warmth. Nothing had ever felt so right.

When she finally pulled back to take a deep breath, he put both of his hands into her hair, spreading his fingers and then pulling gently on the handfuls as he rested his chin on top of her head. His voice was slightly husky when he said, "I was right last night when I said your kiss would haunt me when you went back to L.A. It already does just when I think about it."

Trying to lighten the moment, she gave a small, breathless laugh and said, "LA's not all that far away, plus you'll have all those stinkbugs to keep you entertained once I'm gone."

He expelled his breath through his lips. "Don't remind me about the stink bugs. It will ruin this." He leaned down to kiss the side of her neck gently, his words like a sigh. "LA feels like a long way."

His lips on that tender, sensitive skin gave her chills to her toes, and his breath on her ear made her shiver in pleasure. She wrapped her arms more tightly around him, feeling the muscles in his back ripple under her hands on his shirt. As she rubbed over his back, his hands tightened in her hair and he brought his mouth back to hers with an almost silent groan. Just for a moment, he kissed her almost hungrily, and then backed off to those sweet, mellow kisses again. This time, he pulled away.

He let out a long sigh and tugged gently on her hair one last time. "LA feels like a long, long way." He took her hand again and reluctantly turned back down the path. It was full dark now and they walked more slowly, their only light was that of a few stars in the sky and a lingering lighter skyline behind the ragged pines and peaks to the west. Their walk in the dark became all but dreamy as her eyes adjusted to the dark and the forest began to look silver the nearer they got to home.

As they walked, it took a minute or two to realize that what she was hearing was music and not just the wind in the trees. She pulled up to stand, poised, listening, trying to figure out what exactly it was.

136

Beside her, he whispered, "It's Kit. She's playing at the fire. It's not far ahead, up around that corner." At his words, she noticed the smell of wood smoke for the first time. There was just a hint of it caught on the breeze.

They walked on in the almost mystical darkness, with what felt to A.J. like the music of the fairies playing hide and seek with the night wind. She could easily imagine the mythical woodland people her grandmother had told her about in these magical woods and meadows.

As they walked, the moon came up over the ridge and the landscape was bathed in an ethereal light. Now she could hear the stream too as it tumbled over the rocks and around the boulders in its path. The mist that rose from it wafted away in the moonlight like the music that drifted intermittently through the trees.

As they walked closer, the music became more distinct, and finally, they could hear Kit's voice and her guitar clearly from just up around the bend. She was playing an old Don Williams song and A.J. pulled Sean to a stop before they followed the path around the corner and asked, "Dance with me? One last time? Something for me to remember when I'm back home in reality."

He turned back to her and as he pulled her close, he whispered the question in her ear, "Are the little woodland people watching?"

She smiled and snuggled against him. "I'm sure they are."

They swayed together to the fairy music there in the enchanted forest night. It was even better than dancing in the kitchen. Kit sang and they danced close, and occasionally it was more kissing than dancing, but whatever it was, it was heaven. A.J. didn't even realize when Kit switched songs.

They danced through that ballad too until Kit chose a faster beat. They reluctantly pulled away and turned back to the path. Just as they started to walk, Sean tugged her back and said, "Lexie, there's something I need to tell you."

She tried to read his eyes in the dim light and asked, "Is it going to spoil this perfect night?"

"Possibly." He hesitated. "Probably."

She put her fingertip to his lips. "Then don't. Save it for another time. I want to remember tonight as the perfect mid summer's eve." He seemed to hesitate for a minute and then finally nodded and turned back to the trail.

They came around the corner to find everyone except Ruger and Marti were gathered around a blazing fire, seated on huge logs while Kit sat with them and played her guitar. No one even seemed to notice when they slipped in and sat down. Their logs were a couple of feet apart and A.J. felt ridiculously bereft when he let go of her hand and sat that far away. She laughed to herself to admit she had become disgustingly mushy.

Later that night, after turning off the light in her room, she went to the window and opened her blind. Across the valley she could see his beautiful home. There were lights on in the kitchen window. She turned around and went to bed, mentally bracing herself to leave this place tomorrow. It had been a fun little interlude. One she would probably remember forever. She was sure there were things she'd done here that she would never do again all the rest of her life.

When she thought about dancing with him in the woods tonight, something in her stomach did a butterfly flutter. She wished she could tell someone about it. Even Eric wouldn't understand this enchanted evening. How could he when she didn't? She thought about walking back into her office. She needed to switch back into professional mode. She had to get her thoughts together, find this mysterious architect, and get back to real life. Turning onto her stomach, she breathed a long, soft sigh.

Once Enchanted

Chapter 16

Waking Monday morning was somewhat anticlimactic. He'd told her last night that he had something he had to do early this morning and that he couldn't come and haul her away this time. He'd sounded as disappointed as she'd felt when he'd kissed her goodnight in the shadow of his parents' house and then watched her walk in before going home. It was probably for the best. They'd only known each other since Thursday evening and she'd become unbelievably attached to him in that short time. It was probably good to not encourage anything more because she would be leaving today just as soon as her car was done.

She resolutely got out of bed and dressed in business slacks, a white blouse and heels for the first time in several days. She was heading back out to find this guy in awhile and was determined that today was the day. She twisted her hair back and packed up her luggage, doing her best to focus on accomplishing her assignment and not wondering where Sean was and what he was doing right now.

At five o'clock that afternoon, after driving through a gathering storm that piled the dark clouds against the mountains and buffeted Naomi's Jeep, A.J. pulled into their garage and got out and went into the house. She'd already decided to call Trent as soon as her car was ready and tell him just how little she'd accomplished in the last few days and find out if he still wanted her to stay in Wyoming until she found this guy or come on home.

She'd pounded both the town of Jackson and the newer subdivisions, but no one had been willing to tell her what she needed to know. She was relatively certain that at least two of the guys she'd talked to today had known who she was looking for, but neither of them had been willing to tell her anything. She left her name and Naomi's number with both of them again, and went back into Jackson to the county offices, but had hit a dead end there too.

She'd gotten a list of every project that House Upon a Rock Inc. had pulled permits for in the last year, but had batted zero at every single one. Most of the projects were complete and the few people she did find acted as if they didn't know what she was asking and refused to give her their boss's name.

She knew from the look on Naomi's face as she walked in that she must have looked as tired and disgusted as she felt. Sympathetically, Naomi asked, "Still no luck?" A.J. shook her head.

Naomi took her apron off and said, "Come into my office. Tell me what it is you're trying to find out and I'll start helping you. Maybe some of the people who won't cooperate with you will talk to me since I'm a local." She straightened a couple of things on her desk and then sat down and took out a pad and pencil. "Okay, now tell me who it is you're looking for."

A.J. pulled out the slim manila folder from her portfolio. "I only know his business name, and it's a blind corporation. I don't know who his attorney is, but they've done a killer job of asset protection for him.

I'm the third person Trent's had working on this and this guy's legal stuff is buttoned up to a T. He's apparently an architect who is also a general contractor, and does some marvelous stuff. I've seen his houses and they're works of art! The locals that I've found who know him are incredibly loyal and protective of him. Even this guy's competition seems to admire him." She opened her file and pointed to the paper on top. "The corporation's name is House Upon a Rock Inc."

Naomi sucked in her breath. "Oh my stars!" She sounded horrified and A.J. turned to stare at her. Naomi's face went white, and then red, and then she closed the folder. "On second thought. There are some other things I need to do this evening. Would you mind if I asked Sean to help you out instead of me? I think this is more along the lines of his expertise. In fact, I'm going to send you over to work in his office while I round him up. He's over helping Rob and the boys vaccinate horses right now."

She was practically pushing A.J. out of the room. "Take my car. You've been to Sean's house haven't you?" A.J. nodded her head. "You head on over and get started. Just go right on in. I'll tell him I told you to. His office is right off the front entry. Big, tall, wooden, double doors. You can't miss it. You get started and I'll see to it that he's there within just a few minutes to help you."

Wondering what in the world had so upset his normally unruffleable mother, A.J. asked, "What's wrong? Is there a problem with House Upon A Rock Inc.?"

Naomi looked her in the eye, and said almost as if she was talking to herself, "Oh, I imagine there's a problem all right. But it's one I won't be a party to.

Once Enchanted

Head on over to Sean's and you'll see what I mean soon enough."

A.J. shook her head and went back through the kitchen and was just going through the garage door when she heard Naomi say in a stern voice, "Sean, it's Mom. I think you should know I just sent a very pretty, red headed attorney to your house to work in your office!" There was a pause. "Yes and you deserve it!" A.J. heard her hang up, but she didn't even say goodbye.

Climbing into the Jeep, A.J. backed out of the garage completely at a loss as to what was going on. She parked in Sean's driveway and let herself in the front door with her paperwork in tow. Outside the seven-foot tall double doors, she stopped, almost a little afraid. She wasn't sure what Sean was going to think about this. And whatever was wrong had certainly shaken Naomi up. A.J. pulled open the doors and went in.

At first, she just stood inside and stared around. She'd never been inside a more beautiful office in her life! It was huge, with floor to ceiling, rich, dark, wood cabinetry and bookshelves that took up one whole wall. There was a grand rock fireplace that almost filled another wall and another was all windows that looked out over the entire valley. There were French doors out on to the adjoining deck where there was a stone table.

Before she even looked around, she went to the French doors and let herself outside. There were phone jacks and electrical outlets right on the deck just below a speaker set into the wall. Now this was an office!

She walked back inside. There were two large

Jaclyn M. Hawkes

desks of the same rich wood, one on each side of the room, with a large drafting table in the center that held some tools she didn't recognize and a number of the long white rolls she had seen Sean bring in here the other day. One of the desks held a phone and had some paperwork strewn across it, and was obviously the desk he used. The other one was bare and that entire section of the room appeared to be unused.

At first, she didn't understand and then wondered if he had built a double office with space for a partner or for the wife he someday wanted to have.

The remaining wall was hung with various plaques and framed pictures and she wandered over to look at it. Several of the pictures were of large, beautiful houses or office buildings and a restaurant, and she wondered why he would have them hanging on the wall of his office. One house in particular was familiar and she started to get a strange feeling in the pit of her stomach when she realized it was one of the houses she'd mentioned to Naomi she had seen of House Upon A Rock Inc.'s.

She moved on to the framed plaques. One was an award of some kind. It took her a moment to realize it was honoring the fact that Sean had served a two-year mission to Los Angeles, California.

She couldn't believe it! He'd lived in L.A. for two years! Little snippets of conversation came to her. Naomi mentioning her boys had grown three or four inches on theirs. At the time, she'd wondered on their what? They'd been talking about her youngest son's mission and A.J. just hadn't understood that all of the boys must have served. And Sean, mentioning at the cabin the other day that he had spent a couple of years away from home and had dreamed of coming back.

The mention of traffic, sirens, and jackhammers. If he had spent two years in her town, why had he never mentioned it?

Somewhat floored, she moved on to the next frame. It was a diploma stating that he had a degree in architecture. The hair on the back of her neck began to prickle as she went to the next frames. One was a general contractor's license from the state of Wyoming and the next was a local business license for none other than House Upon A Rock Inc.

She was too stunned to even move! She stood looking at the framed license in a state of shock. And she'd thought he was the most honest, trustworthy guy she'd ever met! That he never played head games! That he really liked her! This whole time he'd been laughing at her! Making an utter fool of her!

She turned around to go start looking for him when she noticed, stacked neatly on the corner of his desk, four of the Post-It notes she'd given out to different men with her own name on them, hoping they would be passed on to the man she was trying so hard to find.

This was the last straw! He'd warned her that she'd be mad when she found out what he did. Well, he was right! She was angrier than she'd ever been in her life!

She picked up the Post-Its as she turned toward his front door. Through the wall of windows she could see him coming across the pasture in the gusting wind. He was on Mamie, the flaxen maned mare she'd ridden the other day, and even mad she couldn't help herself as she watched him come galloping in. He drew up on his side lawn, jumped off and threw the reins as he took the stairs to his office deck two at a time.

Chapter 17

Somehow, when Sean felt the phone in his pocket start to buzz, he knew he was in trouble. He should have made her listen last night. But it had been heaven dancing there in the meadow and it hadn't taken much to talk him out of a more serious discussion. Now he wished they'd talked.

He listened to his mom tell him Lexie was headed to his office and turned to leave without even an explanation to his brothers. He caught up his horse and it took off before he was even all the way up. The way home had never seemed so long.

When he got to his house, he thought to himself that at least it was still standing. That was a plus. He strode in and stopped abruptly when he saw her standing there beside his desk with the Post-Its in her hand.

He should have made her listen last night.

The green fire that came from her eyes could have torched the whole place, but surprisingly, her voice was relatively calm when she said, "I hope you've had your laugh." They stood there staring at each other and then she abruptly turned on her heel to head for the double doors that led to the front of his house.

He caught her arm as she tried to walk past. She turned to look at him and if green fire could kill, he'd have been dead where he stood. "Lexie, I…"

She spun on him. "You what?" Finally, she let go with her anger. "You're such a jerk! A tow truck driver. A tow truck driver!" This last one she said at the top of her lungs. "I'm not gonna like what you do? I wore that stupid dress! I've wasted days! I walked into a smoky bar to find you! I trusted you!"

She strode past him and before he even knew what she was going to do, she ripped the framed business license off the wall and threw it as hard as she could against the rocks of the fireplace where it shattered explosively. She was headed next to the degree and when he realized what she intended he caught her around the waist just inches before her fingers reached the frame.

"Oh, no you don't!" She struggled to free herself, but he was far stronger than she was and she couldn't break his grip. Finally, she elbowed him hard in the ribs at the same time she stomped down on his foot and he let her go just long enough to switch gears and pick her up and throw her over his shoulder. With her kicking and yelling as she pounded on his back, he carried her out the French doors and down onto the lawn. He headed purposefully toward the pond, and he knew exactly when she realized she was going in.

She almost snarled his name, "Sean David Rockland! Don't you dare!" With every stride, she got louder and madder and she was fighting so hard that he almost dropped her just as he made it to the pond's edge.

He paused for a minute. "Are you gonna calm down?" He was winded from carrying her and wrestling her at the same time. She didn't answer him and he set her on her feet, and looked up just as she went to slap him. *Holy smokes!* Before she could

148

connect, he tackled her on the grass, picked her back up, and unceremoniously launched her as far out into the pond as he could throw her.

When she stood up, dripping, but still raging, he said, "Cool off, girl. When you think you can behave like an adult, we'll talk!" With that, he turned and strode back into the house, and slammed the door behind him.

Inside the house, he turned to see what she was going to do and realized that all of his brothers and his dad were sitting on their horses at the top of the hill watching. Even his mom, Isabel, and Joey were standing on the deck of his parents' house. No doubt, they'd all heard her yelling at him and then scream when he'd tossed her in. He could only imagine what his mother was thinking.

He turned to watch Lexie stomp out of the pond, wondering what to do with her next, and darned if she didn't walk right up to Mamie, still grazing placidly on the lawn and climb on her. He came out onto the deck just in time to see her kick her up into a flying gallop and watch her ride away.

It would have been your classic riding off into the sunset, only there was no sunset; only the angry, black clouds of the darkening storm and he instantly went through to his mudroom and grabbed the pack he always took hunting that held his emergency gear. He grabbed a heavy coat and a long yellow slicker and set off for the horse barn on the run. Rossen met him at the edge of the lawn and jumped off to offer him his horse. "You'd better ride, dude! Have you got your phone?"

Sean touched his pocket, then tied the coats onto the back of the saddle, and slung the pack around his waist as he stepped up onto the horse. Rossen slapped him on the leg and smiled and said, "I've been through that hell hath no fury like a woman scorned thing. Only mine didn't have red hair. It'll all work out in the end. Go get her." Sean wasn't quite as confident as Rossen about it all working out in the end as he put the horse to a gallop and tried to keep her in sight on the trail ahead.

Her head start was remarkable and Sean decided she was riding as furiously as she'd been fighting him and he began to pray as he rode into the frenzy of driving wind. What was this girl thinking? She was soaking wet for crying out loud! Moreover, it was getting dark and she was riding right into the face of a storm that promised to be no mild spring rain. Even allowing for how upset she was, this was stupid no matter how you sliced it! He rode on up the trail, sometimes glimpsing her in the distance but mostly just checking the trail once in awhile to see that this was still the way she was heading.

At a fork in the trail, his mouth went dry when he realized she had just chosen the most dangerous place on the entire ranch to ride into at a time like this. The trail was bad and up further it got steep, with a sheer drop off to the side that fell away sometimes for fifty or a hundred feet. It was rocky and a nasty ride for an experienced rider on the best of days.

For her to go up it now, a relative novice, with night and the storm was foolish beyond belief, but she didn't know that. From here, the trail appeared relatively mild. He hurried his horse along faster, wondering what he was going to say to her once he got close enough to get her to stop and turn around.

It was only a bit further on that he came upon her

suddenly. She'd stopped in the trail and gotten off to do something to the stirrups, and the howling of the wind up the canyon had drowned out the sound of his horse. She was still ridiculously angry when she looked up and saw him as she climbed back on and leaned over to adjust her foot in the stirrup. She went to spur her horse off and he caught the bridle in his hand just in time. For a minute there, poor Mamie didn't know what to do. When she couldn't do what either one of them was asking she began to prance and sidestep nervously.

There was still fury in Lexie's voice when she demanded, "Let her go! Who do you think you are playing with peoples lives? Just let her go, and get out of my way!"

He calmly looked her in the eye, but he had to almost shout to be heard above the wind, "Look Lexie. You're mad. I don't blame you. I'd be mad too. Just come home and be mad where you're not going to freeze to death and get lost in the storm and the dark. This trail gets bad up ahead. It's dangerous."

She was still glaring at him and he continued, "Come on, honey. I'm sorry. I should have told you. Come on. I'll make it up to you somehow. I'll positively grovel. I promise. Just don't do this. This is a bad decision. Remember? You're the one who thinks it through and makes a decision based on your best judgment. Think this one through. Please." It was hard to coax against the wind.

Just when he thought she was going to give in, there came a flash and a deafening crash just behind them. At the sound, his horse jumped and he lost his grip on Mamie's reins. Both horses spooked straight forward up the questionable trail. Sean worked to rein

151

in his horse and it was all he could do to keep it from flat out panicking, which was what he was afraid Mamie had just done with Lexie. The light was fading, and spitting rain was starting to fall. All he could do was try to follow her, praying she could get control.

After several minutes, the view ahead opened up and he could see them on the trail over hanging the rocky cliffs below. Lexie was struggling to pull the frightened horse up, but she was losing the battle and Sean's blood froze in his chest when there was another bolt of lightning and the horse reared. He thought his heart would explode as Lexie lost her balance and began to slide sideways off of Mamie, just as both horse and rider went over the edge.

Momentarily, he was blinded by the flash and it was several seconds before he realized that it was only Mamie who crashed and rolled all the way to the bottom of the canyon. The usually sweet natured mare made an almost human sound of fear before it was silenced and then there was nothing but the raging howl of the wind again.

Carefully Sean went on up the trail toward where Lexie had gone off, trying desperately to see if he could tell where she had landed. He had to get right to the trail above her before he could see her there below. She was lying on her back and side about twenty-five feet below the trail. She'd miraculously landed on a narrow ledge, but she wasn't moving and he could hardly breathe as he stood there above her and wondered if she had been killed or only badly hurt. His chest seemed to be made of cement.

Getting off his horse, he hurriedly stripped off his gear and Rossen's rope that still hung there. He pulled out his phone and tried to keep the rain off of it as he punched up Rossen's number. When Rossen answered, he told him as succinctly as possible what had happened and where he was. He ended with, "I'm going to climb down to her with your rope. I'll try to call you back if my phone will work in the storm."

He buttoned the phone back into his pocket and put on the slicker. Knotting the rope around a sturdy tree growing near the top of the cliff, he carefully let himself over the edge. When he got to the end of the rope, he was still a dozen feet above her and had to stop and study the rocks in the gathering darkness to figure out where to climb down the rest of the way, frantic to know if she was alive or not. When he finally reached her and knelt to feel for a pulse, the steady beat that throbbed against his finger was an overwhelming relief.

Instantly the sick tightening in his chest eased up and he could feel himself grow calm and sure. The very first thing he did was utter a very short, very heart felt prayer of thanks and then he placed his hands on her unconscious head and hurriedly gave her a blessing. Never in his life had he been more grateful for the priesthood's power.

He got into his pack to get out a flashlight and began to check her over. He couldn't see anything broken or bleeding right off, but he didn't dare move her for fear of a neck or back injury.

Lightning flashed and thunder rumbled down the canyon and he heard the horse above him spook off as the rain began in earnest. Looking around, he saw that a little further down the ledge there was a place where the rock was undercut. Back against the cliff face it was dry except when a swirling gust blew rain back in. He decided to try to move her even at the risk of injury to try to keep her out of the storm.

At her side, he knelt down and was carefully trying to gather her into his arms when she began to come to. Settling her back onto the ground, he brushed the hair back from her forehead. She moaned and then slowly opened her eyes. They were confused for a few seconds as she looked around and then back to him. When it all finally seemed to make sense to her, she looked up at him and said softly. "I was going to go home with you. I was."

"I know honey. I know. Can you tell me where you're hurt? Is your neck okay? And your back?"

She struggled to sit up, and he helped her. Putting a hand to the back of her head with a groan, it came away bloody, and she leaned forward and he looked at her head with the light. She had a jagged cut that was an inch or two long on the back of her head and it dripped blood steadily onto her wet shirt. He put pressure on her head at the same time that he tried to keep looking her over for other injuries. The blood from her head had spattered on her shirt and in the dark and the rain, it was hard to tell what was what.

The wind was whipping the rain into their faces and he asked her again, "Is there anything broken do you think? Do we dare move you back close under the cliff face, out of most of the rain?" She gave him her hands and he pulled her to her feet and put an arm around her to help her walk. He put her as close under the overhang as he could get her and wrapped his heavy coat around her. "Stay here for just a minute. I'm going to look around here and see if there's any place that's better to sit out this storm." Using his small flashlight, he walked gingerly back down the ledge and then came up and went the other way.

The ledge was only about fifty yards long and only eight or ten feet wide at it's widest. In several places it narrowed down to almost nothing. Working carefully past one of these narrow sections he found a place that was almost cave like. The cliff wall was indented enough that they could sit almost completely out of the rain.

Between her and the bigger overhang, a dead cedar had fallen over the cliff edge and wedged into the rocks. He made another call to Rossen as he worked to drag it back into the sheltered area. They would be all right for the night and then in the morning some of the guys could come up in the light of day and help them climb out when they could do it more safely.

When he came back for her, she was huddled under his coat shivering, with big, tired eyes. He helped her up again and together they worked their way up the ledge to the undercut. He put her back against the cliff wall again and then wrapped her in the coat and solar emergency blanket as snugly as possible, while he worked to get a fire going. The wood was almost all wet and it took him a few minutes to find some dry enough that he thought it would burn and then actually get it lit.

The wind, even under the overhang, was strong enough that even using a lighter and Firestarter stick it kept blowing out. Finally, he got it burning brightly enough that the gusts fanned the flames instead of killing them. Quickly, he built the fire up, then came, and pulled her over to it. She was shivering so hard that her teeth were chattering together. Her clothes were still wet from the pond and he felt terrible about having thrown her in.

Kneeling next to her, he felt the leg of her slacks and her shoes. Her white blouse was all but see through as wet as it was and when she saw his face she looked down and self consciously tried to pull the front of it away from her skin and underclothing. He gave her a wry smile and said, "I know this is going to sound a tad suspect, but I want you to take off those wet clothes."

He took off the slicker, slipped off his button down, and then put the slicker back on over the shirt he had on under it. "I'll turn my back. Do you think you can get out of your things by yourself?" She nodded. "Good. Take them off, put this on and then the coat, then stand close to the fire, and try to get warm. You're already starting to show signs of hypothermia. We have to get you warmed up even before we try to work on your cut." He knelt to help her take off her shoes and stockings before turning around.

As she undressed, he looked out over the canyon in front of them. The firelight flickered and danced on the wet rocks and gave off an eerie glow on the cliff walls far across on the other side. Once off to the left he saw the reflective glow of a pair of eyes watching them. He knew there were mountain lions in this remote area and was even more grateful for the fire.

Behind him, she said, "It's safe to turn around now." Rotating to find her standing in front of the fire wearing only his shirt and coat, he almost wondered if it *was* safe to turn around. They hung clear to her mid thigh, but her long bare legs below glowed in the firelight and she really did look like a fairy standing there trying to warm up.

Her curls were a wet, wild tangle and gave her a touch of the untamed. Even the fact that she was cold and hurt appealed to some deep primal instinct in him that made him need to help and protect her. Coming back to her, he took her hand. It was still like ice, but the fire was burning brightly now and soon its warmth would reflect from the back walls too. He pulled the metallic blanket behind her to reflect the heat back to her, rubbed her hands with his and then her feet, and dug in his pack again.

With the small first aid kit and a bandana, he came around behind her and began pulling her hair away to examine the cut again. He folded the bandana and a gauze pad and as he began to put pressure on it, he could feel her tense in pain and apologized, "Sorry." It killed him to know he was hurting her. "It's still dripping blood and we need to get it stopped."

Her teeth chattered as she said, "It's okay. Actually the cut on my back is bleeding worse I think. I can feel it dripping down inside of your shirt. I've probably ruined it, I'm afraid."

"Where is it?" He wondered how many other places she was hurt that he just didn't know about yet.

She showed him where it was and he pulled the collar of the coat down and then carefully peeled the shirt back off her shoulder. When he saw the cut she was talking about it made him heartsick. The soft part of the back of her shoulder just above her shoulder blade had a long v shaped cut that was already surrounded by a purple bruise. It had blood smeared around it, but a red line from the bottom corner of it still trickled down her skin to disappear into the folds of his shirt.

Shaking his head, he said, "Here. Hold this, can you?" He took her hand to place it on the gauze pad on the back of her head. "Put pressure on it." He took the bandana and another pad and put pressure on her

157

shoulder. This time she winced right out loud. His voice held infinite regret as he said, "Sorry, again." He thought to himself, *what a heart breaking thing to do to such a pretty shoulder.*

He put pressure on her shoulder with one hand and cupped the point of her shoulder with the other to have some leverage to push against. Still the cut didn't stop bleeding for another twenty minutes. With one hand, he rooted around in the first aid supplies until he surfaced with a couple of butterfly bandages. Finally, he carefully pulled the edges of the skin together, secured the stitch like bandages, and asked, "Where else are you hurt?"

She gingerly stretched and moved her head around. "As far as I know those are the only two cuts." He gently pulled the shirt back up, pulled the coat up tight around her again, and nudged her closer to the fire.

She was still shivering and even though the front of her was warm, the part away from the fire was freezing. He built up the fire again, pulling it closer to the back wall and propped her clothing on pieces of wood so they would begin drying. Then he sat down, pulled off his boots, took off his socks, and held them up in front of the fire.

When she looked over at him, he gave her a tired smile. "It's okay to share my socks. My feet don't stink and you already have some of my germs from kissing." He knelt down and she held onto his shoulder and raised each leg in turn while he pulled the warm socks onto her feet.

She sighed with pleasure. "Oh, that feels like heaven. I'll share your socks anytime." She tried to smile but her teeth chattered together.

"Let's try something else. Here, take the coat off."
She took it off and he put it on. "Now come stand right
in front of me and right in front of the fire. He opened
the front of the coat and pulled her snugly to him.
"Now get as close to the fire as you can stand and see if
with my heat at your back and the fire in the front, if
this will make you any warmer."

They were standing almost in the fire and slowly
he could feel her body start to shiver less violently.
Her legs were still cold and so she turned forward and
back from time to time until finally, after what felt like
hours, she quit shivering altogether.

He could tell she was tired. She seemed
completely with it, but he had to wonder how severely
her head was injured to have knocked her out and cut
it that bad. She grimaced when she moved sometimes
and when she fell asleep standing up with her forehead
against his chest he decided to sit down and let her
sleep.

He sat with his back against the wall and his legs
drawn up so she could sit between them. She sighed as
he tucked the coat in around her and wrapped her legs
first in the emergency blanket and then in the slicker.
Within just a few minutes of sitting down, she was fast
asleep again.

He tried to keep the fire going and shift from time
to time so that both sides of her legs were to the flame
without disturbing her too much. Sometime deep in
the night she turned sideways to him and he pulled her
legs up and gathered her completely into his arms with
her head on his shoulder. The rock wall behind them
had finally become heated and even though the storm
hadn't let up, it was much warmer.

Once Enchanted

He'd been moving her clothes around to help them dry and when her pants were ready; he gently woke her and insisted she put the clothes on. He hated to interrupt her sleep, but she needed the extra insulation. She pulled them on under his long shirt and when she came back to sit with him again he wondered if she knew that it was a shame to ever cover up those legs.

This time she sat down in front of him and he pulled her clear onto his lap and held her almost like a child, with her head snuggled into his neck. He wrapped the coat around the front of her and covered her with the slicker again and by the time the storm gained momentum again in the wee hours of the morning, she was sleeping relatively soundly.

He could feel her breath on his skin and smell her shampoo even after her dip in the pond. Occasionally she would moan softly when she moved in her sleep and he considered how lucky they'd been that she hadn't fallen all the way to the bottom. As it was, she was pretty beat up, but she was okay and he was hesitant to even delve into why that mattered so very much to him.

He'd never felt that sense of complete horror that he'd felt when he saw her go off the back of the horse and over the edge. His gut had completely wrenched both then and when he'd looked over the edge to see her lying so absolutely still. Just thinking about it made him hold her tighter to him.

Chapter 18

It was almost four o'clock in the morning when the lightning started again. He'd let the fire die down some in order to let her rest without him moving around so much, and when the first flash came, it lit up the dark like the light of day. She startled awake and when the crash of the thunder followed almost instantly, she clutched at him and hid her face against his chest.

The thunder boomed off the rocks, echoing from side to side, rumbling and growling clear down the length of the canyon. Sean had always loved storms, but being this exposed and this close to the strikes was a bit much, even for him. Flash after flash lit up the night sky and the thunder continued to rumble and boom.

He knew she was awake after the first earth shattering crash, but she didn't say anything, just lay in his arms and hid her face tight when the worst of them came. At length, the storm moved off enough that they could enjoy its unearthly power instead of being so intimidated by it. She raised her head and together they watched nature's glorious show, feeling as if they were almost cocooned here in their little hollow away from the wind.

Later, when the lightning began to fade off down the ridges, he asked, "Lex, are you awake enough that I can start to apologize?"

She still lay in his arms and she leaned her head far

enough back into the crook of his elbow that she could look up into his face. Her eyes were more tired than he could have imagined and she had a deep purple bruise on the side of her face that extended back into her hairline. She was spattered with blood and had mud on her chin and she looked just like she'd fallen over a cliff in a violent storm.

He brought his hand around to gently brush away some of the mud, and then touched the bruise with a tip of one finger. His voice was infinitely sad when he said, "This is all my fault in a way, and I'm sorry."

Her eyes narrowed, questioning, as they filled with tears. "Why? Why did you do that to me? Why didn't you tell me? You were the one person who I trusted the most."

He sighed and leaned his head back against the rock. "Do you remember when I first picked you up and you were so mad at me? Before I even knew you were looking for me, you called me a stupid, hick construction worker. Do you remember?"

Looking slightly guilty, she wiped at the moisture in her eyes. "I remember. But, it wasn't you I was frustrated with really. It was my boss. I'm sorry I took it out on you."

"It was okay. I didn't even know then that I was the stupid, hick construction worker. Then when I realized, I also realized who your boss was and knew I'd never consent to work with him, so it didn't matter anyway. Honestly, I was going to tell you the next day when you left, only that morning when you helped me fix fence, I kind of changed my mind."

He knew he sounded guilty as he continued, "I'd been working beside this wild, feisty, red headed fairy with gorgeous legs, and I knew that as soon as you

162

found out who I was, you were going to leave." His eyes met hers. "I just didn't want you to go yet."

He tugged her back up into his arms. "I'm sorry I didn't tell you. I was wrong not to, and I know what I did was selfish. I hope someday you can forgive me." Pulling her head close to his, he rested his cheek on her hair. "I didn't think it would hurt anything. I was wrong, and I'm sorry. But I wasn't trying to make a fool of you."

She grudgingly admitted in a low voice without looking up, "I felt like a fool when I found those Post-It notes on your desk."

"Lexie, look at me." She lifted her head and he continued, "No one can be around you for more than two minutes and not realize that you are the furthest thing from a fool. You're the sharpest lady I've ever met. If you hadn't had your nutty sense of humor I would have been far too intimidated by your mind to have even come and gotten you out of bed that morning." He paused. "That was before I'd seen your hair down. After the hair I think I'd have braved you, sense of humor or no."

He put his hand into it, gently tugged, and finished, "You were too intriguing. I was willing to chance the anger I knew was coming, to spend a little more time with you. I'm sorry I caused such a huge mess."

She laid her head against his chest again and her voice held the deepest sadness when she said, "I killed your beautiful horse."

Hugging her almost painfully tight, he answered, "I thought you'd gone all the way over with her. It was the most horrible thing I've ever felt. Then when I found you, but you weren't moving . . . " He groaned.

"I'm so glad it was just the horse."

He didn't realize he was hurting her until she made a sound that was almost a whimper. He released her and she gingerly moved in his arms, and then turned to face him and moved back against him. He wrapped his arms around her carefully, making sure not to put pressure on the big cut on her back.

With her face near his neck, she whispered, "Killing Mamie is still incredibly sad. I'm sorry I got so mad and put us all in this situation. I didn't think I had a temper like that. I don't think I've ever thrown anything in my life. I'm sorry."

He chuckled. "I had no idea what to do with you. I knew I deserved it. Heck, even my mom knew I deserved it, but I still had no clue how to fix it. My family will never forget us, I can tell you that. I think they thought the whole thing was a spectator sport!"

Timidly, she looked up at him with big eyes. "Your family was watching? How did they know I was mad?"

"Uh. I think the fact that I left at a gallop to try and do some damage control when she called to tell me she'd sent you over there, was their first clue. Shattering glass was probably their second clue. I think hucking you into the pond, kicking and hollering was just the highlight of the deal."

She dropped her forehead to his chest again with a groan. "How will I ever be able to face them again? I'm supposed to be the poker face of the courtroom. Ms. don't let them know they have you. And now I've gone and killed your beautiful horse and made you spend the night on a cliff, in a raging storm. All because I threw a tantrum like a pouty two year old."

With a serious tone, he replied, "It *was* childish. I

hope you never pull something like this again. But, it was no more childish than my letting you run yourself ragged trying to find me for several days. My only excuse is that I hoped you'd understand eventually and the only harm done would be that your shyster boss would have to pay for sending you on this wild goose chase."

This time she sat right up and kneeled in front of him. "And that's another thing Sean David Rockland. Just exactly how do you know my boss? Could it have been when you spent two years in L.A. and never even mentioned that fact to me? What's up with that?"

He had no trouble meeting her flashing eyes. "I don't talk about the time I spent in LA, Lexie. With you or anyone else. It was the hardest thing I've ever done, and I've put it behind me and try to leave it there." She looked at him, and he could see her trying to understand.

He sighed. "Yeah, I knew of your boss from when I was there. He was trying to cheat some people, a lot of people, out of the homes they'd spent their lives to come by. My mother took the case because I asked her to. That's the stupid part of this whole finding me deal. If your boss had any idea who I was, he'd never want me to work with him anyway. He knows I can't be bought, for any price, and he wouldn't even want me."

He could tell she still had questions she didn't dare bring up and prodded, "What else are you wondering?"

Wheels were turning in her head, he could see them. After awhile she asked, "Why did you do it? Why did you stay? Or even come in the first place, if it was that hard?"

His eyes narrowed. "You want me to quit

something I'd committed to because it was hard? You've got the wrong man, Lex. That's not my style. I stayed because it was the right thing to do, whether I was miserable or not."

"Why were you miserable? What was it that was so bad?" It was an honest question.

He sighed and said sadly, "I lived in east LA, Lexie. The jungle. The place where baptisms weren't cancelled because people changed their minds, they were canceled because they were dead.

"Killed for stupid reasons like which gang happened to be around, or somebody wanted their cool shoes. Where little children learned to be afraid before they could talk and no one was safe. Ever. Our apartment had bars on the windows and doors, and we had to be home, locked in, at dark. Finally, at the end, they pulled us out altogether because it was just too risky. Firefighters and police officers won't even go in there sometimes.

"It's not necessarily a happy place to live. Even you carry a gun and I'm sure you live in a much safer part of town than that. I stayed because they desperately needed the gospel. I don't even know if I did any good, but I stayed. Just no matter how hard I tried, I never learned to enjoy being there."

He looked down for a second. "I hated L.A. I'm sorry, but it's the truth." When he looked up again, he knew that what he'd just said meant their friendship was going to end when she finally did climb into her Porsche and drive away. She knew he wasn't coming out for a visit any time soon. He looked away, for once not willing to look her in the eye.

Turning, she sat back against his chest again and

was quiet for ages. When she finally spoke, all she said was, "I'm going to miss you."

They sat there like that for a long time. He occasionally tossed a piece of wood on the fire, but the wood was almost gone and eventually it burned down to nothing but a bed of glowing coals. After a night that in some ways was much too short and in some ways had felt interminable, the sky in the east began to lighten and ever so slowly, the world began to take on shapes and colors. The clouds that still clung to the highest peaks turned a brilliant fuchsia and lavender. With the light of day he was able to assess the damage more fully and he was appalled to see that she had a number of bruises on her face. He could only imagine what a beating the rest of her had taken.

She was still beautiful, even thrashed and after their last discussion, it almost made him sad. She was almost everything he'd wanted for so long. Almost. Unfortunately, the few exceptions were mountains too tall to overcome. She wasn't a member, she wanted a career instead of a family, and her home was L.A. Any one of the three of them would have stopped him, but it was still going to be awful when she left. As the sky turned into a fiery riot of color, he tried to close the damper on his heart and finally, for the first time that night, shut his eyes and went to sleep.

It felt like only a second later that he was awakened by the sound of his brothers and his dad coming up the rocky trail.

They had an EMT with them who was trained to rescue people from places like this. He roped up, came down to them, and after discerning that Lexie wasn't in any imminent danger, prepared to haul them back up.

This went smoother than Sean thought it would. It

turned out that Lexie was, in fact, a rock climber. They simply lowered a harness and with her help, pulled her right up. It took her less time to climb up the cliff than it took him.

Once at the top, they all looked over to see the mangled body of Mamie lying in the rocks on the canyon floor some hundred plus feet below. When Rossen saw the horse's body, he looked up at Sean. Somehow, he knew not only what kind of night Sean had had, but also how much having her standing there safely beside him meant. That one glance said a lot.

They'd brought extra horses hoping she was in good enough shape to ride back out and although Sean knew she didn't really feel up to it, with his help she climbed gamely on and they had her back home and enroute to the Insta Care within just a couple of hours. She'd wanted a shower, but they finally convinced her that she needed stitches first, even before food. About the only thing they stopped for was to pick up a change of clothes. Rossen offered to drive them and Sean gratefully accepted, knowing he was far too tired to drive them himself unless he had to. He loaded her in, packed with pillows and it wasn't but a few minutes before they were both asleep.

At the Insta Care, they had her change into a hospital gown so she could be examined and then the doctor proceeded to stitch up her head and back. When the doctor went to cut her hair away from the wound Sean talked him into taking the absolute minimal amount. She rolled her eyes tiredly and Rossen grinned from the other side of the room. Sean stood beside her and held her hand through it, remembering a few times in the past being stitched up and thinking some handholding might have been a good thing.

When the doctor moved to her back, Sean was appalled when he saw the cut in the bright exam room light. It seemed much bigger than it had last night and the crusted blood was centered inside a bruise that was nearly black. The other parts of her back that were exposed were bruised too, in a number of places. He'd known she was sore, but he'd had no idea she was this bad! The actual stitching was more than he was up to watching. He stayed by her head talking to her without looking at what was going on until they were finished and the nurse took the pile of bloody dressings away.

Lexie had a neat double row of stitches in a V that pulled her tender skin back together. Sean shook his head knowing she'd have quite a scar to show for her tumble down the cliff.

They checked her head, diagnosed her with a mild concussion, and eventually sent her home with some pain pills and a roll of surgical tape. She was to tape a piece of plastic over the stitches on her back for a few days when she showered to keep it dry.

Back home, he was almost a bit loathe to turn her over to his mom's care to help her shower and get into bed. As they'd pulled in, he'd seen her car sitting in his parents' driveway and, as beautiful as it was, it was the beginning of the end of their time together. They both knew it. When Rossen commented on what a nice car it was, she answered noncommittally and her eyes found Sean's in a long, sad look.

He ate and went home and walked into his office on the way to bed. The broken glass and the mess were still there where they'd left them. Man, he regretted not telling her the other night.

The ringing phone never registered as he slept and

it was almost four o'clock that afternoon before he lifted his rumpled head. What a night! When he was fully awake, he checked his messages and found that Lexie's boss, Trent had left a message for her on Sean's phone. He must have tried it because hers had no reception here.

Sean grinned as he called him back and explained that he was just the guy who'd towed her car and lent her a phone, and that she was indisposed right now. That she had had an accident and been treated and released from the hospital just that morning. When Trent questioned a second accident, Sean just said that he'd heard it was something to do with some guy she was trying to find there in Wyoming. He promised to give her a message that her boss had called if he saw her again.

Stepping into his shower, he chuckled to himself. It'd just serve this guy right to have to pay expenses and sick pay for this whole thing.

She was still asleep when he got to his mom's, so he offered to cook dinner for everyone while he waited. He and his mother worked side by side in the kitchen and she asked him discreet questions. Mostly she questioned if the cliff incident had been her fault.

He turned to give her a straight look. "Come on, Mother. My whole life you've drilled into my head that I'm responsible for my own actions. The same holds true here. She's the one who decided to go rampaging off. No one forced her. But if there is someone else to blame, it's me, not you. When I realized it was me she was looking for, I should have told her." Before she could even ask, he said, "I should have, but I didn't want her to leave." Nothing was said, but when she glanced over at him, he met her gaze, and then turned back to cooking.

When dinner was ready, he knocked on Lexie's door. She raised a tousled head to look at him as he asked, "Do you feel like eating?"

She groaned and then laughed, "For a second there I thought you'd come to get me to go fix fence. I think I may be a little drugged. Yeah, food sounds great, although, I don't know that I feel up to facing your entire family just yet."

"Nah, you're safe. Now if Cooper were here, you'd be in trouble! He'd be having a heyday mimicking you. But he's in South America, so the coast is clear."

When she came out, dressed and with her hair all pinned back she said, "Don't even start on my hair! It's a snarl fest, and honestly, I'm too sore to tackle it just this moment, so lay off!"

Naomi laughed and grinned at him. "Sean, I do believe you have finally met your match." He thought to himself, *that's what it feels like.* But Lexie couldn't be his match. Some big important things just weren't right.

After dinner, he came to her door again. "Bring your hairbrush and come out. I'll help you wrestle that mane down." The look she gave him could only be described as skeptical. He laughed. "Hey, I'm actually pretty good with hair. Okay, so it usually belongs to a horse, but they think I'm great!"

When she came back out, brush in hand, he smiled at her and took her in to sit on the leather couch beside him. Without preamble, he asked, "When are you leaving?" She gave a questioning glance and he added, "I'm not trying to get rid of you. I just wonder what your plans are. How long can we keep you?"

A long, slow look passed between them. Finally,

with a tired sigh she said, "I need to go. I've imposed on your parents long enough. I should have gone a long time ago, before I caused such a mess. That being said, I don't feel so good, and I need to wait at least long enough to let my codeine wear off. Why?"

"Do you think you'd be up to a drive in the morning if I pack you in pillows again? There's something I want to show you." He could tell she didn't know how to take him. It had been that talk about Los Angeles this morning. He'd as good as told her she was a fling and now she had no idea where she stood.

After studying his face for a moment she said, "Sure, I could do that."

Sitting on the sofa with her in front of him, he began to pull the pins from her hair to let it tumble down her back. She was right, it was a tangled mess, and he began to painstakingly separate each flaming curl and brush the snarls out.

He wasn't sure exactly when it happened, but somehow combing her hair went from helping her with a simple task to reveling in the silken, red tresses. By the time it was tangle free, falling in soft curls, he was hopelessly enchanted. She really was a magical fairy. She must be. He felt like he'd been sprinkled with fairy dust and lost all intelligent judgment. He stopped combing and was just feeling it and looking and she leaned back against him with another sigh. It was a happy one this time.

"Thank you. That feels so much better. I hate it when it's like that."

"Messy, or pinned up?"

Without looking back at him, she said, "Both."

Leaning around to look at her, he asked, "Both?

And you still wear it up?"

She nodded a bit sheepishly. "Everyday."

Putting both hands through it, he gently pulled her head around. "You're a nut! Do you know that?"

She smiled and leaned on him again. "You're probably right, but I'm very good at what I do. No one can dispute that. The whole firm is probably in a tailspin without me there to clean up the mess. The only reason I was sent here is I'm the only woman. I carry a lot of the load for them. One of these days they're going to miss me."

He wrapped a long, red curl around his finger. "Me too."

Later he talked her into coming to his house to sit in the hot tub. She moved so gingerly that the soreness was unmistakable and he thought the jets might help. She stepped out of his patio door carrying her plastic and tape to get him to help her cover her stitches. At first, he was entranced by how great she looked in her bathing suit, but when she gingerly sat on the edge and turned around to have him help her, he was appalled.

Every part of her back and shoulders that was exposed was bruised. There was hardly a break between. He drew in a breath. "Oh, Lexie! I had no idea!" He gently folded her into a hug. "I'm so sorry! I never dreamed it was this bad!" The bruises made him completely forget she was gorgeous. All he felt right then was guilt and pity.

"It's awful isn't it? I'm too sore to even be able to really see how bad it is in the mirror. What I can see is pretty ugly."

He tried to lighten the mood as he taped. "You? Ugly? Huh! Not a chance! You're the siren of the entire legal industry, I'm sure! Why else would they

Once Enchanted

keep encouraging you to not be so pretty? They're all just jealous."

As he finished taping, she settled down into the foaming water. "Ah, you were right."

"That you're the siren of all attorneys?"

She laughed. "That this will help."

Chapter 19

The next morning when he came to get her, she asked, "Can we take my car? I think I can get into it easier than your truck, even with your handy little step."

"Sure. How are you feeling?"

"Like I've been driven over by Brandon's tow truck. Will you drive?"

He had to hassle her. "I don't know. That car is professional, ya know. Asking a guy to drive would be breaking the sisterhood, wouldn't it?" He laughed. "Sure, I'll drive your Porsche. I'd love to! Where's your hairbrush? I've been hoping all morning that you'd need help with your hair."

"It's right here. Would you mind? How do you know about the sisterhood? It's supposed to be a closely guarded secret from all things male."

Sitting behind her, he gathered her hair into his hands. In a stage whisper, he said, "I snuck into a meeting of the National Organization of Women. I wore a purple dress and heels and they thought I was Oprah." Naomi and Joey came in just then. Lexie was laughing so hard she was groaning, and Naomi and Joey looked at the two of them as if they'd finally lost it.

Joey said, "What? Did you finally tell her you liked her? What's so funny?"

Still concentrating on her hair, Sean said, "Lexie

just doesn't believe that I have a special rapport with feminists."

Naomi raised an eyebrow. "I wasn't aware of that either. Where did you get this special rapport?"

Sean glanced at Lexie, and she laughingly said, "Trust me. As his mother, you don't even want to know."

When her hair was done and she'd eaten, he gathered the pillows from her bed and a couple of others from the linen closet again and carefully loaded her into her car. She was slow getting in and once he was in the driver's seat, he asked, "Not that I want to spend the day with a zombie, but where are you on your pain pills?"

"I haven't taken anything this morning. I wasn't sure if you would drive or not if I asked to take my car."

His brow furrowed as he asked, "You thought I'd be afraid to drive your car?"

"I can't imagine you being afraid of anything. I just thought you'd give me flack about the sisterhood!" She laughed again as she said it and then groaned. He left her there while he went back in after her pills and a water bottle.

On the gravel part of the road he drove slowly and carefully tried to miss any bumps, and then when they hit the paved he turned north and opened it up. After a few minutes, he said philosophically, "It's lower to get into and a much smoother ride. I'm so glad you thought of this!"

Then he punched it and she laughed at him and groaned again and said, "Do you have to be so funny this morning? Couldn't you be grouchy or something. You're killing me!"

After more than a half hour of driving, she

wondered aloud if he was going to tell her where they were going and he said, "To Jackson. There's something there I want you to see before you go back to California."

Looking out the window, she mused, "You know, my time spent in Jackson wasn't all wasted. I saw some very cool houses. I didn't find you, but I saw some of your homes and they truly are phenomenal. You have an incredible gift."

He glanced over at her. "Thank you. I value your opinion. I just hope it's not your medicine making you loopy. I love what I do. I've wanted to design and build things since I was two I think."

She smiled sleepily. "My medicine doesn't make me loopy. It makes me want to climb over into your seat and kiss you."

"Really?" She nodded. "Well, that's good to know. I can see now why people get hooked." He shook his head, laughing. "You are too loopy. You wouldn't usually say that to a guy would you?"

"That depends on the guy."

"Is there anything else you'd like to divulge while you're being uninhibited?"

"Nope. There's nothing too scandalous about me. Sorry. About the best I can come up with is that I honestly don't sleep in much."

He shook his head. "We should be careful where we let you go on those things."

She leaned her head onto his shoulder. "I think you're right. I'm not loopy, but I'm really tired." In just a few minutes, she'd fallen asleep.

Upon reaching Jackson, he stopped to wake her. She opened her eyes and smiled a tired smile. "Can I come over into your seat now?" He was incredibly attractive behind that wheel. She reached for him.

Pushing her hands back toward her, he said, "That's probably not too good of an idea. You're a little out of it. Are you even going to remember what I'm showing you?"

"Yes. I'm sure of it. I think." She grimaced. "If I don't, you can always remind me. What is it you want me to see?"

He'd pulled the Porsche to the side of the main road leading into the Jackson Hole valley from the south and west. Stepping out, he came around to her side of the car to help her out. They were in the middle of nowhere, and she turned to look at him questioningly.

Pointing to the fields and pastures on each side of the highway, he asked, "Can you see all these fields? All the way to the bend in this direction, and for another mile or two this way? This is the homestead Trent Meyers is trying to take. It belongs to a family here named Blackstone. The grandfather, George Blackstone, is the one whose name is on the deed. I've done some checking. He's seventy-one years old and was born in that farmhouse over there. This ground has been in his family's name since the eighteen fifties. However, his fifth great grandfather was Native American, so in actuality, this land has been in his family for hundreds and hundreds of years. He raises hay and wheat and beef cows.

"See those stacks of hay over there that look like loaves of bread?" She shaded her eyes and then nodded. "Those stacks were made with the same machinery his family's been using since the forties. They just pile the grass hay and leave the top rounded so the rain rolls off. Then they fence off each stack to keep the cows out and when they're ready to use it they just move the fences and bring the cows to the hay instead of the hay to the cows."

Leaning back against her car, he folded his arms across his chest. "The ground has become so valuable to developers that they're having a hard time keeping the taxes paid, so they've applied to have it put into a conservation easement. That means it could never be developed and would remain open space in perpetuity. His family could still farm it and yet not have to always be trying to keep pace with the insane value of real estate around here. They get a one-time, private money payment in exchange for the development rights.

"The problem is it takes a long time to get the conservation easement in place. The government hoop thing. What your boss is trying to do is take this family's ancestral home away. And, if he succeeds in finding someone to declare it blighted, which is insane for how fast real estate is appreciating around here, but you yourself said he could probably find someone crooked. If he succeeds in having it declared blighted, not only will the Blackstones lose their ranch, but they'll never be fairly paid for it either.

"George Blackstone has four sons and fifteen grandchildren. Three of the four sons are in business with him here on this ranch. They all stand to lose everything if Trent Meyers gets away with it." He glanced over at her and ended quietly. "I thought you would want to know all of that before you went home."

Standing in the bright May sunshine, she looked around. It was a beautiful, tranquil cattle ranch and lay tucked into the Snake River valley as if it had indeed been here for hundreds of years. There were log buildings down there that were weathered and gray with age, and a couple of huge, old, classic, red barns with rustic metal roofs.

In the distance, she could see a handful of riders flanking a herd of cows that was being moved through a pasture gate. She came over to stand in front of Sean. "Thank you for bringing me. You're right. I do need to know this before I go home, and I'll do what I can to see that these people aren't cheated. Nevertheless, you need to know, I'm only an employee. Not even one very high up on the totem pole."

Her voice became self-deprecating. "In all honesty, I'm the bottom of the totem pole there. I'll do what I can, but I can't control the outcome of this. I wish I could promise you justice, but I can't. I'm not in a position to control that."

He ran a brown hand through his windblown hair. "I know. I only wanted to make sure you understood what's really going on here." He turned to open her door for her. "Thanks for coming and hearing me out."

Back in the car she asked, "While we're here, do you have time to go all the way into downtown Jackson and let me see some of Kit's work? Isabel was telling me that some of her sculptures are in galleries there. Is there any way I could see some while we're here?"

Leaning across the car, he pulled the seat belt she was having trouble reaching, down for her so she didn't have to twist to get it. She was still ridiculously sore. "I have time, and they're definitely worth it. Kit is amazingly gifted. She's sold stuff to people from all over the world. In fact, she has some great pieces there in California. East of LA, out in the country at Isabel and Slade's horse farm, she did some larger than life size foals bucking and playing around. They stand outside the main gates to the farm and they're incredible. I only saw them before they shipped, while they were still here, but they're awesome. Once you get back home, you should drive over there sometime."

"I definitely will. Wind Dance Farms is famous there. It's famous everywhere I guess, with as many winning racehorses as come out of there. I'd love to just have an excuse to go!" She paused and knew she sounded somewhat sad as she continued, "Mostly it'll just be a matter of finding the time to get away and go. When I get back I'll probably be working those seventy hour weeks again."

"Where would you be right now if you were home?"

She lifted her hand to glance at her watch. "Just about now I'd be in my office wondering if I had time to go get lunch or just make do with an energy bar and a juice." She gave him a sheepish smile. "You asked."

He eased the sports car into a parking space in front of a wood and stone gallery off the main town square. Switching off the car, he turned to look at her. "Why?"

"Why what?"

"Why do you live like that?"

"Like what?"

"The long hours. The commute. Someone else calling the shots. Not even taking the time to eat decently. Why do you do it?"

She could see that he honestly couldn't understand. "Why does anyone work? To make a living I guess."

Shaking his head, he said, "No. That doesn't make sense. If it were just a money thing, you wouldn't be driving a pretty little Porsche. You're smart enough that you could have had the money thing all done up. It has to be something like power or status or that proving yourself thing you were telling me about. People don't pour their whole lives just into earning money unless they're barely managing to feed their families."

Struggling to understand what he was getting at she asked, "What do you mean? Why do you work?"

"For me that's an easy one. At first, it was to make a living, but I got the money thing out of the way. Now I do what I want, when I want to because I love to make beautiful things. For me designing and building is like big boy's art or Legos or something. It's the creation. The challenge. And working like I do, I can arrange my schedule so I can still do my work on the ranch when I'm needed.

"I do it because I love it. There are days I deal with stuff just like any profession, but I work because I believe work is good, not because I want an impressive title and a racy car. And nobody calls the shots. My personal freedom is my biggest thing. I'm sure that will change to a certain extent when I get married someday, but for now, no one pulls my chain but me."

She was wondering how to take all that and knew he could see it in her eyes. She considered for several moments. She was going to give his question some honest thought, instead of just taking offense. Her question, when she finally spoke, seemed to surprise him. "What do you mean; you got the money thing out of the way?"

He shrugged. "When I was little I was awful with money. I could never hang on to it, so I started giving it all to Slade to take care of for me. He was great with money, so I just asked him to handle mine for me and handed every penny I made over to him from about the time I was twelve. I had no idea how much I was worth for years. Finally, when I was signing tax returns, I figured out that he was making me a lot of money and I cranked up earning it to give it to him to invest. He bought a bunch of a small internet company called Hotmail when it made its first IPO. The guy who started it then sold it for four hundred and twenty five million. I only got a small portion of that but..." He shrugged again. "Now I work because I want to."

She added dryly, "And wonder why the rest of the world works through lunch."

"You never did answer my question about why you do it."

"I imagine from your perspective I seem incredibly foolish."

Reaching across and taking her hand, he rubbed his thumb across the back of it. "I know you're not a fool. That's why I asked. Help me understand."

She wasn't sure how to respond and finally asked, "Can I get back to you on that? Some stuff happened last week that had me asking that same thing as I left California, and I haven't come up with an answer yet. I guess in the past I thought that was just part of reaching that elusive success. Being a sharp, young professional who has a satisfying, exciting career. It's taken me a ridiculously long time to figure out that either I've had my corporate ladder leaning on the wrong building, or that it's all a big lie. I haven't figured out yet which one it is. Either way, I've been a fool."

Clicking off his seatbelt, he said, "You'll figure it out Alexis Joy. You're far too sharp a lady not to."

Once Enchanted

Chapter 20

They strolled through the gallery hand in hand, and then he took her to a gorgeous log lodge north of town to eat. They enjoyed an elegant lunch with linen and crystal, beside a huge wall of windows overlooking the breathtaking Teton Range. After their conversation about her career, they didn't talk much. He felt like there were a million things to say or ask and no way to do it, so he just didn't say anything.

On the way back to town, he drove the sporty Porsche to the top of Signal Mountain and helped her out to enjoy the view. As they stood there at the top of the world, not knowing what to say, he turned to her and pulled her into his arms. It was all he could do to be gentle on her bruises. His frustration with knowing their short friendship was soon coming to an end made him want to hold her desperately tight.

He held her close for the longest time, enjoying the feel of her against him and the smell of her shampoo as the breeze blew her soft curls against his skin. Why did she feel so right to him when the circumstances were all wrong?

Before they left Jackson Hole, he encouraged her to take another pain pill. Even if he hadn't wanted her to stay just a little longer, she obviously needed it. She'd stiffened until she literally groaned as she went to sit in the car. He watched her as they drove, wondering what he could do to help her. When they reached the ranch in the late afternoon, he asked her outright and was surprised when she wanted him to take her back to his house so she could clean up the mess she'd made.

"The mess at my house is cleaned up. It's your body that needs taken care of." He gave her a quirky grin. "And other than making you want to snuggle, your medicine makes you tired. Why don't I take you back to my mom's and let you rest."

She sighed and closed her eyes. "You're probably right. Maybe if I take it easy for the rest of the night, I'll feel good enough to face that drive in the morning."

It was the closest they'd been to the whole idea of her leaving and it made something in his heart hurt. Saying goodbye in the morning was going to be hard.

He left her at his parents' house with a gentle kiss and went home to work in his office for the rest of the evening. He'd gotten behind on his design work while she'd been here and tonight it was a good thing. He needed something to occupy his mind or he was going to be certifiably lonely.

In his office, he just stood looking around for the longest time. Even raging mad, she'd been beautiful. Wild, but beautiful. He worked straight through dinner. Not because of their conversation of that afternoon, but because he wasn't in the mood to face his whole family again. It was the first time since she'd been here that he'd felt that way.

At almost ten fifteen that night, he heard a car pull into his driveway. Probably his mother again. Sometimes when he didn't show up at her house for dinner, she showed up at his just to be a mom. She'd come and they'd talk about inane things for awhile and then she'd leave with him knowing how much she loved him. He looked out the office windows wondering why she hadn't pulled all the way into the garage. She had an opener.

It wasn't his mother, it was a little champagne Porsche and he saw Lexie slowly climbing the stairs to his office deck. He opened the door and came out to greet her. "What are you up to at this hour of the night? I thought you'd be fast asleep, gearing up for your drive." His eyes searched hers.

"I've been sleeping off and on since you dropped me, but now I'm wide awake. What are you up to? How come you missed dinner?"

He leaned on the rail and looked out across the sleeping valley. "Just not in the mood for it I guess."

Coming to stand beside him, she said, "Your mom knew I was restless. She asked me if I would come over and check on you. She's the most motherly person I've ever known. I still can't believe she's a practicing attorney."

He didn't look at her as he said, "Being an astute business woman doesn't have to preclude being a great mom. Her family is her life's work, but that doesn't mean she can't do other things she wants. She's a killer attorney. That's just not where her heart is. Her passion."

Lexie mused almost to herself, "I wonder if it was always that way. Did she always know that was what she wanted? How did she make it all the way through law school without having a passion for it?"

"I don't know for sure. I obviously wasn't there at the time, but she hadn't met my dad or joined the church until her last year of law school. She'd been raised in a pretty rough home and at that time, she

187

didn't even think she should get married and have a family. She thought she wouldn't know how to have a decent home life after the way she'd been raised and she didn't want anyone else having to go through what she had gone through as a child. So I'm going to assume that she put her heart into law school because that was what she planned to do for the rest of her life."

He looked up at her with a smile. "My dad threw a little kink into her plans."

"I imagine he did. She seems to like him a smidgen." She laughed. "Sometimes they're so chummy it's almost embarrassing!"

He chuckled and took her hand. "Come inside and talk to me while I work. There's this girl who has occupied my mind lately and I'm a little behind." Inside she sat in the leather settee and he went back to making measurements and taking notes on the set of plans he'd spread out on his drafting table.

Lexie took up where they left off. "Your mother really grew up in a less than ideal home? I would have thought she came from perfect parents the way she parents all of you."

Looking up from his plans with a wicked grin, he said, "You should have seen her when she had a house full of six little kids who were only nine years apart in all! She was motherly all right!" He laughed softly to himself. "I think I'm personally responsible for teaching her to swear. I really was the rebel of the family. I still am."

Lexie looked shocked. "Your mother swears? No way! I can't even imagine her cussing! What did you do? For that matter I can't imagine you doing anything too terribly outlandish."

"I'm pleading the fifth, but I will tell you that the first time I remember her swearing I had a horse in her living room. She was *not* impressed!

"The thing about that time was I wasn't even trying to make her upset. I was like six and just wanted her to help me fix something on my saddle and it didn't occur to me that she'd mind the horse being inside. After that though, I'd pretty much figured out that I could get an entertaining response out of her if I pulled something outlandish, so I think I started doing it on a regular basis. By the time I was in high school, she had one way she disciplined the rest of the kids and another for me. I was by far the most harrowing of her children. Although Cooper has been known to challenge my rebel standing. She doesn't really have gray hair, but she blames me for giving it to her anyway."

Lexie's eyes were big. "You took a horse into her living room? I can't believe she didn't kill you! Please tell me that you made it back out without any terrible events occurring inside her house."

He gave her his most heart-stopping smile. "We'll, no, not exactly. Why do you think she swore? Not only did we have a rather green incident, but he stepped through the sub-flooring on the way back out. Like I said, she was not impressed. Maybe that's why I became a builder. I've had to repair a few things from time to time."

Giggling she said, "You'll probably get one just like you! Paybacks, you know!"

"I'm way ahead of you. My living room floor is strong enough to withstand any horse on the place! But you're a fine one to talk. You'll probably get one just like you, and you'll have to hide all the projectiles

189

Once Enchanted

and have all tempered windows!" He laughed. "Did
you play softball in school? You'd have made a
ripping pitcher!"

She looked so guilty that he added, "I'm just
kidding you, Lex. And even mad you still looked like
an enchanting fairy. A very angry, enchanting fairy,
but still enchanting all the same!"

He rolled up his plans, slipped an elastic around
them, and put them in the basket with the others
beside his desk. Then he took his notes and sat down
at his computer and for a few minutes typed stuff in
and then the huge printer in the corner kicked into life.
He came over to her and offered her a hand. "Come
with me into the kitchen? Are you hungry? I still have
to eat dinner."

"No, I wouldn't care for anything, thanks." She
followed him to the kitchen and sat on a bar stool at his
counter watching him while he worked. He pulled
eggs and veggies out of the fridge and chopped the
ingredients up for an omelet, whistling while he
worked. Finally, he went over and turned on the
sound system at a wall pad, and then sang along to the
quiet radio.

When he was finished he took out two plates, set
them on the table, and came over to take her hand
again. "I know you said you didn't want anything, but
you have to at least come sit with me or I'll feel stupid
having you watching me eat."

"Give me a little bit and I'll eat with you. You're
quite a cook. Where did you learn to chop like that?"

He pulled out her chair to seat her. "Isabel taught
me that. She's the one who's quite a cook. I like to
cook, but she's a wizard! She cooks fancy stuff like
soufflés and twelve layer tortes, and hollandaise from
190

scratch. She's been a very rewarding addition to the family! Do you want to say the prayer?"

It was a matter-of-fact question and she said, "Sure," and prayed without seeming to think a thing about it and they ate in companionable silence for a few minutes.

Looking up, he caught her watching him with her wide green eyes and asked, "What are you thinking?"

"Just how wrong I was about you the night we met when I thought you were a smart alec tow truck driver. I still think you're a smart alec, but that night I wouldn't have guessed you could cook."

He grinned. "Just don't tell the stink bugs. I mean you can tell them I'm a smart alec, just don't tell them I can cook."

After they ate, he got up, took their plates to the sink, went to the freezer, and came back with the tub of lemon sorbet and asked, "Could I interest you in some dessert?"

Their eyes met and held across the table. "Only if it includes dancing in the kitchen. That's the reason I came over here tonight, you know."

"You came because you wanted dessert?"

She hadn't looked away. "Yeah, I was really hoping for some lemon sorbet."

"Cool!" He helped her out of her chair and handed her the tub and a spoon, and then went and fiddled with the radio. "I was hoping you were hoping for lemon sorbet."

They began with their heads together eating straight from the tub, laughing and teasing each other, but a minute later, when she leaned over to wipe some off his upper lip, the dessert was forgotten. He pulled her to him in a gentle embrace, and kissed her for a long, slow moment. When he eventually backed off, he licked his lips and gave her a lazy smile. "You taste really good." His voice was slightly husky.

She came close again and smiled up at him. "I'll bet you say that to all the girls."

They stood there like that for a long time, talking and eating sorbet and snuggling. When the pint was gone, he turned off the kitchen light and pulled her close to dance to the slow music in just the glow of the porch light shining in through the window. This time they didn't talk much.

Most of the time their lips were busy and even if they had talked, neither one of them knew what to say. They both knew she was leaving first thing in the morning to go back to L.A. It loomed between them emotionally, so they didn't go there, and instead just basked in being in each other's arms and tried to ignore the question of each other's heart.

Finally, she sighed. "I should go. It's after midnight and I'm a guest in your parents' home."

He left her mouth and leaned to kiss the soft skin of her neck. "I know." He continued to nuzzle her and after a few more moments, she gently pushed him. He looked down at her and kissed her mouth one more time. It was long, sweet, and slow and it felt like goodbye. He hugged her to him, rested his cheek on her soft curls, then took her hand, and slowly walked her out to her car.

As they went out the door, she said, "I'm going to miss this kitchen." He knew she was trying to smile, but it wasn't working very well.

He held the door of her car for her. Before she got in, she looked up at him for the longest time, but neither one of them knew what to say, so at length, she hugged him again and got in and drove away.

Chapter 21

The next morning he didn't show up for breakfast, but he came in a few minutes after, dressed in his boots and jeans and helped her carry her luggage to her car. The rest of the family except Naomi had already left to start moving a herd of cows to a different pasture, and when she went to tell Naomi thank you and goodbye, she felt silly that she wanted to sit right down and cry. Professional women didn't cry.

She hugged the older woman tightly and struggled to say, "Naomi, thank you for everything. You'll never know what these few days here have meant to me. I feel like a different person since I came here."

Naomi did have tear bright eyes as she said, "I hope you're not a different person. We thought the person you were when you showed up was great!"

"I don't know how to thank you yet for taking me in. I'll think of something. I've never been around a family like yours. I've loved every minute of it here."

Smiling, Naomi said, "We've loved having you here. Some of us more than others." She glanced up to where Sean was loading the car. "You don't need to do anything to thank us. You've done more than enough pitching in. Just email my son from time to time so that his heart doesn't bleed to death while he works to get over you."

At that, Lexie teared up in earnest. She wiped at her eyes, embarrassed. "He hasn't mentioned wanting to be emailed. I think he'll be just fine without me."

Naomi didn't say anything; she just looked at her with those incredibly wise blue eyes. Finally, she said, "Honey, we women can't always wait for the men of this world to get their acts together and get the ball rolling. I'm sure you know that by now." She smiled her kind smile. "Get going. You drive safe and if you're too sore, pull over and get a hotel. There's nothing that won't wait if you feel lousy." She pushed her toward her car. "Good bye Alexis Joy. Good luck in your life."

Walking to her car, brushing at whatever it was that was irritating her eyes, Lexie saw that Sean had a saddled horse waiting for him. Resolutely, she squared her shoulders and when she met him at the open door of her Porsche she felt like she had her emotions reasonably under control.

They just stood looking at each other again for the longest time. This time they didn't even try to say anything. When she worried that she was going to get emotional again, she leaned over and gently kissed him. She looked back up at his stormy blue eyes and knew she would never, ever forget them.

Feeling like there was something in her chest that wouldn't allow her to take a real breath, she looked away, climbed into her successful car, and drove off without looking back. If she did, she wasn't sure she'd make it out the big gate.

She drove carefully on the gravel road. Whatever was bothering her eyes had really begun to make them water now. She could hardly see to drive.

From the house, Naomi watched Sean close the door of Lexie's car and when she drove away without looking back, she saw his broad shoulders slump just for a moment. He walked over to his horse and with one last glance at the plume of dust left hanging in the air over the gravel road, he stepped into the saddle and loped away to catch up with the others and the cows they were moving.

For a few minutes, Naomi thought he was actually going to be able to do it. To just walk away, and though she had to respect his character strength, she knew that he cared more for the girl in the Porsche than any other girl in his life. She watched him gallop across the valley and her heart was breaking for him. At the last minute, he turned his horse at a ninety-degree angle and rode to the top of the notch to look over the ridge into the next valley where the road went through. He rode to the crest of the hill and stopped and just sat his horse for a few minutes, and then, finally, slowly turned and walked his horse back down.

Once Enchanted

Chapter 22

When Sean made it home that night, he was tired. They'd moved cows and then he'd volunteered to fix a hole they'd found in the fence as they turned the herd in. The others headed on home and he mended the fence and then rode the rest of the fence line to double check. Occasionally he got down to fix a weak spot, wishing he'd thought the whole fence-fixing thing through better.

He'd only wanted to do it so he could keep himself busy and his mind occupied. At the time, it hadn't occurred to him that the image of her in her shorts and tank top would dog him the whole day. He couldn't even bend over the fence without picturing her in his mind.

Once he was convinced the cows were well contained, he mounted up and headed for home. As he passed the trail to his cabin, he turned off. The little log structure had been the site of a great deal of peace for his heart over the last years as he had dreamed of it and then actually constructed the dream. Usually the calm and tranquility of this place could overcome any stress that troubled his life, but on this afternoon her presence was like a ghost that haunted the place. A beautiful fairy ghost, who whispered through the enchanted forest glade and swirled in his head like an angelic auburn haired mystical wraith.

Thoughts of her brought an almost physical heartache. But it was a good pain and he lingered on the little porch letting the memories wash through his heart and brain. Maybe he could get past this in one hard, fast, heart-wrenching purge. That was his plan. She'd been here such a short time. He should be able to get over her as quickly as he fell for her.

He knew there were certain things he needed when he finally found "her". Lexie had been missing a couple of the most vital and he wasn't an emotional guy. All he had to do was come to grips with the cold hard facts and the sappy stuff would take care of itself. In the mean time, he just had to stay busy.

He left the cabin and rode more fence lines on the way home, tightening wires and replacing stays until the shadows grew long and the hunger pangs in his belly became more demanding than the images in his head. Arriving after dark, he put his horse away and went home to eat a sandwich and go into his office to continue trying to exorcise the enchanting fairy from his mind. He was hard at work designing a new small office complex when he heard his garage door go up.

A few minutes later, his mom came in carrying a plate in each hand and said, "Isabel made a stroganoff that was so over the top I thought I'd better bring you some for when you finally get caught up with whatever project deadline your trying to meet tonight. Oh, and there's banana nut bread too." She came up behind him to look over his shoulder at his computer screen. "Is this the new doctor's office? I love the rock work. You have an incredible gift."

He mumbled, "Thanks Mom," as the phrase echoed in his head. Lexie had used those exact words.

She went on, "The house feels a little empty tonight with Alexis gone. I wonder if she made it home okay."

He looked up and met her eyes. "I know where you're going with this, Mom, and yes, we need to call and check on her, but you need to do it, not me. You and I both know I just need to back away on this one."

After a long glance, she sighed. "I know, but it makes me sad. She was adorable."

The smile he couldn't help felt good. "She'd say that was a very unprofessional word. You know that don't you?"

Waving a hand at him, she punched up a number on her phone. Even just hearing half of the conversation was bitter sweet. He did need to know that Lexie was okay. She'd been thoroughly hammered to start such a long trip. Nevertheless, he had to get started forgetting her and getting on with his life. After only a week, he was already in way too deep.

His mom discreetly didn't mention him as she made certain that Lexie had gotten to wherever she was going safely. After she hung up, he didn't ask. He just kept on working. This was the first day. That was the only reason this was so hard. Tomorrow would be better and in a few days, he wouldn't even remember what that flaming hair looked like.

As she went to leave, his mom came over to stand next to him until he looked up at her. When he did, she said, "Try not to be too much of a stranger."

Getting up from his computer, he gave her a hug. "You know me. I can't live without you for long. I have a lot to catch up on, but I'll be around."

He walked her to her car in the garage and said, "Bye, Mom. Thanks for always taking such good care of me." On his way back into his office, he sent up a silent prayer of thanks for being blessed with the ultimate mother. Even though he'd given her fits sometimes, she was always there for him when he was struggling.

At four o'clock the next morning, he finally called it a night and headed for bed. Even then, he found himself lying awake in the dark looking at the ceiling, wondering if the same ghost that haunted the enchanted forest had taken up residence in his house.

Chapter 23

Lexie arrived at Eric's house in the evening and almost had to be extricated from her car. She'd stiffened on the drive until she was completely miserable. Initially she'd intended to drive all the way home, but enroute had decided she wasn't up to it and detoured to Flagstaff. By the time she was in Arizona, she knew she was going to need more down time than she'd thought.

Eric peeled her out of her car and put her to bed with a heavy dose of pain medicine. When he'd helped her tape up her back so she could shower first, she thought he was going to be sick on her when he saw it. His hug had been long and gentle and she'd broken right down and cried. She never cried, and she'd done it several times already this day. It must have been either the injuries or the medicine. That was her excuse.

She slept until almost eleven o'clock the next morning after taking more medicine in the middle of the night. When she finally dragged her hammered body out of bed, both babies were down for naps and Eric's wife Josie was grocery shopping.

They sat at the kitchen table over a plate of blueberry muffins catching up on each other's lives. He'd gone to hand her a cup of coffee, but for some reason she declined. She hadn't had any in a week and the headaches had finally stopped. She'd had to admit she'd been addicted to caffeine and it bothered her. It hadn't ever seemed like a big deal to her before, but now hot cocoa just sounded like a better idea.

He got her some and said, "You need to take another pain pill. You keep grimacing."

Nodding, she said, "I think you're right." When he handed it to her, she smiled and told him about how the codeine had affected her when she was around Sean. Both of his black eyebrows shot up. They talked at length, and she was honest with him about her work troubles and how her heart had hurt as she'd driven away yesterday. They'd never had secrets.

He knew her better than she did herself and she wasn't surprised when he cut right to the chase and asked, "Why don't you quit your job and go start a practice in Jackson Hole?"

She *was* surprised when that question made her lay her head on her folded arms and begin to cry as if her world had come apart. She was so mixed up. He pulled his chair over next to hers and patted her arm. He went to rub her back and she winced and he said, "Sorry, Lex. Sorry for hurting your back and your feelings. What can I do to help you? We'll work on this together. We've been able to figure everything out together so far. We'll figure this out too."

When Josie came back in to find them buried in a deep discussion about what was truly important in life, she took one look at Lexie's tear stained face and went into the other room to keep the babies entertained. Lexie was completely embarrassed to be caught crying. It was as if the tears that had been dammed up for so long had sprung a leak.

The conversation flowed from the work situation

she had to change, to the experiences she'd had in Wyoming that had her questioning what she really wanted out of life, to the principles she had learned in church on Sunday.

When she told him some of the stuff she'd heard that day and then got the copy of the Proclamation to the World out that she'd folded and placed in her Bible, he was markedly interested in hearing what she thought about it all. She asked him if he'd ever considered why God didn't have a prophet on the earth anymore, and his answer floored her.

"I guess I've always thought that there really was a prophet here somewhere and that we just hadn't found him yet. I don't know why God wouldn't talk to his children. He's the same yesterday, today and forever, remember? I'm sure there have been times when there weren't prophets on the earth, but we need counsel for our day. The world needs more than just the Bible and the imperfect reasoning of men. God wouldn't just leave us to sink or swim on our own forever. Somewhere I'll bet He has a man who's a prophet just like Moses or Abraham of old. Why do you ask?"

For a minute, she was speechless. "Why haven't you ever said something like that to me?"

His smile was gentle. "Lexie, you've been slightly preoccupied with that career of yours. Would you have listened to your nutty brother's deep philosophical thoughts on God? I'm the brother you think is a tad eccentric, remember?" He squeezed her arm. "I just had to wait until you needed to figure some things out for yourself before I could venture something like that."

She looked into his eyes and hers teared up again.

"I don't deserve you, do I? You've always been the wise one while I was the Chicken Little, fussing around about stuff that doesn't even matter in the long run." She spoke almost to herself, "Sean reminded me the other day that we need to stay focused on the goal. I asked him what the goal was and this big, gorgeous, competent man didn't hesitate for one second when he said to return to our Heavenly Father with honor. It was a wake up call, I can tell you. Can you imagine one of the guys at work saying something like that?"

Eric smiled and nodded. "I think I'd really like to meet this Sean who reminds you about the real goal and then throws you in a pond to make you cool your temper off. He sounds like a man of wise judgment to me! Are you going to keep seeing him?"

At this, the tears started down her cheeks again. She wiped at them, embarrassed. "Sorry, I have no idea where these tears are coming from." She tried to smile, but her heart was obviously sad. "Actually, I left there yesterday without any plans to even contact him again. He's a Mormon who lives and works in Wyoming, and wants to marry and have a family someday. And I'm an attorney in LA, the place he hates even when he tries not to. How in the world is there any point in staying in touch?"

Eric shook his head. "Lexie, Lexie, Lexie. You've just been sitting here telling me that you had your best time ever with this guy and his family in Wyoming. And that you're honestly questioning whether you even want to stay in L.A. You and I both know you'd like nothing more than to have a family. Other than saving up enough to be able to quit work for awhile so you can just be a mom when your babies are small, what's the problem?"

His voice softened and he went on, "What do you

have to lose? Just your jerk of a crooked boss who you're always having to dodge his inappropriate advances. I think you ought to seriously consider starting your own firm. If you can handle a huge portion of the load where you're at for someone else, why not work for yourself and actually keep some of the profits you earn? Honest attorneys are rare and valuable things. Go out on your own! Give it a shot! What better time than now, when you have no huge responsibilities and you're frustrated already?"

She shook her head. "You make it all sound doable. Do you know that? As far as Sean goes though, he never said even one word about ever seeing me again. He was great, but he wasn't interested. I was just a fun week's distraction for him."

Eric was skeptical. "Someone who tries to remember that the goal is to return with honor doesn't sound like the kind of guy who uses women. And it wasn't like he was trying to get you to hand over your body. He kissed you. You said you felt like you could trust him. You have good judgment in people. I've always felt that your ability to judge people's character was one of your gifts. Do you honestly think you were a fling?"

She thought about it at length and then shook her head. "No, he was honest with me. Other than the whole not telling me who he was thing. And even in that he was honest when he said it was because he didn't want me to leave. And he *was* respectful."

"Well then, it sounds to me like the question isn't what he wants, but what you want. You're going to have to pin that down for yourself. Someday you're going to have to actually go for what you decide is the most important, and my advice is to decide soon.

You're twenty-seven years old, and not getting any younger." He teased her to try to make her smile. "I happen to know exactly how old you are, you know. We have the same birthday!"

She stood up to come around and gingerly hug him. "I know you have the same birthday. You're my birthday gift from God. You're His way of helping me get through this life without self-destructing, and I would be absolutely lost without you. I love you. Thanks for letting me bawl on you. Can I ask you another favor?"

"Sure. What now?"

"Will you help me find out if the man who Sean said was the prophet, really is?"

He put an arm around her. "Absolutely. After you wake up. Right now I'm putting you back to bed."

Chapter 24

Two days at Eric's had her feeling strong enough to face the drive home and the men in her office. She wore her power suit the first day back. She needed the confidence personally that she could face I-5 and the corporate head games.

Her face was still bruised, although some of the bruises were turning from black and blue to yellow and green. She did the best she could to cover them with foundation, but the tinges showed through. Before she left Eric's she'd had him bandage the stitches on her back loosely. Her clothing irritated them and she wondered how she was going to manage when she couldn't reach them herself back home. Now the bandage was a distinct bulge under the fabric of her suit, but it couldn't be helped.

She pulled her hair back tight for the first time in almost a week and as she secured it, she remembered that first morning in Wyoming when Sean had plunged his hands into it. This morning her hair almost felt like her own little secret that she kept from all those manicured wimps she worked with. It was kind of fun to know that none of them had the slightest clue who the real Alexis Joy O'Brien was.

She parked her car, and carrying her portfolio, pep talked herself all the way up the elevator to the seventeenth floor. Stepping off, she caught her reflection in the metal trim across from her and knew

Once Enchanted

she looked the part of the polished young professional woman as she steeled herself to face Trent first thing and get it over with.

She didn't even go into her office first, but went straight to his. It was a pleasant surprise when he seemed glad to see her, and honestly concerned at the condition of her face. She waved off his effusive attention before he could get any chummier and sat in her customary seat pulled up close to the front of his desk.

Rubbing his hands together in anticipation, he said, "Well A.J., knowing you, I have no doubt that you accomplished what I sent you out there to do. What have you got for me? Did you succeed in bringing this guy on board?"

She almost felt sorry for him. Almost. She wasn't sure if the massage oil she detected was in her head or if he'd been to the spa already this morning, but either way it reinforced her determination to end his stint as her boss. "I found your man, Trent, but you're not going to like what I have to say."

She got straight to the point without candy coating anything. "Do you remember a few years back when you had some trouble with a young Mormon missionary named Rockland? He's the one who brought in Naomi Rockland to litigate for the property owners of that highway project that fell through?"

A guarded look appeared in Trent's eyes. "I vaguely remember an obnoxious, young, idiotic missionary. Yes. What's your point? I want to know about the architect in Wyoming."

"I hate to break the news to you, but that missionary and the Wyoming architect/ builder are one and the same man. His exact words were, 'Your boss won't want me because he knows I can't be bought for any price.' I daresay I believe him. I don't think you can talk him into being any part of a scheme that smacks of corruption, but you're welcome to try."

She smiled sweetly and handed him the file. "Here's his office phone number. He told me unequivocally no to being part of the project, but I don't have the clout you do. Maybe you can talk him into it." She stood up to go. "Do you want me to get back to the cases I was working on when I left or do you have something else you want me to do?"

He must have detected a change in her demeanor from before she left for Wyoming, because he looked at her as if she'd shocked him. Indeed, she probably had, by not even trying to hide the fact that she believed his scheming to be less than above board. The pallor of his face had turned a rather pasty shade of gray. "Rockland? Naomi Rockland? How in the world did they find out about this and come in to try to throw a monkey wrench into this project? I wonder who hired them."

Lexie shook her head and said, "I don't think they had to come far. Their family ranch is not far south of Jackson Hole. I believe he told me they had been there for five generations now. They haven't just come in. What do you want me to get working on today?"

He was still mumbling almost to himself, obviously disappointed that she'd failed. Watching him, she had to wonder why she didn't feel the least bit bad that she'd failed in her mission. Honestly, she was quite pleased to see her boss stymied, at least in this project. She tried not to let that show in her face as she said. "I'll just get back to working on my previous agenda. If you have any changes let me know." She left him in his office, looking dazed and wondering what had gone wrong.

Stepping through the door of her own office, she looked around and decided it was all going to be okay. She really did like being an attorney, and she was very good at it. The people she was working with left something to be desired, but then a lot of attorneys had literally been trained that everyone was dishonest to a certain extent, so personal integrity was optional.

She knew some people believed it, she accepted it, and came to the conclusion that that meant being honorable was all the more important and precious. There had to be the good guys to try to negate the effect of the bad. What she did wasn't the problem. Where she did it was.

She dug into the pile of work she'd left behind and that had been added upon in her absence, and focused for the morning on clearing as much of it away as possible. In fact, she made a sizeable dent in it before lunchtime. She knew after her talks with Sean that working through lunch wasn't going to happen much anymore, but while she was here, she made the time count. When she picked up her purse and walked out to go down and actually eat lunch, she met Trent in the front lobby where he asked her, "Where are you headed?"

"To lunch." She said it cheerfully as she breezed past him and went out the door without giving him a second glance. She had the impression of a large mouth bass as she looked back at him through the heavy glass doors into the office as she waited for the elevator. He was standing there looking at her with his mouth standing open as if he couldn't believe she actually needed nutrition. She'd definitely poured too much of herself into this man's enterprise.

It was fun to know she was going to be out of here in the not too distant future. Her attitude had already lightened up considerably. Stepping into the elevator, she made a mental note to start getting her resume out just as soon as she had it updated.

After lunch, before she started back into her paperwork, she called a friend and arranged to go to the symphony that weekend. That was another thing that was going to end. She was no longer going to spend her nights and weekends toiling in her home office.

She knew she made less than the men around her and she wasn't going to fall for what Sean had called the unfortunate circumstance working women found themselves in, as far as being treated differently than her male counterparts. She would give the firm an honest day's work for an honest day's pay, but from here on out, it ended when she walked out those doors at night. With that in mind, she hustled through the afternoon and then on the stroke of five, straightened her desk, shut her computer down and walked out. In the parking garage, as she walked toward her car, she wished she knew how to whistle. She felt like trying it.

Her spirit was strong, but her body was sore, and stopping at the grocery store on the way home was as industrious as her evening got. She had ibuprofen and a Lean Cuisine from the microwave for dinner and headed straight for the shower and bed. As she lay down and tried to find a position that didn't make the bruises on her back ache, she mentally went over her day. This would work. If she just kept her mind constantly busy, she'd soon forget all about the tall blonde man with the brawny shoulders in Wyoming.

Once Enchanted

Day two didn't go quite as well as day one. The morning commute was a nightmare and she was already somewhat frustrated when she walked through the glass doors of the front office fifteen minutes late. There was a handful of the guys standing around talking and laughing with seemingly nothing much pressing to do, so she was surprised when she got to her office and found a fresh pile of work on her desk topped with a post note with the single word "Urgent". She dug in, telling herself that she'd handled stuff like this before without letting it get to her. She could keep it up. She turned her Ipod on to listen to music as she worked, and tried to just focus and plow through.

She was doing all right until, at almost three o'clock that afternoon, the old song came on that was playing when Sean had taken her in his arms to dance in the kitchen that first evening at his house. The memories slammed down on her heart and her working mindset dissolved into a melancholy that took the last bit of air out of her spirit. The ache the song brought on was almost physical, and for a moment or two, she listened and relived that sweet night in his kitchen.

That was the way life was supposed to be. She was sure of it, even though nothing like that had ever occurred in her life to make that seem familiar. Still it was. It was like coming home. Being in his arms had felt so right. Somehow, she needed to find that feeling again here in her own life. There had to be a way to feel that and still be the woman she was here, didn't there?

Looking around at her stuffy office piled with cases

212

she wondered how to reconcile the two. There had to be a way, but she sure didn't know what it was.

She changed the music to up beat rock and roll and tried to push back her feelings and finish her workday with enough drive to call it a worthy effort. It took all of her self-control.

At four thirty, Trent paged her and she picked up a notepad and headed to the boardroom for an impromptu meeting. At least everyone was there when she got there and she didn't feel like she was being singled out for a bigger load. That comfort was short lived however when a half hour later, it was just her and Trent again. She fielded his passes for the next forty-five minutes as he arranged for her to do the research and briefs for some litigation he would be handling personally, as well as her other responsibilities.

Heading back to her own office, she tried to tell herself that she should be complimented he wanted her to be the one. He was trusting her with a portion of his professional standing. It worked to a certain extent. She was gratified that he wanted to work with her; she just hoped that keeping his hands and personal thoughts to himself was a bigger deal to him than it had been in the past. She didn't want to strain their relationship any further by telling him exactly what she thought of his innuendos.

That night she was tempted to take a whole briefcase full of work home, but she didn't. She was still tired and sore and she needed to do better at having a life, no matter how much she was handed here. She left carrying only her purse, still determined to get back to the vision of having a great lifestyle and being successful at the same time.

Settling into her luxurious car in the parking

garage, the stitches in her back pulled uncomfortably when she leaned back into the leather seat. They were starting to truly heal, but were too dry and had become more tender. She wished she could reach them better.

The freeway on ramp was still a few blocks ahead when her phone rang and she picked it up to hear Kit's voice on the other end say, "Hey, Alexis. It's Kit Rockland. How are you feeling?"

Lexie was surprised at how nice it was to hear her voice. "I'm doing well, thank you. How is everything back in Wyoming?"

"Actually, I'm here in L.A. for a couple of days working, and this time I didn't bring Rossen. He had some government report he had to do right now and Mimi was sick, so it's just me this time. Where are you and have you already had dinner, or can I treat you?"

The two young women determined that they were within a reasonable distance of each other and Lexie met her at her hotel to eat together. Walking through the revolving doors into the hotel lobby, she felt more upbeat than she'd felt all day. Kit had begun to be a true friend in the few days she was there and it would be great to see her again.

When Kit actually did see her, she gave her a gentle hug and commented on the bruises Lexie still sported that didn't want to stay covered with make up. "You still look like you fell over a rocky cliff in a raging storm. How are you feeling, really?"

This time Lexie was more honest when she admitted with a self-conscious smile, "Like I fell over a rocky cliff. Honestly, I'm not nearly as tough as I once thought. Coming back to work full time has been pushing it."

They sat down at their table and opened their

menus and Kit said, "It's too bad that you couldn't take a little more time. I wish you were self employed and could call all your shots. Is there anything I can do to help you?"

"In fact, there is. Would there be any way you could help me reach the stitches on my back to put something on them to soften them up. They're so dry they're pulling and I can't reach them. Sometimes living alone isn't all it's cracked up to be."

Kit smiled. "I'll bet it's down right peaceful after being with the Rocklands. I remember the first day I ever came there. I couldn't even imagine a family that big and rowdy. Cooper was there then too. You don't know him, but he's the character of the bunch."

"They're all characters. They were thoroughly entertaining. I actually went to my brother's house for a couple of days on my way home. He has two babies, so I was acclimated to the quiet in stages. But my condo does seem pretty dull after last week."

Their food came and they ate and talked. Sean was never mentioned by either of them. It was almost like an unspoken agreement, but they discussed all kinds of other things. Lexie asked several questions about the church, and when she commented that she wished there was someone nearby that she could learn from Kit laughed and said, "Alexis, not only are there missionaries everywhere, but there are wards all throughout the world. There is a ward right here where any neighbors you have who are LDS go. You probably already know some of them."

Lexie was stunned. She had had no idea there were that many Mormons. Kit told her how to get online and find one near her so she could check it out and then reached across the table to touch Lexie's hand.

"I hope you do check it out. The gospel of Jesus Christ is my greatest treasure. It has been the best thing that ever happened to me. I love it even more than my family because I know that without it we wouldn't even be an eternal family. I hope you'll love it too."

Her voice was so quiet and pointed that it touched something in Lexie's heart. It was hard to equate the rocker chick she knew Kit to be, with the beautiful sincere woman across the table from her, speaking her deepest feelings. However, there was no doubt that she was indeed a famous rock star when a few minutes later, several young people approached their table for her autograph.

After they ate, Kit took her up to her hotel room where she dug out some antibiotic ointment, smeared it on Lexie's stitches for her, and then covered them up with her bandage again. They arranged for Lexie to come have lunch with Kit again the next day. She would come right to Kit's studio so she could meet some of the other people Kit worked with and get to see what the inside of a recording studio was like. Lexie left her with a hug.

Somehow, visiting with her that evening had been very comforting for her. She knew from the way Kit avoided the mention of Sean that he wasn't in the picture as far as Lexie was concerned, but she was glad she didn't have to completely walk away from the other friends she'd made in Wyoming. She'd grown to love the whole Rockland family in her time spent with them and it would be great to still be able to stay in some contact with them.

The next day Lexie called and offered to bring the lunch for everyone. When she was escorted past a set of security guards into the building where she was to meet Kit, she was floored to be greeted by one of the biggest recording stars in the whole country. The dark and handsome man who opened the door was none other than Nick Sartori, rock and roll super star. He greeted her as if he was thrilled to meet her and then introduced her to the members of his band and the others who were working there in the studio that day. Meeting him in that setting, with Kit at her side, made it all seem perfectly normal and they had an entertaining lunch together before Lexie headed back out to work.

Lexie shook her head and smiled as she pulled her car back into the parking garage. Kit had just invited her to the most astounding lunch ever, but it had been no big deal. Kit was still just sweet, savvy Kit, and Nick and the others had been friendly and funny, and she'd felt right at home. His drummer had been particularly entertaining. Lexie couldn't remember when she'd met someone that animated. Walking past the others in the lobby, she truly felt like she had a fun secret from them this time. Her determination to continue to have a real life was coming along.

Kit went home and Lexie's body healed. On the tenth day, she went and had her stitches taken out and all she had to show for her stint in the wilds of Wyoming was a couple of pink scars and a heart that struggled to forget. She was going to be okay. She kept telling herself that at those times when she couldn't make the memories stay neatly stored away.

She went on with her job, and did her best to be fulfilled by it. She'd put her resumes out, and, in fact, had been offered a number of positions at different firms around the area. Each time she had discussed the offer with Eric and they'd prayed about what she should do. They'd never felt good about any of them, so she was still with Meyers and Meyers and Victor, wondering what her Father in Heaven had in mind for her.

She'd gotten on line as Kit told her and found a church nearby she could attend, as well as one near Eric so he could check it out with her. She'd just begun to show up and had been going for a couple weeks before anyone understood that she wasn't a member and was just checking things out. When the bishop realized that, they encouraged her to take a more basic Sunday school class that taught fundamentals, and arranged for her to have a set of missionaries come and teach her too. She and Eric talked back and forth about what they were learning every few days and it brought them closer than ever.

She was relishing having the true gospel, but other than that, the energy had drained out of her life like she'd sprung a hole somewhere. The weeks dragged on seemingly interminably, and still, she dreamed of Sean night after night and then woke up tired and discouraged. Even doing her very best to forget him didn't tarnish the memories that haunted her.

He'd been right. Time did help. Okay, so it had been months instead of days, and the fairy had only gotten faintly less distinct, but at least her image was slightly less haunting than it had been. He'd been working insanely long hours trying to keep his mind occupied, and to a certain extent it was working. At least he was getting a ton done. He'd designed and built more in the last couple of months, than he'd done in the year before that.

At first it had been so hard to go where he'd been

with her that he could hardly face his mom's house or even his own kitchen. On about the fourth day of not showing up at his parents' house for meals, the whole family had arrived at his house for dinner, complete with the meal in tow. They'd been so nonchalant about it that he'd had to laugh and he made it a point to put in an appearance at least once every day or two after that. He knew they loved him and they probably understood. At least as much as he did.

What was there to understand? She'd been here a total of six and a half days. That was nothing! He'd be done being haunted any day now.

The days had turned into weeks and then months and he still worked long into the nights to try to ease the images in his mind. Days weren't so bad. He was at different job sites she'd never been to, and he was around people who had never known her. He could stay busy and focused and make it through, but the nights had been hard. Harder than almost anything he'd ever done.

The only thing that helped him sleep was to get tired enough that his body shut his brain down. He'd spent about a million hours in his home gym, working his body to exhaustion to kill the frustration, and he'd spent seemingly another million in his office to keep his mind busy. That was the only way he could go to bed and have any hope of getting any real rest.

When it became obvious that this wasn't an infatuation that was going to go as easily as it had come, he'd begun to have long talks with God, trying to understand why he'd fallen so hard for someone who was so incompatible. He'd never really come to understand his feelings, but he'd gotten closer to God, and had come to trust that somehow he would make it

Once Enchanted
through this in one piece.

So, every morning he just kept getting up and going to work, waiting as patiently as he could for the fairy with the fiery hair to go away.

Work was work. Try as she might, Lexie was having trouble finding the passion. She didn't dislike working, and she liked the actual litigating. It was just that ever since that morning after her all-nighter, when she'd known she needed to make some changes, she'd never once since then felt like part of the team at work.

That was probably a good thing when, late one Friday afternoon in early August, she came across some documents in some paperwork Trent was having her sort that she clearly understood were the go ahead for the project in Jackson Hole. She was working in Trent's office for the afternoon so she didn't have to haul the files back and forth. He was in and out, mostly out, so she was able to work relatively straight through. He had, in fact, found a planning commission member there in Wyoming who would declare the Blackstone's ranch blighted and was poised to take the ranch using eminent domain.

Lexie was appalled enough that she sat in shock for a few minutes, and then made copies of the documents and went straight home, praying all the way. She had no idea what she should do, but she felt strongly that she needed to do something. She struggled to decide if this had any attorney client privileges attached to it and finally decided it was simply information dealing with his real estate company and it would be okay to blow the whistle.

The remainder of the afternoon was spent trying to

figure out exactly what she could do ethically and, at length, she packed an overnight bag and went to the airport. The only flight she could find that night flew into Salt Lake City, but she took it anyway, then rented a car and hit the road east on I-80 for south western Wyoming. Still unsure of what to do, she put in a call to Naomi even though it was now ten thirty at night. Naomi was wise and would understand the situation, and Lexie knew she could trust her.

They talked all the way across the sage flats almost until Lexie reached Evanston. They decided Lexie would continue on to the ranch. First thing in the morning, they would find someone in the county who could figure out what was going on and, hopefully discreetly, put a stop to the whole deal.

As it turned out, Naomi recommended Lexie go to Sean. He was the one in the family who worked the most closely with the county planners and they both knew he could be depended on to keep Lexie out of trouble as much as possible, but still have a vested interest in preserving the Blackstone ranch.

Talking with Naomi had helped immensely, but knowing now that she would be seeing Sean in the morning had Lexie completely undone. All the thoughts and feelings she'd worked to squelch for months came rushing back with a vengeance. It was as if all the struggle to put his face, and voice, and laugh out of her thoughts and heart had been a trick of her imagination. The memories had been there all the time, waiting to flood back as soon as her defenses were down.

At one o'clock in the morning, California time, she drove through the locked gates at the guardhouse and up the gravel road to the ranch. She still had no idea how she was going to deal with Sean in the morning. Tonight she was too tired to figure it out. Maybe she'd be suddenly inspired. As of right now, all she knew was that she wanted to see him more than she could even fathom. She was just glad she had a valid excuse.

Chapter 25

He'd been dreaming about her, he was sure of it. He lay awake wondering what had awakened him this early on a Saturday morning. Working so late made it harder to get up some days, and this morning something seemed out of place. That was what it was. Some idiot was ringing his doorbell.

He'd never actually heard it ring since he'd installed it, and he didn't think whichever brother was ringing it today was all that funny. As he climbed out of bed to go chew out whoever it was, he tried to think if there was something he'd agreed to do today that he'd forgotten. It wasn't like the door was locked.

They'd given up on the bell and started knocking and he growled as he reached his entry. "All right, all right already! What is it?" He yanked open the door, ready to trounce someone.

Whatever he had been going to snap died in his throat when he saw Lexie standing there on his front porch. She was wearing the zip off shorts again with a stretch t-shirt this time, and her hair hung around her face in the auburn curls of last night's dream. He didn't know what to say, couldn't even speak, and apparently, she couldn't either. Self-consciously he ran a hand through his tousled hair and looked down at his own rumpled t-shirt and cut off sweats, embarrassed.

Finally, he decided a man can only take so much and he reached out to her and literally pulled her inside and shut the door. Without letting go of her hand he went back down his hall and through the bedroom he'd recently vacated, and into the adjoining bathroom. He dropped her hand, pulled his toothbrush out of the holder on the counter, and began to brush his teeth. She looked at him as if he'd lost it and finally spoke to ask a question.

"What are you doing?"

His words were full of foaming toothpaste as he tried to answer her with the brush still in his mouth. It was garbled, but he tried to say, "Brushing my teeth."

She was obviously lost. "Why did you drag me through your house and into your bathroom so I could watch you brush your teeth?"

He spit and wiped his mouth with the hand towel as he turned to answer her. "So I could kiss you." He gathered her into his arms almost ferociously and proceeded to kiss her more thoroughly than he'd ever dreamed of kissing her. And he'd dreamed of kissing her a lot.

He finally pulled his mouth away and hugged her tightly with his cheek against her hair. "First I thought you were one of my brothers, and then I thought you were a dream. You are a dream. What are you doing here?"

She pulled away from him far enough to look up at him and say, "You don't so much as even email me! Not even once! And then kiss me like that, the second you see me? What is up with you?"

He could see the hurt in her eyes, and it killed him. He ran a hand through his hair again with a sigh. "I shouldn't have kissed you, I know, but I couldn't help

224

myself. I'm sorry." He took her hand to lead her back out of his bathroom and bedroom. Once safely in the hall he turned back to her. "No, I'm not sorry. I loved kissing you and I want to do it again." He was watching her, wondering what she was thinking as she was looking back at him. He could tell she was hurt and confused.

His arms came around her gently as he pulled her to him and admitted softly, "I've missed you. I've missed you incredibly. I'm sorry I haven't told you. I thought it would be better that way. I've spent the last months trying so hard to forget you." She looked up at him, her eyes sad and questioning and he added with all the discouragement he'd been fighting, "It hasn't worked very well."

"Why have you been working to forget me? What's wrong with us being friends?"

His eyes searched hers. Did she really think being just friends was an option? Maybe it was for her, but it wasn't for him. He'd cared way too much, way too fast, to ever be able to be just friends. He turned away and brought her with him into the kitchen. As he started to pull things out to fix breakfast, he said in a voice that held infinite sadness, "I guess I'm not as tough as you are Lexie."

She got right in front of him. "I'm a little lost here, Sean Rockland. I knew when I left that you had no intention of staying in touch with me. And I dealt with that as best I could, understanding that I was just a week long fling for you, and that you wanted it that way. But those kisses in there didn't feel like I don't matter to you, so what's going on? Why does the thought of remaining friends make you sad?"

Once Enchanted

For a minute, he had no idea how to answer that. He didn't think he could bare his heart to her. Finally, he asked, "Did those kisses in there feel like I want to be just buddies?"

Hesitantly she replied, "No, of course not. Why?"

"That's my point, Lex. What I feel for you is never going to be just friends."

"Okay. So now I'm more lost than ever. You like me, so we can't keep in touch with each other at all. Is that what I'm understanding?" He didn't answer her, but he was watching her as he grated cheese and she went on, "So how does kissing me like a caveman fit into all of this? We can't be friends, but kissing is okay?" She looked confused and he had no idea what to say.

Finally, her face brightened, and her tone was more upbeat when she said, "Okay."

"Okay what?"

"Okay, so we'll say we aren't friends, and we won't keep in touch, but I can come here and we'll kiss like we really matter. I can live with that. Come kiss me."

He shook his head and started to chuckle. "Between the two of us, we're both nuts. You haven't by any chance been taking narcotics this morning have you?"

She smiled. "No. Why do you ask?"

"Just, the last time you said something like that you were pretty drugged. How is your back, by the way?" He came over to her and gently pulled her shirt aside to look at her scar and let out a breath. "That was the hardest thing for me. To not call and find out how you were." He tried to tell her with his eyes how much that had troubled him.

226

She turned around toward him again. "It was hard for me too. I was hammered. Kit is actually the one who helped me a lot with that. She helped me put salve on it and bandage it when she came to town. I couldn't reach it by myself."

He stared down at her. "Kit saw you when she came to LA? She never mentioned it to me."

Lexie just gave him a sad smile and put her arms around him. "You were going to kiss me, remember?" He was suddenly worried and she must have known it because she said, "You weren't afraid of me awhile ago in your bathroom."

He put both hands on her shoulders. "I must have been half asleep and caught off guard. I didn't have the good sense to be afraid of you. Now I do, and I'm scared to death."

She moved closer to him and whispered, "Funny, I can't imagine you afraid of anything." She stood on tiptoe to reach his mouth before he finally dropped his head to hers with a long sigh. Kissing her was the sweetest thing he'd ever known. He knew this was going to kill him later, but he didn't even care. She felt like heaven here in his arms. He kissed her with all the pent up frustration of the last months and she kissed him back the same way.

When they finally ended the kiss, she stayed there in his arms and said all too innocently, "I've missed this kitchen."

They ate and she explained why she was there, and asked what he thought could be done without implicating her enough to have her disbarred, saying, "Your mom thought it would be okay if I tried to get someone to look into it, as long as I kept as much distance as possible. Can you think of anyone honest who could delve?"

Nodding, thoughtfully, he mused, "Ken Terry is the head of the planning commission. He actually invited me to his ranch the other day to help brand calves. I told him I didn't have time, but maybe I'd better show up this morning and see if he has any more to do." He turned to look into her eyes. "How long are you going to be here?"

"I have to be back at work on Monday morning so no one knows I came." She obviously hated to even admit it to him, and she looked down and said, "I'm sorry."

With a gentle voice, he said, "It's okay, Lexie. You can do what you need to do without feeling guilty about it. Can I have a date with you tonight?"

"Yes, please. Can we do something that won't be too obvious in case there's an investigation into who blew the whistle on this thing? I'll face the music if I have to, but I really think it would be better to not have anyone know I came here."

"I was thinking of taking you line dancing, but that might be too public. What would you like to do?"

"You don't have anymore chinking to do, do you?"

She said it with a grin, but he couldn't return it. His voice was subdued when he answered, "Honestly, I haven't been back to the cabin since the day you left. I don't even know if it's still standing."

Sobering, she asked, "Why haven't you been there?"

He got up to start clearing the table. "Just busy I guess." He tried to meet her eyes, but was afraid she'd see what he was thinking if he did.

The mood lightened again when she asked, "No dessert? I came all the way from California for some lemon sorbet, you know."

228

He dug in the freezer. "No lemon, but I do have some chunky fish. Will that do?" He didn't tell her that he hadn't been able to face lemon sorbet since the day she'd left either.

"If I pass on the chunky fish for breakfast, can I still have the slow dancing in the kitchen?" She came up to him again. "No strings attached, I swear." She raised both hands as if to emphasize her point and he took them in his.

He pulled her close and gently put his hands into her hair. "No strings attached. Fat chance." His mouth came down on hers.

A little while later she said, "We completely forgot the music. No wonder we forgot we were dancing."

Leaving her to go meet the head of the Teton county planning commission was hard. He knew she'd be gone again the next day and he wished he could just spend the whole time with her, but this had to be done. He took the paper work she'd brought and left her standing on his driveway next to the Trailblazer she'd rented in Salt Lake City.

When he got to the ranch, Ken was surprised to see him, but acted as if it was perfectly normal for him to show up just after breakfast on a Saturday morning. He took him out to show him a new bull he'd just purchased, and when they were alone, standing at the side of a pole corral he turned to Sean and with a smile in his eyes, asked him what he really came for.

Grinning, Sean asked, "How did you know I had another agenda?"

Ken laughed. "You'd be surprised how many people show up here like this who need something or other. Usually, it's some hot shot developer and not a nice, upstanding, local boy like yourself, but you get the picture."

"You're right and I'll get right to the point. First off, what I'm here about is a rather delicate matter. The person who brought this to my attention this morning is in a bit of a bind and would prefer this be kept as discreet as possible. Are you familiar with the Blackstone ranch just south and west of Jackson?"

"George Blackstone's?" Sean nodded and Ken turned back to lean on the poles and said, "Yes, I'm very familiar with it. We've been in the process of having it put into a conservation easement for over a year now. Just last week we got the final approval. The paperwork should be complete within the next two weeks."

"Then you're completely unaware that one of your commissioners has declared that piece blighted, and approved a plan to have it condemned and developed by one of those hot shots you were just talking about, through eminent domain?"

Ken nearly exploded away from the pole he was leaning on. "What! What are you talking about?" Sean handed him the official county document that showed its blighted status. Ken studied it for a moment as his face got red and the veins became prominent on his neck. "What in tarnation is going on here?" He was shouting at Sean like it was all his doing.

Sean chuckled and turned back to look out at the bull and said calmly, "Can I assume that this will be looked into from your end? It would be a shame for the Blackstone's to lose a ranch that has been in their family for a couple hundred years. Not to mention all your hard work. And making the county look ridiculous." He smiled as he emphasized this last.

"Darn tootin' right this will be looked into! Somebody's head is going to roll with this one, and I can just bet who it is! This county is being taken over by foreigners. Out-of-staters who have no sense of how we do things honestly in this state! Mostly it's those dang movie stars! They think because they have gobs of money they can do whatever they want! These new scallywags think nothing of bending a few ethics to line their own pockets. I'll bet that's what's going on here. If money changed hands on this, there'll be criminal charges pressed!"

Sean turned to head back to his truck. Smiling, he said over his shoulder, "I know a couple of good attorneys. That's a fine bull, Ken. If you decide you want to sell him, call me."

Ken called him back, "You'd better take this with you." He handed him the paper. "Monday morning I might just accidentally do an internal audit on any unusual projects and find the same information you just showed me without letting on that any outsider at all brought it to my attention. That way your whistleblower will remain out of the picture and I can have all the credit." He slapped Sean heartily on the shoulder. "Good of you to stop by. Always a pleasure to show a fellow cattleman an exceptional new bull!"

On the way back to the ranch, after grabbing a burger in Jackson, Sean drove faster than he probably should have. He was glad Ken had taken over as easily as he had. It was unlikely that either he or Lexie would have to do much more. He couldn't wait to see her again. He knew that was incredibly foolish after what he'd been through these last months, but today he didn't even care. She was even more beautiful and captivating than he remembered.

He thought about what they should do this afternoon as he traveled. What he really wanted to do was get her on a horse again. She needed to do that as soon as possible to keep her from becoming afraid of them after her last experience. It should have been done before she left the last time, but she'd felt so lousy. Maybe he could talk her into going for a nice, easy ride. He still hadn't figured out what to do with her for their date tonight. He'd let her decide.

When he pulled into his parents' yard, he saw that his dad and Rossen had had the same thought he'd had. Rossen had Lexie in the arena on a sweet old horse riding in circles, while his dad watched from the rail. As Sean got out of his truck, his mom came up to him for a hug. She leaned back to study him, and he met her gaze openly as she asked, "Well?"

"Well what?"

"Don't give me that. You know exactly what I'm asking. How are you?"

He gave her a grin as he ducked through the fence. "Right now I'm great! I don't even want to think about Monday morning."

When Lexie was through riding, she came over to him where he stood near the rail next to his father and it was the most natural thing in the world when she slipped in next to him and he put his arm around her shoulders. They stood there talking for a minute until his dad took the reins of the horse and went off to put it away.

She looked up at Sean and asked, "How did it go?" The words were calm, but he could see the strain in her eyes.

With one finger, he rubbed at the tiny grimace between her brows. "Good, I think. Ken was totally

232

disgusted. The conservation easement on that piece had just barely been approved, so whoever pulled this had blown off a huge amount of time-consuming paperwork and negotiations. He said he would get to the bottom of it as discreetly as possible and if someone had been paid off, he was going to press charges." Sean grinned. "I told him I knew a couple of good attorneys."

She laughed. "Oh, that'd be discreet."

"What are your plans for this afternoon? Will you do something with me?"

The smile faded from her face as she studied his. "What did you have in mind?"

"I have no idea. I didn't know you were going to be here, remember. I was actually going to work all day today."

"On Saturday? I would have thought a guy like you, in a place like this, would be off fishing or something. You don't usually work weekends, do you?"

He didn't meet her look again. "I have lately. It's been extra busy."

She came around to stand in front of him and looked up into his face. "You're self employed. Nobody pulls your chain, remember? Why all the long hours? You call all the shots."

He almost felt evasive when he answered, "I've just been calling a lot more of them lately. That's all. Do you fish?"

She let him change the subject. "A little. It's been years and years, but my dad took us a few times when we were kids."

He turned to begin walking toward his truck. "Did you like it? Or did you go just to please him?"

"I liked it. I wasn't a die hard like he and Eric were. I think the whole need for predation is a guy thing, but I loved eating them. When I got tired of fishing, I just read a book on the bank while they finished. We were all happy that way."

"Does Eric still fish much?"

With a laugh, she said, "Eric has a two year old and a newborn. He says this is his season of parenting, and he takes it pretty seriously. He's having a ball with them, but I doubt he fits in much fishing."

Sean was watching her talk about Eric's family. She sounded happy when she did. He wished he dared ask her why Eric wanted a family and not her, but he didn't want to mar their short time together. Instead, he asked, "Would you like to fish today? The river should actually be great right now."

"Can we take some wooly buggers?" She laughed when she asked it.

"I think we can handle that. Do I dare ask how you're feeling after riding? How sore are you? Do you want to ride horses or take the truck?"

Her blush made him chuckle as she said, "No horses. Please."

At his truck, he stopped and turned. "Are you afraid of them now? Since your cliff wreck?"

She shook her head. "I actually was a bit at first, but Rossen and Tillie helped me over that. No. Now I just have bruises in unmentionable places. By tomorrow, I'll be walking funny as it is. The stink bugs will think you're nuts to be seen with me." She smiled up at him. "Maybe we could take a four wheeler."

Heading out toward the river just up the road in Slade and Isabel's valley, with her arms wrapped around his waist, Sean decided the four-wheeler was a great idea, and he was glad she'd requested it. It brought back memories of their first morning together, but today she wasn't hesitant to hold on to him like she'd been that time, and he loved the feel of her against his back.

At the river, he rigged her up with the requested wooly buggers. She'd laughed and said they just looked like a regular bug to her. When she had no idea how to cast a fly rod and either tangled her line with wind knots or flogged the water, undoubtedly scaring any nearby fish clear into Montana, he came up behind her to help her.

She obviously enjoyed his rather intimate instruction, and then learned how to cast so quickly, that he almost had to wonder if it had all been a ploy to get him close. He thought about that and decided it was okay by him.

He stayed with her and helped her for awhile, inordinately pleased that she had no qualms about wading in the river in the old tennies she'd borrowed from Joey for the occasion. Of all the places they'd been, she looked the absolute best standing there in the Salt River with the water rippling against her calves and the sunlight glinting off her hair.

She hooked into a fish and he came and helped her unhook it and then carefully slipped it back into the green and gold water. At first, he didn't know what he'd done when she put her hands on her slim hips and gave him the look and said, "Sean Rockland! I was gonna eat that fish! What did you go and turn him loose for?"

He had to laugh at her. "Sorry, I just assumed this would be catch and release. Can't we just fish and you can keep one when we're ready to go home?"

She shook her head adamantly. "You can catch and release if you want to, but not me. That would be tantamount to getting pleasure from hurting their little fish lips and I'm not going there. It's bad enough to hurt them to eat them, but God says that's okay, so I can handle that. But only that. If it's big enough to keep, then I don't want to turn it loose."

He grinned at that and she went on, "You can laugh all you want, but I'm not facing a bunch of accusatory trout when I reach the other side! I'm in big enough trouble as it is without that." She laughed again and admitted, "But I don't think it will matter all that much. It will probably take me all day to catch my dinner anyway."

"Accusatory trout? You ought to be an attorney or something." He shook his head still chuckling. "In the interest of conserving the trout with the little fish lips, I'll just go ahead and catch and release and let you be in charge of procuring the meat for the table. In which case, you'd better keep two. Is God okay with that?"

Working to keep her line untangled, she said, "Hey, you're the aficionado on God here. You'll have to ask that. But I will accept the responsibility for helping you to not go hungry, if I must."

A half-hour or so later she hooked into another one and he began to wade over toward her to help her with it, but she said, "Don't even think about turning this fish loose!" She was so serious about it that she cracked him up. "It's big enough for both of us, so I only have to catch one. That's much better than having to kill two of them. I hate that part."

He handed her the wriggling fish after he'd removed the hook and watched her wade closer to the bank and try to whack the fish's head on a rock. After several tries at braining the poor thing unsuccessfully, he came and took it from her, picked up a stick laying half out of the water and quickly put it out of its misery. He tried to hide his wide smile as he handed it back to her, and went back to fishing. Her attempt at being kind hearted had been positively torturous, but he wasn't going to mention it.

She put the fish on a stringer and put it in the water to keep, and then went and sat on a huge boulder out in the current. With her feet still in the river, she began to watch him. She played in the water with her hands and then eventually laid back to look up at the sky. Within minutes she'd turned on her side. She lay with her head on her arm and her legs curled up and he realized she'd gone to sleep on a boulder smack dab in the middle of the river. This time she looked like a mermaid or rusalka laying there in the sun with her fiery hair falling across the rock. He could see why the sailors had been enchanted to their deaths.

Even though she was fifteen feet away from him and asleep, she was still with him, and he fished there beside her, at peace for the first time in months. The serenity of this down time was the healing his heart and mind had needed with an almost choking desperation. The sun on his back, the light breeze, and the sound of the water, rejuvenated his spirit in a way he hadn't dreamed possible.

As peaceful as it was, he was still inexplicably drawn to her. At length he broke his fly rod down and left it and his vest on the bank, then waded out to her rock to sit on it beside her silently, with his back propped against the boulder. She was beautiful laying there. She looked like a very untamed version of one of the porcelain dolls Joey had collected when she was little.

The sun turned her skin to silk and her hair to living flame. It was all he could do to let her sleep, and he reached out a finger to one long red curl. It was amazing how soft it was for how wild the curls were. It was bright burgundy with highlights the color of a new copper penny and gold bullion. He'd never seen anything like it. He wound his hands through it gently and then felt guilty when she stirred. She must have had a long week and a short night.

She woke up just enough to flash him her sleepy green eyes and move her head up onto his thigh as she turned over, spilling her hair all the way across his lap. Settling back to enjoy her while she napped, he had to wonder if he'd dreamed this day up. With her hair in his hands and the sound of the river all around him, he leaned his own head back and closed his eyes. The way he felt with her, how could she not be the one he'd been looking for, for so long?

His entire life he'd never questioned whether he would marry a girl who was a member of the church. He'd dreamed of the day he would be sealed in the temple for time and all eternity. He'd seen someone there across the altar from him in white, he'd just never seen a face, but it was so easy to picture Lexie's there now. What a mean twist of fate that the face he saw couldn't be there in the temple with him. Still, he had to wonder why Heavenly Father would let him have that vision and feel this way, if it wasn't right.

For just a moment, he wondered if he could marry her even if she was of another faith. She was a good person. He knew that without a doubt. She had a wonderful spirit about her, and he'd never questioned whether she was trying to do what she thought was right. That had been obvious from the time she'd tried to keep him from shooting that stupid elk. But just the thought of forgoing his lifelong goal made him mentally squirm, although it was a thought he wanted to take out and examine. There was always the chance he could convert her wasn't there?

He drifted off to sleep determined to talk to her about the church the first chance he got. There was still her career and L.A. to deal with, but the sweet smelling jumble of riotous curls in his lap made those obstacles feel smaller than they had felt in the past.

Once Enchanted

240

Chapter 26

Waking up, realizing she was sleeping with her head on his thigh on a rock in the middle of the river made her smile. That was definitely the way to wake up from a nap. She thought back to first thing that morning when he'd yanked open his front door. Even as late as she went to bed last night, she'd slept poorly knowing she was going to see him today. It was like trying to get to sleep on Christmas Eve.

Finally, seeing him standing there with his hair tousled and in his cut off sweats was even better than the dream. He was even sexier than she remembered. He looked brawnier than he had in June and there was a leanness to his face that made it look like it had been carved from stone. The blue flames that had flared in his eyes the moment he saw her had been the best part of it all.

She smiled remembering that kiss in his bathroom. Just thinking about it made her stomach do somersaults. She'd never dreamed of a kiss like that. She'd never let herself. He was the only one in her life who she dreamed of kissing and these last months she'd known letting her heart and mind go places like that would just hurt.

This afternoon, looking back on this day, and how easy and comfortable being with him had been, her whole mindset was heading in a different direction.

Once Enchanted

He could try to forget her all he wanted, but that wasn't going to change the look in his eyes. She wasn't sure what it was that she saw there, but it was something that smoothed over the wrinkles in her heart and calmed the turmoil in her mind.

She had no idea where this relationship was going. She only knew that it was right and good, and that this man was as much of a rock in the river of her life as the boulder they were sitting on right now. Eric had been right when he'd known immediately that somehow Sean was different that first time she'd told him about him. She rolled over to look up at him as she made the discovery that she was going to go with the flow here and see where this friendship that couldn't be a friendship ended up.

As she turned, she realized he had both of his hands in her hair. Moving made it pull almost uncomfortably, but she still reveled in the way he felt about it. Before they'd even really gotten to know each other he'd made no secret of the fact that he thought it was marvelous. No one had ever made her feel beautiful the way he did. It was an incredibly heady feeling. Knowing she was desirable to him made her feel this sweet, very female sense of power.

He opened his eyes to look down at her for a long, slow moment before gently brushing the hair back from her face. "Short night?" His voice was a bit husky.

She rolled back over on his thigh, afraid he'd be able to see the way she felt in her eyes. "Short night after a long week. Sorry I fell asleep on you."

"It's okay, I was tired too." He pulled her back around and lifted her up into his arms and cradled her with her head up on his chest. "I just thought I was

242

Jaclyn M. Hawkes

fishing with a rusalka. I was waiting to see if you were going to wake up and lead me down to the river bottom to keep me a slave to your feminine powers." There was a smile in his voice. The steady beat of his heart was reassuring in her ear.

For awhile, they just sat there like that, enjoying the closeness and the peaceful setting around them. Finally, she said, "There's something I need to tell you."

He didn't move, just gave a mellow, "Hmm." His breath on her skin felt warm.

"I'm joining the largest women's organization in the world. I thought you should know, since it's all your fault."

He pulled away to look at her and she couldn't help her smile as she looked back and he asked, "Which women's organization have I driven you to?"

His eyes held hers almost mesmerized. "Uh. It's a big one. More than ten times bigger than the National Organization of Women."

She felt him tense against her and his blue eyes sharpened. "What do you mean your joining?"

"I'm getting baptized in a couple of weeks." His eyes narrowed as he looked at her, trying to understand what she was telling him. She sat up and knelt in front of him. "I really am. I wouldn't joke about this. I'm joining the Relief Society. When I went home, I had to find out more about the prophet. I had to know for myself. I've been going to my ward there and taking the missionary lessons and I'm getting baptized. Thank you, by the way. We've been looking for the true gospel."

She could tell that he still wasn't sure that what he was hearing was what she was really saying and she asked, "Sean, are you okay? Aren't you going to say

243

something? This is a good thing isn't it? That whole worth of a soul thing. Aren't you happy for me? For us? Eric and his wife are getting baptized too."

"Slow down, Lex. What are you telling me?" She wasn't getting through to him very well.

She spoke slowly and distinctly, "Sean David Rockland, will you baptize me a member of the Church of Jesus Christ of Latter Day Saints?" This time he was thoroughly in shock. She took his slack jaw and tried to move it up and down. "This is where you say yes, and act like you're happy for me. You are happy for me aren't you?"

Finally, he understood. She saw wonder dawn in the deepest part of his eyes. "You're getting baptized! Really? Aw, Lexie that is so great! I had no idea. You've been going all this time?" He touched her hand with his own brown, calloused one. "I wish I'd known. I mean, I know it was my fault that I didn't know, but that's such a great thing! I would've liked to have been excited for you."

In a serious tone, she said, "No. Being completely apart from you was a good thing in this. I checked this gospel out knowing that you and I weren't an issue. I had to do the whole study the facts and think it through. If you'd been in the picture it would have been harder to know if this was a Jesus Christ thing or a Sean thing. This way there was no doubt. Does that make sense?"

He smiled and tugged her back down to sit by him. "That makes sense. You're an incredibly wise woman. Do you know that?"

Leaning her head against his shoulder, she sighed happily. "I don't know about that. I have my moments. But you can tell me that as much as you'd
244

like anyway." After a minute, she leaned back around to look at him again. "You didn't answer me. Will you baptize me?"

For some reason, he was watching her mouth. "Lexie, I'd love to baptize you, but there are a couple of missionaries back in California who have traveled a long way from home to teach you the gospel. Don't you think they'll be terribly disappointed if they don't get to baptize you after they've helped you to know this is Christ's church?"

"Oh. You're so sweet." She patted his cheek with her hand. "You're very thoughtful, but they were sister missionaries. They can't do the actual baptism anyway. And as far as conversion, that was mostly you. I trusted your judgment; I just had to make sure for myself. And Kit and Rossen were a big help too. Mostly the missionaries have helped me to understand the principles and the correct doctrine."

"Then I'd be honored to baptize you. When do I need to be there?"

She was watching his eyes. "You'd come to L.A. to do it?"

"Of course, Lex. This is a big deal. I wouldn't miss it." He put a strong arm around her shoulder. "Have you set a date?"

She looked down and shook her head. "I wanted to talk to you first and see if you'd do it and when you'd be available."

"I can come anytime. Would you be offended if my family came too?" She looked up surprised. "I'll bet they'd all like to be there."

"I'd love it, but I don't feel like I can ask them all to travel that far. I'm already so much in all of your debt." She paused for a minute again. "Speaking of debt, you never cashed my check for the horse."

He was quiet while he thought for awhile and then said, "She was insured, so you didn't need to pay me. Accidents happen."

"Sean." She reached over and turned him to face her. "I was responsible for her death. I need to be honorable about it. It's the least I can do after causing that whole mess. I feel even worse since your mom told me she was your best broodmare and bred to a champion stallion. Cash the check. It's the right thing for me to do."

Looking at her long and hard, he finally said quietly, "Okay. I'll cash the check. How many more of my family have you been keeping in touch with?"

Without looking away she said, "All of them. I haven't heard from Treyne, or Ruger or Marti, but everyone else."

He considered this at length and then asked, "If you hadn't found that information about the Blackstone's ranch, would you have still asked me to baptize you?"

She looked down at her hands. "I'd like to think so, but I don't know. You'd made it pretty clear that when I left, I was gone. But I'd thought about it a lot. Let's just say that I'm really glad I felt like I needed to come here this weekend and leave it at that, shall we?"

"Was it all me? You haven't contacted me either."

Her heart was a little sick at his question. Knowing more about the church now, she could understand why he wouldn't have wanted to date a non-member, but honestly, the fact that he hadn't even tried to get a number or an address had killed her. It had definitely been all his idea that they not keep in touch, but she wasn't brave enough to tell him that and said instead, "Nothing is ever all one sided is it?"

Facing the fact that he'd planned to forget her and probably still did, kind of put a damper on her afternoon. She stretched and slid to the edge of the rock to climb down, giving herself a lecture that she'd be leaving this man again tomorrow and that other than her baptism, she'd probably be leaving him behind with no strings attached again. She didn't understand him very well. He acted sometimes as if he adored her, and then sometimes like he was walking straight away. She tried to bring back her resolve of a little while ago to just let things flow, but still, the day had lost some of its sparkle. This wasn't the way she thought she'd feel when she told him she was joining the church.

They gathered up her fish, climbed back on the four-wheeler, and headed home. Holding onto him was still wonderful and when he stopped the bike on the ridge top to watch the sunset again, it was easier to enjoy right now and try not to worry about the future. She watched the glorious reds and oranges fade to purple, and azure, and gold as she breathed in the clear, sweet sage and pine scented air.

Still, for a relatively intelligent woman, she sure didn't have many answers.

Once Enchanted

Once Enchanted

Chapter 27

Back at his house, Sean taught her how to clean her fish in the big utility sink in his garage before going out to light the grill. He'd felt her emotionally pull away from him and knew it was his fault, but there was nothing for it. It was wiser on both of their parts to try to keep their heads, in spite of the physical attraction that frissioned between them like a living thing.

She was going to be a member of the church, but she was still obviously committed to her career and fully intended to go back home to L.A. He couldn't blame her for either of those two. It was her life and she had the right to live it as she chose. He just couldn't reconcile himself to giving up the thoughts of the family that he'd always hoped for, even to be with her.

Well, he could have, but he was torn. The time spent with her this afternoon on the river had been heaven, but he knew that families were part of God's plan and he couldn't bring himself to consciously veer from that plan even if it meant being haunted by an exquisite fairy forever. Lexie ranked huge, but God was God.

He came back into the house just as Rossen walked in the front door carrying a watermelon. Sean slapped a hand to his forehead. He'd completely forgotten the family was having dinner at his house that evening.

He looked at his watch, and realized he had just twenty minutes. How had he forgotten? Lexie had him way too preoccupied. He turned to face her and could tell she knew just what was going on by the little smile on her face. She confirmed that when she said, "Would it be okay if we included your family on our date?"

He came over and gave her a hug, laughing. "I'm sorry. Dinner at my house completely slipped my mind. Could you hurry and help me make a pasta salad?"

"That's pushing it for me. You'll have to tell me what to do." They hurried to pull the dinner together. He put water on to boil and took a huge bag of steaks out of the fridge that he'd put in to marinate the night before, and went out to put them on the grill that luckily was already heating. At least almost everything was prepped. Only dessert was missing. They'd just have to have hot fudge sundaes.

As everyone came in, he put them to work chopping various vegetables for the salad while he fried pieces of smoked sausage. He was floored as one by one they all came in and greeted Lexie. Some even hugged her, and it was obvious they'd all kept up their friendships with her without him even knowing. Mimi greeted her with a huge happy hug and tickle. Sean couldn't even believe it. When had Mimi gotten that friendly with her? Lexie and his mother were talking about her up coming baptism and he wondered how long his mother had known. And why hadn't she mentioned such a big event? How had he missed all of this?

Dinner came together miraculously, in spite of his absentmindedness. And then several of them decided to stay and watch a movie down in his home theater.

Lexie saved him from another awkward situation when she asked if he would mind if they stayed and watched with them. He made popcorn and took it down to find that they'd chosen to watch Willow.

Somehow it was very apropos to have a beautiful warrior girl with wild red hair who turned into a gracious queen on the big screen. Lexie had never seen it and she watched his family cheering the Brownie characters on and quoting the movie as much as she watched the show. She hadn't said much about the theater room, but he caught her looking all around as she settled into the double recliner beside him.

He was glad he'd seen the movie. Otherwise, he wouldn't have known what was going on. His mind was far more on the girl next to him than the film. He hadn't noticed that she smelled like some kind of fruit on the river today. Some kind of fruit and then some perfume that was much more exotic. It seemed to cloud his brain, because he was having a hard time remembering to keep his heart safely at a distance. Mostly he just wanted to snuggle her close and breathe her in. When the movie finally ended, he wished it had lasted longer.

It was after eleven and he was torn. He could see that she was tired, in spite of her nap in the middle of the river, but she was also leaving right after church the next day and he wanted to enjoy having her while he could. She was watching him and he thought she knew what he was thinking. When she arranged to ride back to his mom's house with Joey anyway, he was ridiculously disappointed, even though he'd been with her for almost thirteen hours already that day.

He was a mess. One minute he wanted nothing more than to be with her and then the next he was

251

trying to mentally push her away. Everyone filed out, but he caught her arm before she went out the door and pulled her back in and closed it. He wasn't even sure what he was doing, but he knew he needed more of a goodbye than a friendly smile and hug. He pulled her to him almost roughly and buried his hands in her hair as he kissed her. Geez, she felt like his woman.

Some of his frustration must have come through because she pushed him away and licked her lip and he knew that he'd hurt her. His remorse was instant and he pulled her back and kissed her this time as if she was made of glass and whispered how sorry he was against her lips. Joey was honking and he wanted to swear.

Lexie looked up at him with those vivid eyes that he couldn't fathom right then and said, "Good night, Sean. I'll see you in the morning." She gave him one last, long look before turning to walk out and shut the door behind her. Her habit of not looking back was gonna kill him.

He spent forty minutes on his speed bag and universal gym working at a frenzied pace before his body gave out. This time he was physically done, but his mind hadn't even begun to ease up. This day had been heaven, but he knew he was going to regret it forever anyway.

It was late enough in the night before he got to sleep that Sunday morning his alarm didn't even register. It rang for more than fifteen minutes before it finally woke him, and he had to rush to dress and get over to his mom and dad's. They were almost finished with the family breakfast and he grabbed a muffin and a glass of milk while he waited for Lexie to come back out of her room. She'd already eaten and disappeared.

When she did show up, wearing a deep emerald suit dress that exactly matched her eyes, and carrying not just a Bible, but a Book of Mormon too, she rocked him to his toes. His feelings were strong enough to actually scare him. For a minute he wondered if he'd be better off staying away from church today, knowing he was going to pay for it for years to come. How was he supposed to use his head when she looked like that? There was no way.

She walked up to him almost a little hesitantly. She had a pink spot on her lip that made him feel terrible. He touched it gently, feeling infinitely guilty. "Sorry." He leaned down to kiss it softly, oblivious to the rest of his family standing nearby. She glanced quickly around at them, and he took her hand to hustle her out to his truck.

Pulling down the step and helping her up in was bitter sweet. This morning even the happy memories filleted him. She hadn't said a word and he was hopelessly mixed up and wondering what she was thinking. Then she slid over to the middle of the seat before fastening her seatbelt, confusing him even more. He put his arm around her and kissed her gently for a long minute before starting up and pulling away down the gravel road.

They'd been on the road fully ten minutes before either of them spoke. A couple of times she'd looked up at him with big quiet eyes, and he'd looked back, not knowing what to even think, let alone what to say. Finally, he said, "I'm sorry I hurt you." He squeezed her hand gently.

It felt like a long time before she said, "I don't understand you, Sean." The words were so quiet that he almost couldn't hear her.

He sighed as he ran a hand through his hair. "That makes two of us, honey. That makes two of us."

Priesthood felt like it lasted for days, and then when he finally got back beside her, being there was almost painful. Neither one of them had much to say during either of the meetings and when they stood up to go fifteen minutes before the end of sacrament meeting so she could get on the road to Salt Lake to catch her plane, his heart was in shreds. At his parents, he loaded her overnight bag into the back of her rental car and they stood looking at each other wordlessly beside it. Geez, it was hard to say goodbye. Finally, he asked, "Can I drive you to Salt Lake?"

Even then, she just looked at him for a second, the obvious hanging there between them. He'd have to find a way home after turning in her rental car, but he didn't even care. She looked down as she quietly asked, "Do you think that's wise?"

He was obviously frustrated when he answered, "How should I know? Probably not, but I can't do this. I can't just put you in this car and shut the door and watch you drive away without looking back again." He couldn't even look at her as he said it.

"I'd love it if you drove me to Salt Lake. But, we should go right now. I'm going to miss my plane."

His smile was sad. "That's not a very good argument, is it?" He held her door for her and then went around and got in the driver's seat and peeled out, spraying gravel in their wake.

He turned the radio on low. She was listening to a playlist of Celtic music and the flute floated quietly through the car like a thick mist that coated his heart and mind with lead. It was plaintive and soulful and the loneliest sound he'd ever heard. They rode the entire two and a half hours without talking. They held hands, sometimes almost desperately, but speaking was taboo, just as it had been before she left the last time.

At the airport, they turned in the car and crossed into the main terminal as if walking to the executioner's. He stood in the line for security with her hoping they'd have a hijacking or something that would shut the whole place down so she couldn't leave. It didn't happen, and eventually they got close to the front and he had to tell her goodbye. He still didn't feel like he could do this.

She turned to him and buried her face in his chest, hugging him tightly. He wrapped his arms around her and held on. Finally, she looked up at him and he leaned down to kiss her, watching her eyes the whole time. The person behind them cleared his throat and Sean pulled her out of line. He kissed her again trying not to let the unbearable frustration through and then pushed her gently back into line. Neither one of them said goodbye. She turned and went through the security station and then hesitated for just a second, but she still didn't look back before she disappeared on up the concourse.

He took a shuttle to one of the hotels near the airport, walked inside his room, and literally kicked the door closed. Then he felt stupid. His dad would have been disappointed that he'd done something so petty in violence.

He pulled his tie all the way off and tossed it on the chair, and then threw his jacket on the bed and went to stand at the window and watched the planes coming and going at the airport. He watched the one he thought she was on until it was a speck in the clouds and finally disappeared and he felt like kicking the door again.

He showered and then laid on the bed, exhausted, but not the least bit sleepy. Punching the pillow into shape, he turned on his stomach. What was up with him? Man, he needed some serious stock taking.

He tried to make sense of the way he'd been feeling the last forty hours or so, but only ended up with an emotional roller coaster ride which made absolutely no sense. He went back to the window and stared out without seeing anything but her slim figure in the sleek green suit walking away from him. The stupid thing about it was that even though he was completely mixed up in his own mind, the only thing he knew for certain about what was in her mind was that she readily accepted his affections, but then could just as readily leave him. When they were together their friendship was effortless and the physical attraction was outrageous, but neither one of them could talk about feelings or the future. What a stupid way to be!

At length, he again faced the truth that he wasn't up to doing this alone, and went and knelt beside the bed. He poured out his heart and then asked for help in getting through this. The last three months had been awful, and this time losing her was worse by far. He needed divine intervention. Even though he knew that God knew all about what was going on, he still told him his troubles in depth, hoping he'd be able to work something out in his own mind. Eventually, exhausted, he still had no answers, but found a measure of peace of mind and went to sleep.

His phone ringing woke him up in the evening. It was Brandon. When he found out where Sean was and that he didn't have his truck, he laughed. "Dude, you're a mess! This girl has you wrapped around her finger and it's almost funny to see the great king of the heart breakers finally getting a taste of his own medicine!" When Sean didn't laugh back, he paused for a moment and then said. "I'm coming to get you. Which hotel are you in?"

Sean sighed. "Don't come get me. I'm not up to facing my mother yet. Give me a day or two."

"Your mom is the reason I'm coming. How do you think I knew you were gone? If I don't come get you, she'll call out the Federales and show up herself and you'll end up feeling like a marshmallow momma's boy. And what would you do in Salt Lake without wheels for a day or two?"

Sean finally worked up a hint of a smile. "Meet girls?"

Brandon laughed. "You're a sick man, Rockland, but I like that about you. Do you want me tonight or tomorrow afternoon? Those are your only two choices. Angie has plans for tomorrow night and Tuesday's booked solid."

"Let me sit for tonight and come get me tomorrow. Maybe by then I'll be better than a puddle of adolescent emotion. And can I ask you another favor? Call Rossen and tell him I'm just hanging out in the city for a day, so the word will get back to my mom before the Federales hear from her."

"Will do. I'll call you when I hit the state line. Get out of that hotel room and get a breath of fresh smog. It'll do you good!"

"And you think I'm sick. Thanks, man. I owe you."

"Actually, I'm the one who got you into this whole mess by the last favor you did me. Now we're even."

"Not by a long shot."

"Hey, I've had my moments in the sun with heartburn over a female. I thought Angie was going to kill me before we actually got our act together and got married."

Sean didn't have an answer for that and finally just said, "See you tomorrow, knowing as he did that he and Lexie didn't have the happily ever after in their future like Brandon and Angie had found.

He took Brandon's advice and took the train in to Temple Square. He walked around the visitor's center and went to the Christus until they closed and locked the doors, then he went back to his hotel and dug out the Book of Mormon that was with the Gideon Bible and settled down to study the story of the stripling warriors. It was his favorite part of the Book of Mormon and even today, it made him feel like he could handle anything. Reading about someone else's troubles made his own seem not so insurmountable.

He finally dropped off to sleep and woke up feeling not as trashed as he'd expected to be. He showered and went back down town and spent the morning doing some much needed shopping he'd been neglecting. He truly did try to dig up an interest in some of the women he saw, but it was frankly pathetic. Compared to Lexie's vibrant beauty and polish they all looked drab and slightly dense.

He did find one store clerk who had some potential until she came around the counter and he noticed her bellybutton ring. He left the store disgusted. He hated this whole meat market thing!

Brandon was as good as his word and showed up mid afternoon and hauled Sean's halfhearted body home. He'd looked at him and blatantly told him he looked like something the dog had thrown up. It worked wonders and Sean laughed until he felt much better. When Brandon dumped him off in his driveway, he had enough gumption to try to get on with his life again.

Once Enchanted

Chapter 28

He threw himself into work with a renewed vengeance and made it through the next two weeks until it was time to fly out to California with his family to baptize Lexie. Everyone was going except Marti. She had a race meet at Wyoming downs where she'd committed to be the attending veterinarian.

Sitting on the plane, Sean ran the gamut of mixed emotions. He was so excited for Lexie to become a member, and while he couldn't wait to see her, he almost dreaded it too. He'd begun to feel like a dog having its tail docked an inch at a time.

Moreover, going back to L.A. was something he'd sworn he'd never do. Some of his mission he'd loved. He'd learned to truly love the people, even when some of the stuff they did was brain dead. And some of his companions had become his closest friends, but he'd never get used to that huge, smelly city. Just thinking about it made him feel like he couldn't breathe.

He knew his mom was watching him and leaned his head back and closed his eyes trying to feign sleep. He'd been honest with Lexie. This really was a big deal and he wouldn't miss it no matter how uncomfortable it made him feel.

It was Friday afternoon and Lexie's baptism was the next morning. They all came off the concourse and were headed toward the rental car counter when

Rossen and Kit exclaimed at recognizing Nick Sartori's limousine driver. It turned out that Lexie had arranged to have him pick them all up and she and Nick were waiting outside in the limo to greet them. They were obviously having such a good time hanging out together in the limo that it almost made Sean melancholy.

She greeted them all enthusiastically, and then explained that her brother Eric wouldn't be coming into town after all, because his children had come down with the chicken pox the day before.

Apparently, Lexie viewed this as the opportunity to pay back their hospitality and had arranged for their hotel and gotten tickets to a musical for all of them for that night. She volunteered to watch Mimi and only hesitated a second or two before accepting Sean's offer to stay home with her and send Nick or one of his friends in his stead. He didn't necessarily mind the theater, but it didn't hold a candle to spending the time with Lexie.

At first, she was somewhat stiff with him at her condo with the toddler and she never did really loosen up. He wondered if she was having as rough a time being without him as he was without her. They didn't actually get truly comfortable with each other until it got late enough that they were too tired to be wary and just then his family stopped by her building to pick him and Mimi up. He left Lexie at her door, with a gentle hug but not even a kiss, hoping things would go more smoothly in the morning.

She looked celestial in her white dress. Seeing her like that made him wonder how things couldn't work out between them. She seemed more perfect than ever, and her face glowed when he helped her back up out of the water after baptizing her. He'd baptized a number of people in his life, but nothing came close to having the chance to baptize her. All of his brothers and his dad stood in the circle with a handful of the elders from her home ward to confirm her.

Afterward, watching his family hug her and shake her hand, he felt that sense of rightness again. She belonged there with them all. She felt as much of a sister as any of the other Rockland women did. A sister to all of them except him. She would never feel like just a sister to him. Even in her sparkling white dress, he wanted to kiss her.

That afternoon they all went to the beach. It was the one part of his mission that had truly fascinated him, even though going in the water had been forbidden. Nick had arranged for them to have access to the private gated beach he owned part of, so they had the whole thing largely to themselves. Sean went out into the ocean and the stress of the city seemed to wash off. The sea was magical. He could see how the myths and fairy tales had come to be. There really was something enchanting about it all.

Body surfing out in the waves with his brothers, he turned to see Lexie on the beach with Mimi. They were skipping out into the surf and then turning and running, trying to escape the waves as they spilled up on the sand. He could hear their squeals over the sound of the breakers and the seabirds overhead.

He knew exactly how the sailors must have felt when they'd tried to follow the mermaids only to find that they couldn't really have them and that their fascination would come to mean their very lives.

Once Enchanted

Watching Lexie was like a deadly seduction that he knew would eventually kill him. At least that's the way he felt when he thought about being without her again.

Actually leaving her this time was easier. The whole family was running behind and there wasn't a chance to have a long, painful goodbye. They had to rush just to make it onto the plane. Finally, seated on the plane, waiting for it to taxi away he looked back at the airport. It still hurt even though he was the one leaving her this time. At least he had looked back at her.

🐎

Back home he tried to truly just get on with his life. She was officially a member now, and he was aware his family stayed in touch with her, but he was going to do better at getting past this. He honestly thought that, and for weeks he struggled along okay, until the day he got a card from her in the mail. It had a photograph on the front of a beautiful winged fairy with long, curly red hair. The photo was misty and she was almost hidden in the trees and flowers of a lush woodland. It was such a lifelike photo that he had to wonder how it had even been created.

It took him several minutes of staring at the face that could have been her on the mythical, winged girl before he even opened the card to see what it said inside. It was short. It simply said, "I thought of you when I saw this, Lexie".

His stomach clenched when he read her pretty, bold signature. He'd treasure the card, but it sure didn't make putting her out of his mind any easier. He put the card on the edge of his drafting table and tried

264

to go back to work, but every few minutes his mind and his eyes would wander to the enchanting fairy in the mist.

A couple of days later he found a tiny fairy figurine hanging from the curtains over his kitchen window, the sun sparkling off her iridescent wings. He found it in the morning and for just a second had to wonder how it had come to be in his house during the night. He wanted to ask who had put it there, but decided not to. He didn't want his family to think it was a big deal.

He wasn't sure how to respond to either the card or the figurine. His reasoning argued that he shouldn't respond at all and just move on and let his heart heal, but that felt so brutal, and they somehow helped the heartache. Finally, one morning he sent her a simple text. "There are fairies here. Where are you?"

Later she texted him back. "Work (w/ L.A. stink bugs). You?"

That night after working until his mind was positively weary he wrote back, "Kitchen/ dessert/ lonely". He shouldn't have said it, but it was true.

After that day, they texted or emailed back and forth almost everyday. He always asked her where she was. For some reason he needed to know where she was and what she was doing that was so much more fulfilling than being where he was. It was a little morbid, but he always wondered. Nothing was ever said about the future, but at least he knew she was thinking about him, and him, her. He got bits and pieces about how work was going. Not much, but enough to know that she was still frustrated with the status quo. He didn't know why she stayed there. He'd probably never understand.

About every week he found another fairy somewhere in his house. They'd be peeking out from behind something on his bathroom counter or hiding in the spices in his cupboard. He was really beginning to be intrigued with how they were appearing. They were all tiny, colorful, winged creatures with beautiful faces and incredible deep copper hair that tumbled around their shoulders and invaded his dreams.

One day, almost as paybacks, he asked Kit to do him a favor and take a tub of lemon sorbet to Lexie when she went to L.A. on her next trip. He'd figured out that Kit and Rossen were staying with Lexie at her condo these days when they went. Kit had laughed. She had no idea why he asked that, but she was willing to comply. He didn't hear from Lexie for more than two days after that and wondered if he'd offended her. When she finally wrote back, it was a simple, "Sorbet excellent, dancing lost in transit. Dang!". He'd laughed until his heart felt better. From then on he sent sorbet every time he found another fairy somewhere in his house. There were eleven in all.

Chapter 29

The first time Kit came to see her in her office, the whole firm came unglued. All the guys standing around talking instead of working had been speechless for once, and then they'd been just about salivating as Kit went back through to leave. When she was gone, they all piled into Lexie's office to find out what was going on.

Kit had brought a small tub of lemon sorbet packed in dry ice and beautifully gift-wrapped and Lexie had been speechless too, when she opened it. She wasn't sure whether to be happy about it or sit right down and bawl. She missed him like she'd miss oxygen. Ever since the evening she'd hit that stupid elk she'd been an emotional mess. Being madly in love with someone so unattainable and so not there, was a good way to scramble a heart.

When Lexie told Kit about all the commotion in the office they'd laughed, and after that it got to be almost a standing joke to see who they could get to deliver the ever-mysterious lemon sorbet. Nick had brought it the next week and the office had been in enough of an uproar afterwards that Trent's dad, Spencer—the big boss, had come out and tried to get back some semblance of order and sent people back to their offices to work.

Bryan Cole, a country music super star, had been

the courier the next time and when Spencer came out again, he gave Lexie a rather pointed look. She just gave him a shrug as if to say, "Hey, it's not my fault." and took the neatly packaged ice cream back into her office to stash in her little fridge. Every time she opened the delivery to see Sean's frozen proffering, she'd remember his delicious kisses and her tummy would do its somersault thing. Then, the rest of the afternoon, she'd daydream about dancing in the kitchen.

Sometimes it made her so lonely that she felt like he was being cruel and she almost resented them, but she still lined up the empty tubs on the edge of the shelf inside her office closet so that on rough days she could look at them and know that at least he was thinking about her.

The hassles of working where she wasn't happy and being perpetually lonely week after week were beginning to wear on her. There were times she wondered if she'd ever truly feel like smiling again. She doubled up on her vitamins and started to spend almost an hour every night in the exercise room of her building trying to see if the almost violent physical activity would somehow counteract the ache in her chest.

She resolved to honestly try to get on with her personal life and accepted every date she thought she could possibly deal with from the men in her singles ward, and even asked Eric to set her up on the odd weekend she was down there. However, so far, all that had come from it was that they'd made Sean look better than ever and she'd had to turn down two marriage proposals. Still, she doggedly tried. She wasn't going to feel like this forever. Not if she could help it.

One weekend was the worst of all. She knew she was hormonal and that she was an emotional mess, but there wasn't much she could do about it, and when Nick showed up late in the day Friday with a pretty box, she didn't even crack a smile. He noticed her less than exuberant countenance and quietly shut the door to her office and asked, "You okay?"

She couldn't even answer him for fear of losing the fragile control she had on her emotions. He walked over and wrapped her in a hug and the very gentleness of it made her break down and cry on his shoulder until it was wet through. Afterward, she felt more embarrassed than she'd ever felt in her life and was incredibly grateful when he made some silly comment about crooked lawyers that made her laugh through her tears. He dried them with a tissue from the shelf behind her desk and laughingly told her she needed to fix her mascara before she got back to suing people.

Walking him back out with everyone staring and coming up to him, she had to wonder if the constant attention from people all around him ever got old.

At the door, he turned to her and said, "Yeah, sometimes it gets old, but mostly I'm just grateful. I try to always remember that it's the fans who have given me my success and lifestyle." She turned to stare at him, stunned that he appeared to be able to read her mind and he smiled and said, "Don't go home and cry alone. Take yourself out shopping or dancing or something. At the very least call me, and we'll go up the coast highway in my Maserati. That always helps me when I've bawled all afternoon. There's something about going a hundred and twenty that's very therapeutic."

She laughed at the thought of him bawling all

afternoon, which she was sure was exactly what he'd intended. He gave her his rock star smile, and gently touched a tendril of hair that had escaped its pins. "I have no answers as far as romance goes, Lexie. I'm a hopeless failure in that department. Mostly due to those heart throb Rockland boys, but I do know they're good men and worth the hassle. Hang in there. You're tough. Chicks are durable, ya know. You'll figure this out and live happily ever after." He pulled the red curl and let it spring back and then left through the firms huge glass doors.

When Lexie turned around to go back to her office she saw that Trent had been watching through the doorway of his office. She nodded to him and went into hers, thinking about all the things Nick had said. He was incredibly good looking, and she knew he was attracted to her. She wondered why she knew there would never be anything more than friendship between them.

She finished out the afternoon and then went home and took a long bath. Nick and her cry had helped her immensely, but her heart and her spirit were still unbelievably tired. She lay in the tub with the jets going and wondered what was so wrong with her as far as Sean was concerned. None of the other men she came in contact with seemed to have a problem becoming attached to her. She was invariably trying to field one come on or another.

It was just Sean. The one guy she would have done anything to be with, wanted nothing to do with her. Well, not nothing. She knew when she was around him that the blue fire in his eyes could get hot enough to torch things within seconds. That wasn't a lot of consolation when he made no bones about the

Jaclyn M. Hawkes

fact he wanted to forget her when she wasn't in his
arms.

She tried to take Nick's advice and not go home
and cry alone, but when she closed her eyes, she could
feel the tears slip down her face. It was just the steamy
bathroom. It couldn't be that she was twenty-seven
years old and miserably alone in a city of millions of
people.

She was out of the tub and eating a carton of
reheated Chinese food in front of the TV when Eric
called. The first thing he said was, "Hey Lex. You've
been on my mind a lot this afternoon. Are you all
right?" The tears that she'd believed all cried out
started up again with a vengeance and he waited on
the line until she got enough control to speak.

Finally, he said, "Lexie, quit your job. Sell your
condo and move away from there. I'm sure that's why
you're not getting a yes from God about the other job
offers. None of them are right. Just do it. Either come
here to work or go to Wyoming, but get on with it.
One thing we do know is that what you're doing right
now isn't working. You get more miserable by the day.
I'll come out and help you move. What d'ya say?"

She sniffled as she tried to reassure him, "I'm okay.
Honestly, I am. I'm just hormonal. Sorry." She told
him about crying all over Nick that afternoon and they
laughed together at her sogging out a famous guy.
They spent over an hour talking and by the end of the
phone call; she'd decided he was right. She'd known
for months that she needed to make some changes and
it was time to just do it. Maybe a change of scenery
would help. But somewhere far away from Wyoming.
She didn't think she could take knowing Sean was
close and still out of reach.

When she went to hang up, Eric said, "I've always

271

wanted to ride in a Maserati."

Monday morning she put in her two-weeks notice and decided while she was at it, she'd sell her car and buy something more practical. When she mentioned to Rossen and Kit, who were in town, that she was going to move, they asked if she'd already sold her condo. When she said no, they offered to buy it on the spot. They worked out a deal where they would even buy all her furniture and dishes so she wouldn't have to move everything, and could just buy new when she finally decided where she was going. When they left, she was thrilled to have dealt with that huge hassle so easily and yet crushed to know that Sean's family was so much closer to her and more concerned about her than he was.

Chapter 30

He rode up to the cabin one afternoon with a string of pack horses carrying the stovepipe and the fireplace box he was going to install. When he got there, he found a fairy peeking around a post on the front porch where they'd eaten their lunch. She had a baby with her and it rocked him to his toes. He was stunned and had no clue how to take it. He wished he could just call Lexie and ask her straight out what it meant. This one was almost a bit strange. None of his brothers had ever been out here that he knew of. He took out his phone and texted her. "Cabin enchanted. How? Where are you?"

After dinner that night, when he went into his office to work, he found a long real email message from her. Her boss had gotten word that day that the blighted status of the ranch in Jackson had been reversed and the commissioner he'd been working with had been indicted over the deal and was being criminally charged with corruption, extortion, and racketeering. Trent Meyers had been subpoenaed and was livid about the whole thing.

Sean couldn't really tell how she felt about it all. It was hard to get her tone in writing. He wished again that he could just pick up the phone and call her. Hearing her voice would solve so many things.

That night he had to work late to have any hope of sleeping.

The next morning he found a fairy again. This one was on his bedroom dresser and he could have sworn it hadn't been there when he'd come to bed at almost three thirty. He picked up the tiny figurine and studied it, marveling at the workmanship and the incredible likeness to Lexie's features. How in the world had this gotten there? He was almost beginning to think there really were little woodland people here.

He couldn't get her out of his mind that day. Not for two minutes. He'd been trying to design a new house and finally, just before lunch he called it a day, took his fly rod, and went out to the river. He never even made a cast, just waded out to Lexie's boulder and sat there thinking about her. It was late September, and the world around the ranch had turned brilliant red and gold and yellow. She'd been haunting him night and day for almost five months. Sometimes he wondered if he was going crazy.

He sat on her rock for hours and then went home and into his bedroom to pray. He poured out his heart one more time, then got up, squared his shoulders, and headed back out to his truck to go to one of the homes he was building. Maybe he'd do better at a site than he'd done in his office. He was headed down the gravel road when he met Joey's little SUV coming in and pulled over to roll down his window to say hi.

She rolled down her own window and studied him and without hesitating asked, "Are you as hammered as you look?"

He thought about that for just a second and said, "Yeah, I think I am. How 'bout yourself?"

She didn't even laugh. "Why don't you just marry her and be done with it? How long are you going to keep doing this to yourself? It better not be much longer. She'll find somebody else."

Jaclyn M. Hawkes

The thought made his heart stop just for a beat and a long sigh accompanied his discouraged answer. "It's not all that simple, Joey. We're not exactly Mr. and Mrs. Compatible. Do you want me to go live in LA? Or her to agree to have a family she doesn't want?"

Joey looked taken aback. "She doesn't want a family? That's hard to believe as much as she loves Mimi and Maire and Patrick. She really told you she doesn't want a family?"

"Of course she hasn't told me that. Does she need to say it, when it's so obvious? And who are Maire and Patrick?"

Joey threw her SUV into park and shut off the engine. "You've got to be kidding me! You haven't even asked her? You're just assuming she doesn't want a family and that's what's keeping you apart? That's the dumbest thing I've ever heard! Sean David Rockland, get your butt on a plane and go talk to that girl! Of course she wants a family. What in the world would make you think she doesn't?"

"Joey, would she be a hard core professional woman in the middle of LA, if marriage and family were all that vital to her? Think about it."

Joey just looked at him and shook her head. "Sean, you're such a dork! It takes a husband and father you know. Until she finds him, what? Do you just want her to stay home and knit tea towels? How brain dead are you? Are you not even going to give her the chance to say yes or no? Who do you think you are, making all the decisions without even giving her a chance to weigh in? You're a jerk! A big, stupid, unrighteous dominion jerk! You don't even deserve her!"

She started her engine back up, pointedly rolled up the window in his face and sped off. He could hear the gravel she was throwing up hitting his tailgate. He stayed parked right where he was, trying to assimilate what she'd just tossed at him. A dork and a jerk. A big, stupid, unrighteous dominion jerk.

She acted as if he was being all high handed or something. Of course Lexie didn't want a family. Would she keep going back there to work so hard if that wasn't what she truly wanted to be doing? He looked in his rear view mirror at Joey's SUV receding into the distance and realized there was a fairy sitting beside one of the headrests on his backseat. He turned around to stare at it. *How in tarnation?*

He reached back and picked it up and asked it, "Am I missing something really important here?" The woodland creature had no answers for him. It just looked at him with those big green eyes that were so like Lexie's. He sat there for a few more minutes and then turned his truck around and went back home.

He lined up all the fairies on his drafting table and looked at them. Why was she sending them to him? What did she want? What did the baby one mean? Would she send them if she didn't want him to think about her? If he was honest, that's why he was sending her lemon sorbet. He'd been hoping she'd remember how much they'd enjoyed each other's company and want to come back to him. No, he'd never actually asked her to come. But couldn't she just tell that he needed her more than anything?

He sat there and began to feel guilty. This wasn't really about how he couldn't live without her. This was about the fact that he didn't really love her enough to be willing to pull up stakes and move back to L.A. He thought about that long and hard. Yeah, he did. He absolutely loved her enough to take a chance on
276

trying to talk her into a family, even if he had to live in Los Angeles to do it. It had just taken Joey being brutally honest with him to make him see that.

He stopped himself for a minute. What if she really didn't want a family at all? It was a thought that made his heart ache. Nevertheless, he had to know. He couldn't live like this anymore. He went back into his room to pray for more wisdom.

All evening long and way into the night he struggled to hear an answer. He needed to know if it would be going straight against God's plan to be with her, even if she didn't want a family now, in hopes that someday she would. He felt good about it and wished he could be more sure of what God was trying to communicate to him.

Was he okay with this because it was what he wanted? Or was he really getting the answer that his future lay with a spitfire redhead in California? He finally fell into a restless sleep and dreamed about those stupid, never letting him be at peace, fairies.

When he woke up the next morning in the bright light of day, it was as if the actual sunshine had revealed what should have been obvious to him from the very start. He'd thought he needed to ask God every time, when in truth, he also needed to ask Lexie. God was good with this decision. He had no doubts about that now. Joey was right. He was a jerk to not even give her the chance to turn him down. He packed a bag and hustled to his truck, whistling for the first time in forever.

Once Enchanted

Chapter 31

Her stomach had just started to tell her that she shouldn't have skipped breakfast when she'd come in that morning at five a.m., and that she couldn't skip lunch when her cell phone buzzed that she was getting a text. She was deep into writing a brief, but she glanced at it anyway. Her heart rate quickened just a hair when she saw it was Sean. She tried not to let herself react that way, but no amount of self-discipline could make her heart behave.

She always felt that little jump and then invariably felt a let down after thinking about him and knowing he wished he could forget her. All the text said was his usual question. "Where are you?" She had to chuckle. Where did he think she was at eleven o'clock on a Thursday morning?

She texted back, "Where do you think? And you?"

Two minutes later, Elise, the receptionist at the front desk paged her and said, "Ms. O'Brien, The Rock is here to see you, but he's blonde. Shall I send him in?"

"I'll come out, thank you." What had Kit done this time? The Rock? He wasn't even a singer, he was a movie star! Why would a black guy dye his hair blonde? She was just going to get up and go out to meet him when her door opened. She looked up and for just a second or two couldn't breathe.

It wasn't The Rock. It was Sean. Then she got it. He was built just like The Rock, only he was blonde, and wearing a gorgeous business suit. That's what Elise had meant. Even with all of her concentration, she couldn't seem to get her mouth to move.

Finally, he said, "Hi, Lex." She was still just looking at him in shock and he came around her desk, slid her chair back and took both of her hands to pull her to her feet. Then he kissed her again like he had that morning in his bathroom. At first, she just let him kiss her, but when the shock wore off, she couldn't help herself and started to kiss him back. Then she came to her senses and decided she ought to push him away. Before she got around to it, she heard a gasp at her office door, reluctantly pulled back and turned her head to look over and find Elise standing there, shocked.

"Sorry, Ms. O'Brien. I just wanted to make sure he found your office okay. He didn't want to wait for you to come out."

Straightening her suit, Lexie smiled. "Uh, he found it. Thank you."

Sean went over, shut the door and came back. He went to take her into his arms again, but she put up a hand and he slowed down. He didn't stop and still obviously intended to kiss her again even as she asked, "What are you doing?"

He laughed as his arms tightened around her. "I'm kissing you. What does it look like?" After a few minutes, he pulled barely away and whispered, "I've missed you." He put his forehead down against hers. "I've missed you so much."

She was still just looking at him in silence. She couldn't even believe what she was seeing, and was
280

incredibly lost. Finally, she asked, "What's going on? What are you doing here?" She searched his eyes trying to figure it all out. Not only was he here, but he was acting as if they were a couple without all the issues that had been swirling around them from the start. Incredibly lost was actually an understatement.

He backed off just far enough that he could really look at her. "Aren't you glad to see me?"

This was really strange. He was too happy and too cuddly for her to fathom this. She felt almost a bit wary. "I'm not sure what to be." She asked him right out, "Why are you not trying to stay away from me?"

He sighed and touched a tendril of her hair. "I deserved that. I can't stay away. It was hopeless anyway. I can't live without you. So I'm giving up and giving in and just enjoying you instead. If you'll let me."

All of this was so unnerving that she didn't even think to object when he started pulling the pins out of her hair and letting it down. He put his hands into it and tugged on it while she was still just looking at him. Finally, in a gentle voice he said, "I'm sorry I surprised you so badly. Have you already eaten? Can I take you to lunch and talk to you?"

His gentleness got through to her and she struggled to pull herself together. "Yeah, sure. Just let me get to a point that I can save this." She sat back at her computer, finished her work and powered it down. While she was turning it off, she asked, "What are you doing in LA? I didn't think I'd see you here again." It was a casual question, but she was burning to know what had gotten him here after the way she knew he felt about it.

Watching her eyes, he said, "It's kind of a long story. Can we talk about it over Chinese? I know a great little restaurant not far from here."

When the computer made its shutting down sound, he took her hand and headed out of her office. Still slightly shell shocked, she just followed him. In the lobby, they met Trent and several of the other guys. She got the impression that Elise had been talking about her because they all stared at her and Sean as they walked on by. She heard one of the guys comment on her hair as she went past and she realized Sean had let it down and she'd just left it. As she got to the door Trent said, "Oh, A.J., I forgot to tell you I need you to meet with me at twelve thirty to go over some notes for tomorrow's stuff. Maybe you'd better stay in the building today."

Sean didn't skip a beat. "I'm sorry. Ms. O'Brien has prior commitments this afternoon and won't be able to make that meeting. It's too bad she didn't know sooner. You'll have to reschedule. We'll be back about one." With that, they both calmly walked out the door and she was proud of herself for not even gasping when he'd talked to her boss like that. Of course, Sean was about four inches taller and sixty pounds heavier than Trent and it was blatantly obvious that none of it was fat, so Trent hadn't even thought to push it, but still.

In the parking garage, he handed her into a rental car and when he came around and got in beside her, he turned and apologized. "Sorry for talking to your boss like that. It ticked me off that he thought he could just order you to stay in the building. We really can stay if you want to. He's still as much of a weasel as he was years ago."

282

That made her nearly panic. "You knew him? Did he know you?" This could be bad. Trent was still furious about his Jackson deal gone south and she really didn't want him to wonder if it was her doing.

With a humorless laugh Sean said, "I'm sure he had no idea who I was. He didn't bother to notice me years ago and I've grown about six inches and put on like seventy pounds since then." He glanced over at her. "You said you handled a lot of the load there, but if those pretty boys in the lobby were the best he's got, he's in trouble. No wonder you have to produce!"

She almost got the giggles. They would have been so offended if they'd heard him say that, but it was exactly what she'd been thinking from day one. And Sean was right. Trent was in trouble. Spencer Meyers, Trent's dad, was actually quite an astute man and had offered her a huge raise to try to keep her from leaving. But it had been too little, too late, and she'd been honest with him that while she appreciated the money, she didn't intend to stay. It was too bad Trent couldn't have been a chip off the old block.

Sean took her to a tiny Chinese restaurant she'd never even known about, although it was quite close to her office. They went in the door and were seated, and then he got up and went through the kitchen doors into the back. A second later Lexie heard a veritable squeal and could hear a woman chattering in some language she didn't recognize.

The woman was obviously excited and a few minutes later a tiny elderly Asian woman burst through the kitchen doors and came to her table, with Sean at her heels. The little woman gripped Sean's hand and then greeted Lexie with positively effluent enthusiasm. She was still chattering away and though

283

Lexie had no idea what she was saying, it was very apparent that she knew Sean and was overjoyed to see him.

Finally, she calmed down somewhat and with the utmost dignity, she spoke to Lexie in broken English, "Welcome to my restauran, Miss Elder Rockland. Am most happy meet you." She gave a subtle bow and Lexie looked at Sean to know how to respond. He laughed and wrapped an arm around the tiny woman and she smiled up at him again. It was interesting to see how much he obviously loved this little woman he must not have seen much in the last few years.

"Alexis Joy, I'd like you to meet Sister Chan. Sister Chan, this is Lexie O'Brien. She lives and works here."

The little woman reached up to pat Sean's cheek and said, "You sit. Talk. I bring much food." She bustled back into the kitchen and Lexie laughed, feeling like she had been through a minor windstorm.

"She's priceless. Apparently you met her on your mission?"

His smile receded until it didn't reach his eyes anymore. "She's the one who mothered me enough to help me handle this town. She spoke almost no English and I hadn't figured out Mandarin and for awhile there, it was just the international language of love, but it was what I needed. I'm not sure that I'd have survived without her."

Lexie watched his face as he spoke. Even after several years of being home, talking about his experience with living here still came at the cost of his smile. It indeed must have been a time of struggle for him. It made her wonder all the more what had brought him back this time.

Again, she decided to just ask him right out. "Why are you here? In LA, when it makes you so unhappy?"

He hesitated and Sister Chan burst back in from the kitchen with heaping plates of steaming Chinese food that smelled like heaven. Lexie was disappointed to be interrupted, but she was starving and dove in with relish. It was by far the best Chinese food she'd ever tasted and she regretted not having known of this place for the last couple of years. It was a shame she was just discovering it as she was leaving.

They ate and tried to talk, but every time they seemed to be getting somewhere, Sister Chan would reappear with more food. Finally, Sean said, "We need to go before she brings us all of this month's profits in one meal. He stood up and went back into the kitchen for a few minutes and then paid the bill.

Sister Chan came back out and her eyes filled with tears as she and Sean hugged for a long moment. She said another string of fast sentences that Lexie missed and patted his cheek again. This time he spoke back to her in the same foreign language and Lexie was floored. She hadn't understood that he really spoke an Asian tongue. Sister Chan was speaking again and this time she gestured to Lexie with a teasing smile. Sean looked slightly embarrassed as he answered her, and Lexie had to wonder just what the conversation that she was missing entailed.

At length the little woman came to her and gave her a gentle hug. Pointing to Sean, she said, "He good Elder. Hold on!" Sean laughed and Lexie blushed and Sister Chan gave them both a sweet smile as they walked out. Lexie went back to the car in a daze. Sean spoke Chinese! At least she assumed it was Chinese.

He was quiet on the way back to her office, and she followed suit. She still hadn't found out why he was here, but it was almost one o'clock and she had to get back. She only had today and tomorrow to finish the cases she was working on. She could leave whether they were completed or not, but she wanted to have everything buttoned up if at all possible. She wanted Trent to have no doubts that she'd been an honorable employee.

After arranging to meet her at her condo for dinner, he walked her back up to her office, kissed her goodbye, and then left. She went back to writing her brief, but was hard put to concentrate. It took all the self-control she had to put him out of her mind and focus for the next few hours. As she left that evening, Trent watched her walk out, and though he didn't say anything, she knew he was dying to ask who the guy had been. She was glad he didn't.

She climbed into her new Mountaineer and pulled the pins back out of her hair. She was seriously considering never wearing it up again when she left here. She hummed to herself and thought about going straight home without picking up her dry cleaning for the last time, but decided she had to have it if she was going to be able to leave tomorrow as scheduled as soon as she was off work.

She was so at odds within herself. Half of her was so happy he was here and wanted to see her, and half of her wanted to run away from him and protect her heart from being mangled any further.

At her building, she saw him leaning against his rental car in the garage as she pulled in, but he didn't realize it was her until she got out and spoke to him. As she did, he did a double take and checked out the Mountaineer again. He was carrying a box in one arm, but came to help her carry her briefcase and dry cleaning with the other. "Nice car. Where's the
286

Porsche?"

For some reason she was hesitant to tell him. She wasn't sure if it was because she was admitting defeat at being a professional here in the big city, or if it was because telling him she was pulling up stakes and moving but she still wasn't exactly sure where to, left her open to total rejection from him.

It leaned pretty seriously toward the latter and she hedged a little as she answered, "I sold it."

"Why?" He made it hard to hedge.

"I decided I needed something less sports car and more sports utility. I like it a lot. I can see out better."

He didn't reply as she unlocked her door, but then, when they stepped inside and she saw him looking around at the packed boxes and suitcases by the door she knew what was coming. Walking into her bedroom, she hung the clean clothes bags in the almost empty closet and turned back around to meet his gaze. It was almost a hint cool. He asked, "So what's going on?"

Stalling, she asked, "What do you mean?"

"Why are you packing everything up here in your condo?"

In a matter-of-fact voice, she said, "I sold it too. To Kit and Rossen, furniture and all."

She tried to walk past him to go into the kitchen, but he caught her arm as she walked by. "What's going on, Lex? Why have you sold your house and your car? Where are you moving to?" She looked up at him, but didn't want to talk about it, especially not with him. She could feel the discouragement and tears of a couple of weeks ago settling into her heart again.

How could she admit to him that she was lonely and miserable and felt like she was growing old

287

without any of the things she wanted most in life? Trying to explain the reasons she was leaving sounded suspiciously like, "I'm in love with this big, handsome man in Wyoming who only wants to forget me and I'm packing up my broken heart and my things and running away."

She shrugged out of his grasp and continued on into the kitchen. Trying to make her voice nonchalant, she said, "I just needed a change of pace. Do you want pizza or lasagna? Sorry, I'm afraid those are our only two choices." She began setting out dishes. He didn't answer her and she turned to look at him.

He was watching her as if he thought she was either going to vaporize in front of his very eyes or bolt. She almost wished she had those choices as she reached into the fridge and took out a bag of salad and a tomato. She nearly accidentally stabbed him when he went to take her hand at the same time she tried to reach for a paring knife.

He took the knife and set it down, and practically dragged her back to the living room, gently pushed her onto her couch and then sat down beside her. The tired note in his voice was her undoing. "Is there anyway you could let me in on what's going on here?" Meeting his eyes made her want to cry all the more as he added, "Please?"

She shook her head. "I don't really want to talk about this, Sean. It was just time. That's all. It was just time."

The wheels were turning in his mind, she could see them, but she knew he didn't understand. How could he, when she didn't? "Time for what? Where are you moving to?"

She decided to just be honest. It didn't matter

anyway. After tomorrow, she'd never see him again. What would it matter if he knew the truth? "Just time for a change of scenery and, as of right now, I don't know where I'm moving to. For a few days, I'm going to visit Eric. Maybe I'll end up there. I don't know."

"Why?"

It was a simple question, but there were so many answers. "Lots of reasons, Sean. None of which are important right now. Tell me what you'd like to eat and it can be cooking while we talk. But let's talk about you instead of me. You never did say why you're here?"

He got up and put out a hand to stop her. "Stay there. I'll put the lasagna in. Don't move. I'll be right back." Thirty seconds later he was sitting in front of her again. He met her eyes for a long moment before he said, "I came here to rent an apartment. I'm moving here."

She wondered if she'd heard him right. This time it was her turn to question, "I thought you hated L.A. Why are you moving here?"

Softly he said, "To be by you."

She didn't understand. This had to be another one of his cling to her as if he couldn't live without her and then turn around and pull hard away moments. How was she supposed to take this? Or feel? It was all too much. Her spirit was too tired. Her heart too trashed.

She put her face into her hands and began to cry. She tried to be quiet, but the tears dripped through her fingers and onto her skirt. She felt him come to sit beside her, but instead of turning toward him, she turned away. She was too tired to play head games right now.

He came around to the other side of her and

289

gathered her into his arms. "Please talk to me, Lexie. Why does my coming here make you sad? Help me understand." She sniffed and he handed her a handkerchief. It smelled like him and made her cry all the harder.

Chapter 32

When he told her that he wanted to be by her and it made her start to cry like her world was coming apart, Sean was completely at a loss. He'd never seen her lose her composure more than the time she'd barely teared up. He wasn't really sure how to deal with her heartache except to hold her and even then, she'd initially turned away from him. He held her and stroked her hair as he listened to her cry and wondered what he'd been missing in her life that had her completely uprooting.

She got up and went to the kitchen and pulled a couple of tissues from a box that was partially packed. He started to follow her and she turned on him. "No!" She put her hands out. "Stay over there. It's too hard to think with you beside me."

Going back into the living room to stand next to her fireplace, he said, "You can use the handkerchief. That's what I gave it to you for."

She sniffled into her tissues and looked embarrassed as she wiped at her tears with his handkerchief. "Tears are okay, boogers are disgusting, but thank you." She turned her back on him across the room and he wanted to go to her in the worst way.

Just as he was about to walk over to her again, whether she wanted him close or not, there was a loud thump outside. Then there was the distinct sound of keys and he realized someone was unlocking her door.

He glanced up at her, but she didn't look at him.

Presently the door opened and a man leaned down, picked up a couple of nested boxes, and walked inside. He was as tall as Sean was, but had short, coal black curls like the mythical Adonis and a neatly trimmed mustache and goatee. He was wearing long shorts, Tiva sandals, and a tie-dyed t-shirt that stretched over his arms, shoulders, and chest. He nudged the door shut with his knee and advanced into the room.

Tossing his keys onto the counter, he dropped the boxes and went straight to Lexie, completely unaware of Sean's presence. It was obvious that she'd been crying and he put an arm around her shoulders and pulled her close, then kissed her tenderly on the forehead. He pulled her chin up to look at him and asked, "Hey, you okay?" His voice held infinite concern and it made Sean's gut tighten sickeningly.

Joey had warned him about another guy if he didn't hurry. Lexie turned into the man's arms and let him hold her, just the way she hadn't let Sean, and Sean's heart landed somewhere in the pit of that gut with a thud.

He must have made a sound because Adonis turned and saw him standing against the mantle. Their eyes met over her shoulder and for a second there it was like two boxers across the ring, just before the match started. Sean wanted to cross the room and bust the guy and tell him to stay away from her, but it was obvious she was right where she wanted to be.

The black haired man's striking eyes mellowed and he pulled back from her, looked down and said, "I'm gonna go down to the sports bar around the corner and grab a sandwich and catch a few minutes of the

Dodger's game. I'll be back in awhile." His voice was gentle and he kissed her again, this time on the top of her head before glancing over at Sean as he headed back out the door.

For a few seconds after the door latch clicked there was absolute silence. Finally, Sean said, "Why didn't you just tell me there was another guy instead of bringing me home so we could be a cozy threesome?" He sounded bitter and he knew it. Seeing her in another man's arms was the most awful thing he'd ever experienced.

She blew her nose and turned away from him. "That was Eric."

Understanding dawned slowly, but when it did, it was an unbelievable relief. Just when his world righted itself again, she continued sadly, "There's not another guy Sean, but there's going to be. I'm sorry, but that's the reason I'm leaving. I don't want to live like this anymore."

He started toward her and she turned and put up her hand to stop him again. "No. Hear me out. I can't do this Sean. I love you, but I need more than a long distance, three word a day friendship with a guy who needs me desperately for a few hours when I'm around to kiss and then flip-flops and does his level best to forget I exist.

"I'm going away. I'm going away from work and being used, and this lonely city, and away from your memory. I'm putting it all behind me. It's my turn to forget you now. I'm going to find a guy who likes me whether I'm a professional or not, and who loves me consistently, even when I'm not right there with him. And I'm going to get married, and settle down, and have a handful of babies, one right after another before

I'm too old. I have too many important things in my life that are glaringly missing and my heart is too tired to play games any more."

She shook her head. "The physical attraction is huge with us. It is. But there's more out there. I know there is. Eric found it with Josie, and I saw it with your parents and brothers, and I'm not willing to settle anymore. So, I'm sorry you came all the way here to see me, but you'd better just go back home. I'm leaving tomorrow, and the time's past for romantic dabbling anyway."

He knew she was trying to tell him to go away and leave her alone, but he couldn't help the smile that was steadily growing on his face. In one short spiel, she'd solved all the major troubles of the world as far as he was concerned. She loved him. She'd just said it right out loud without even hesitating. Heck, he wasn't even sure she knew she'd said it, but she had, and she'd meant it.

That would have been enough to keep him flying for the rest of his life, even without the fact that she said she was leaving LA, and wanted to get married and have a family. He'd been wondering if being without him was as hard on her as the reverse was on him. Apparently it was. She was sufficiently miserable to thrash her entire life to make changes. His smile was big enough that he worried he was going to offend her and tried to tone it down.

She made a sound of disgust and went off, "You are such a jerk! Here I am being as honest as I can be with you, and you're laughing at me." Turning toward her bedroom, she said over her shoulder, "Just leave. Go back and have dinner at your hotel. I'd rather eat alone. You can see yourself out." The bedroom door slammed with a crash just a second or two before he yanked it back open.

She turned toward him, eyes blazing. "What are you doing? Get out of my bedroom! While you're at it, just get out of my life!" She continued on toward her bathroom, but he caught that door before she could slam it. She spun on him. "You're not taking a hint very well, Sean! Go away. What do you want?" At first, she'd sounded angry, but it mellowed to sounding tired at the end.

Gently, he said, "I want to know where you're going tomorrow."

"To Flagstaff, Arizona. Why?" He had her practically pinned against her bathroom counter.

"Because I'm going to follow you there. And if you leave there, I'm going to follow you again. I'm going to keep following you. I'm going to haunt you just like those little monster fairies in there have been haunting me! I'm going to be your shadow, because you're wrong if you think I can flip flop and put you out of my mind, or that I forget you when we're apart."

She wouldn't look at him and he reached down and gently pulled her chin up until their eyes met. Softly, he said, "I can't go two minutes through my day without dreaming about you. I love you, Lexie. I love you enough that I came here to live in L.A. and forego having a family to be with you. I thought you loved it here and didn't want a family, and I still had to come and try to get you to marry me." Her eyes flew to his and he asked, "Is there any way that I could marry you, wherever you are, and volunteer to be the dad?"

Her brilliant green eyes widened until she looked almost frightened. Finally, she smiled through the remnants of her tears. "Was there a proposal in there somewhere? What are you asking?"

He gave her a daring smile. "I'm asking if you'll marry me and if we can have several babies together. Cute, little red heads with feisty temperaments and beautiful green eyes. Smart, talented, fun babies just like their mother."

He could tell she wasn't sure how to take him and continued positively, "Come on, Lex. This is a good decision. Think about it. Study the facts and make an intelligent decision. Just know that I adore you and have since that first night in that hot dress, when you killed my trophy elk.

"I did try to forget you. I thought we were all wrong. I tried everything. But there was no way. I love you too much and I can't live without you. I'll go anywhere you choose, we'll have exactly the family you want, and you can work or not. I'll leave it up to you."

She didn't say anything right away and he went on, "I'm a nice guy, Lex. I'll be a good husband and father. I promise. Scout's honor. Cross my heart and hope to die." He gave her his biggest smile. Finally, that toned down and he pulled her into a hug, put his cheek against her hair and whispered, "Being away from you is awful. Please say yes."

Her voice was low when she asked without raising her head, "Tomorrow are you going to have second thoughts and want to try to forget me again?"

"Lexie, look at me. I wouldn't be here if I hadn't already decided that I was going to be with you forever if you'll let me. Those babies were a problem, I'll admit it. I want a family. I really want a family. And I thought you didn't and I know that families are part of God's plan for us, but I needed you enough that I had to take the chance that someday you'd change your mind. Even if you didn't want one and were staying here, I'm never going to want to forget you. That was the dumbest idea in the world. There's no way! Who in the world could forget you? Once enchanted, always enchanted."

He wound down and just waited, watching her. He could tell that she wanted to believe him. There was hope in her eyes, but there was doubt too and he said gently, "I honestly do love you, Lexie. And I do want to marry you and be with you forever. If you can't answer me right now, can you at least think about it? I'll wait forever for you if I need to." His blue eyes held her green ones.

Sighing, she said, "I'd love to marry you, Sean. I'd love to have you be the dad, but I don't know that that's a very good idea. And I'm so mixed up that I don't even recognize myself. What do I do now?" It was an earnest question. He took her hand, led her out of the bathroom, back into the living room, and sat in a recliner that rocked and then pulled her onto his lap.

With her securely nestled in his arms, he said, "I don't have all the answers, honey. But if you're asking me, I think you should marry me and we'll live happily ever after." He breathed in the scent of her hair and wound a long, red curl around his finger.

Lying against his chest, she asked, "If you didn't know I was moving, what made you come here today?"

"That darn baby fairy made me nuts. I had to know what it meant. And then yesterday Joey laid into me. She called me a big, stupid, unrighteous dominion jerk for not asking you to marry me and letting you have the option of turning me down. Somehow, I'd never thought of it that way. I thought you were doing what you wanted and that you didn't want marriage and a family. I'm sorry. I didn't mean to be a big, stupid, unrighteous dominion jerk. Will you forgive me?"

She smiled sadly. "You're not really a jerk. But sometimes you're so, so hard to understand. What did you mean, that darn baby fairy?"

He kissed her forehead where it lay against his chin. "That second to last little fairy has a baby with her. Talk about haunting. They were on the cabin porch. I didn't know anyone else in my family had ever even been to the cabin. The fairies have to hang out with you for awhile. I can't even sleep. They're making me crazy."

She twisted to look up at him. "What in the world are you talking about?"

Her buzzer went off and he gently pushed her off his lap to stand up and walk into the kitchen. As he rummaged for hot pads, he nodded at the box he'd brought in. "The fairies. I brought them to you to watch over for awhile. They do make me think of you, but I have to have some peace." He pulled the lasagna out and set it in the middle of the table, and came over to stand beside her as she pulled the fairies out and lined them all up on the edge of the counter. There were sixteen of them now, including the fairy baby.

She was looking at them closely as if they fascinated her, and then looked at him and said almost reverently, "Trooping fairies! These are incredible! Where in the world did you get them?" He did a major double take to study her intently.

"What do you mean, where did I get them? Didn't you send them to me?" She looked up at him, genuinely surprised. She acted as if she had no inkling

298

about them.

"I didn't send them. I've never seen anything like them. I wish I had. They're phenomenal!" She had the baby one cradled in the palm of her hand.

He put an arm around her waist. "You had to have sent them. Who else would send me fairies? I've never talked about a fairy with any one else in my life. You wouldn't tease a guy would you?" Looking into her eyes, he could tell she was being honest. "Holy smokes! Who in my family did you tell that we had a fairy thing going back and forth?"

Her green eyes looked up at him blankly. "I haven't told anyone but you about the Irish legends. It must have been you who told them." Her proximity was blowing his mind.

The fairies weren't nearly as fascinating as her mouth and he asked, "If I kiss you, are you going to think that all I want from you is kissing and that I don't honestly love you?"

"Possibly." Her face was serious, but she added, "But I think you should chance it."

They were still kissing when they heard Eric come back in the door. He commented dryly, "You're not crying anymore anyway. That's a good thing." He walked over and offered Sean his hand. "I'm Eric, by the way. And I'm assuming you're Travis. Right?" He glanced at Lexie and then laughed. "Just kidding. It is Sean isn't it?"

Sean met his handshake. "Sean Rockland. And you're Eric. She told me you weren't red, but you're really not red. Are you two honestly twins?"

"We have the same green eyes, and curls, but other than that, we're polar opposites." He wrapped an arm around her shoulders. "That's probably why we like each other so much." He looked down into her eyes. "I'm assuming that you've worked through whatever had you so upset awhile ago."

Sean and Lexie looked at each other, but neither one answered. Eric looked from one to the other. "So do I need to go back and watch the rest of the game? The Dodgers were up three runs just FYI."

Shaking his head, Sean said, "No, you don't need to leave. She's not crying, but she needs your advice right now. I'll go back to my hotel so you two can talk. But you should know, I asked your sister to marry me. I love her and I'll go wherever she wants to move, if she'll have me. Or if she wants to stay here, I'll come here, or she can come back to Wyoming and work there if she wants. The county is looking for another attorney. I'll follow her wherever she feels like she needs to be. She just doesn't trust that I'm serious."

He looked steadily at Eric. "I've never been more serious in my life. I swear it. I'll go so you can talk, and she can think this through. I know she values your wisdom and judgment. Maybe you can help. It was good to finally meet you." Sean turned back to Lexie and kissed her gently. "Pray about it. I love you."

With that, he walked out the door, praying harder than he ever had in his life.

Chapter 33

When Sean left so abruptly, Lexie was surprised. And worried. She looked up at Eric and all but wailed, "Now what do I do?"

With a laugh, Eric teased her, "You sound like this is a terrible turn of events, but he didn't look all that bad to me. You're in love with the guy. What's so devastating about a marriage proposal from him?"

She went into the kitchen to cut the tomato and set the salad out. As they sat beside each other at the table, she sighed and asked, "How did you know that you should marry Josie?"

"That was simple. It ripped my heart out to leave her at her apartment and go home to mine at night."

"I feel that way too, but he'll probably go back to his hotel and decide this was all a mistake and that he should try to forget me again." They bowed their heads and he prayed, hardly even interrupting their conversation.

"Has he ever told you why he's hesitated this long when he obviously loves you?"

"I'm sure at first he hated the fact that I wasn't a member. And honestly, he was right to. Tonight he told me that he loved me enough to marry me even if he had to live here in L.A. and even if I didn't want a family. He hates it here. He served his mission here and was miserable. He's definitely a wide, open spaces kind of a guy. I have no idea why he assumed I didn't want a family, but I think they were the kickers. L.A. and foregoing children."

Eric chewed thoughtfully and then said, "Being willing to agree to not have a family sounds like he's definitely serious. That's a big deal to most people. I can't imagine making that hard of a sacrifice, no matter how pretty and intelligent, or fun and talented a woman. You did tell him you want kids, didn't you?"

She blushed. "Several actually. He volunteered to be the dad."

"No way!" Eric busted up. "He really did? He said that?"

Feeling slightly embarrassed, she added, "That was just after I called him a jerk and told him to see himself out and go back to his hotel and eat alone. He's remarkably patient with me."

Eric just shook his head. "You can say that again! You make him sound like wonder boy. I think he was being honest when he said he loves you. You say he's kind and honorable, and hard working and wealthy. That he's handsome and funny and gutty enough to say something like that. I don't know. Maybe you'd better just walk away from this one. At first glance, he just can't cut it."

He was smiling widely at her, and then became serious. "How do you feel, Lex? You're a smart lady. What does your theory of think it through and then make your best decision tell you? Could you wake up beside him everyday for the next seventy million years?"

She stabbed a bite of lasagna and then twirled her fork to catch the trailing cheese. "Wondering if I like him enough has never been the issue. I'd have stayed in Wyoming the first time if I'd thought he wanted me to. And actually, I think he did want me to, but he never even asked for my phone number. It was like there was this unspoken rule that we couldn't keep in touch. Even after all these months, we've touched base every day or two, but somehow we aren't allowed to talk about the future or us. Today's the first time he's ever been like this. I mean speaking wise. If we're together, I always know he loves me and wants me physically. I can see that in his eyes when I'm with him."

"And so . . . "

"And so you're right, I think I'd better just walk away."

He choked on his salad. "You lost me. You love him, he loves you, he has all the right qualities, so you're going to walk? I don't follow you." He'd been playing with his food and now he pushed his plate back completely.

She pushed hers back too. "Eric, you don't understand. When we're apart he does everything he can to forget me. He's told me that himself. By this time tomorrow he'll probably be back home in Wyoming trying to work me out of his system. With me, it's out of sight, out of mind for him. I can't agree to marry someone who wants to forget me most of the time. This isn't about how much I love him, or even how much he loves me. You and I both know that having a decent marriage takes effort. I'm sure even the best marriages have their moments, and we both know what a bad marriage can be like. For me to do this I'd have to know he wanted to be married to me one hundred percent of the time, not just in his weaker moments."

Once Enchanted

He was quietly watching her, and finally said, "Okay . . . So, you can't agree to marry him. Your decision is made then. Do you feel good about that?"

She shook her head and sighed. "No, I hate it. But it's what I should do." She pulled her plate back and started to eat again, as tears welled in her eyes. "Maybe the move and some new faces and less negative at work will help me learn to forget him. I have to get on with my life."

Chapter 34

Sean knew the minute he heard his phone ring at ten thirty that night, California time, that it was her. He was honestly a little afraid to even answer it, and when he heard her voice, he knew that what she was going to say wasn't going to be what he wanted to hear. She sounded tired to the bone and thoroughly discouraged. In a way that was actually good, because he knew she wasn't happy about calling him and turning down his marriage proposal. At least she wasn't glad she was ripping his heart out. When she finished telling him that she didn't think it would be wise to marry him, he had only a one word question for her.

"Why?" He wanted to at least know that. "On second thought, don't answer that right now. You can tell me when I pick you up for lunch tomorrow. I deserve to be told to my face, don't I?"

She agreed that he did and they arranged to have lunch. Then both of them went to bed in their respective rooms and spent long hours studying the shadows on their ceilings and wondering how it had come to this. They didn't know it, but they were both praying at the same time for the same wisdom and peace.

When he was finally able to fall asleep, he had the most pervasive dreams ever. The entire night was filled with trooping fairies, dancing around their fires, laughing and teasing and singing. All of them had babies with them now, and they were no longer just auburn headed. There were black haired ones and blonde ones and brown ones, and by the time he awoke, he was more tired than when he'd gone to sleep.

Stepping into her office door unannounced this time, the fact that she'd had a rough night too was apparent. She was still drop dead gorgeous, but there wasn't a hint of the usual sparkle in her pretty eyes. When he came and pulled her chair back again and pulled her into his arms, it was a bit awkward for both of them. He looked down into her eyes and studied them for what felt like a long time before lowering his head to kiss her gently, but with all of the emotions he felt. There was desire and hesitation and sadness and determination, and a deep and abiding friendship that last night hadn't put a dent in.

This time it was Trent who busted them kissing. For a minute, they didn't know he'd opened the door, and even when they heard him clear his throat, it took a moment to acknowledge him. When they looked up and pulled apart, Sean didn't waste a whole lot of time in taking her hand and pulling her toward the door as Trent attempted to get her to work through lunch this time. She assured him her workload would be complete by day's end as they breezed past him with her trying to replace the pins in her hair.

In the elevator she started to laugh. Sean hardly let the doors close before he began kissing her again, and then didn't really want to quit, although it stopped at another floor. She smiled when the people waiting to get on looked in and then changed their minds and said they'd wait for the next one, and he turned to her again before the doors had shut. By the time they reached the parking garage she was breathless and seemed somewhat lost again about what in the world their relationship was. He could see it in her eyes.

Helping her into the passenger side of his car, he went around and got in the driver's seat and when he went to kiss her again she stopped him with a raised hand. "Sean, wait. You do know that I said I wouldn't marry you last night, right? We don't have a misunderstanding here, do we?" He smiled as he watched her watching him.

"No, I didn't misunderstand. But I don't want you to misunderstand me either. I love you Lexie, and I'm not going to give up. You love me too, I know you do. I can see it in your eyes and you still like me to kiss you. Just try to deny it! I don't blame you for not trusting me. I haven't had that great of a track record deserving it with you. I'd hesitate too, if I were in your shoes. So I'm going to earn your trust or die trying. You're going to have to tell me to get lost a thousand times before I'll quit trying to talk you into marrying me. Speaking of marriage, why exactly did you turn me down?" He still leaned into her to kiss her.

When she could finally answer him, she looked somewhat guilty and began, "I, um, I, we, Eric and I, talked about it last night and we, actually I, felt it would be foolish to agree to marry someone who loved me passionately one minute and tried his best to forget me the next. I think that when we're together the physical attraction takes on a life of its own, which is very nice, but I need to marry someone who remembers he adores me even when I'm not around. As attractive as you are, you have to admit that you have a bit of an issue with that."

Starting up the car, he looked over at her. "I know you think that, but it's only because you couldn't see how miserable I've been without you. I never told you how I felt, but that doesn't mean I wasn't thinking about you. Lonely beyond belief. I *did* try to forget you for the longest time; I thought we were totally incompatible. We're not exactly Mr. and Mrs. Everything In Common. It just took me a long time to figure out that it's far more important that I be with you than that we're just alike.

"I would have been here sooner except that I struggled with going to God and telling Him that, even though his plan included families, I needed to forego that because I loved you. I felt like I was directly going against him. I prayed for peace a thousand times instead of asking what I should do. Finally, I asked if it would be okay if I took a chance that I could talk you into wanting a family and I finally got the answer.

"I'm sorry. I do love you Lexie, but God still outranks you. I couldn't just ignore his plan. But that didn't help my heart. I've missed you more than I can say." He kissed her again gently. "I'll show you. Even if it takes me years to make you believe me, you'll understand someday. I honestly do love you. Now, what do you want to eat?"

That night he helped her and Eric load the last of her stuff into their SUVs and, after telling her he was going to fly home and pick up his truck and then drive down to Flagstaff to find an apartment there, he kissed her goodbye again and watched her head out of L.A. for good. This time she looked back.

Chapter 35

He hadn't been back home for ten minutes when he heard his garage door go up and his mom came walking into his bedroom where he was packing up his clothes. She hugged him tightly as her eyes filled with tears. He didn't know what to say to her, just tried to tell her that he had to do this. She didn't say much either, simply started helping him load the cases with tears streaming down her face. When he was finally ready to go, he never dreamed it would be that hard to say goodbye.

In Flagstaff, he checked into a hotel as near as possible to Eric's house and then spent the next day and a half persuading Lexie to help him look for an apartment. He didn't even try to be subtle, just told her he wanted her to like it because he was hoping that she'd marry him and come live with him in it as soon as he could talk her into it. She watched his eyes a lot, but she didn't give him any encouragement. And when he asked her what she wanted, she didn't weigh in with any ideas that were important to her.

They'd been to six apartment complexes before she gave an opinion at all. She just wrinkled her nose and shook her head when the manager wasn't looking. He started to pick at her, and when she gave any sort of hint, he picked up on it and went from there. After five more buildings, she said, "Sean, are you sure you want to do this? These places seem dumpy after your beautiful home. Won't you be miserable in a cramped little apartment?"

From across the truck he smiled at her sadly. "Not nearly as miserable as I've been in my big house without you. Should I rent a house instead? Would you like that better? It'll only be until I can find some ground and build us a house here, but that takes awhile. What do you think?"

"What about your house in Wyoming? You wouldn't sell it!" Her face was horrified.

"I'll sell it to Joey, or Treyne, or Coop when they get married. Would you rather live in a house here than an apartment?"

Without realizing it, she began to give him ideas. "No, let's look a little more. There has to be an apartment here somewhere that feels like home. Let's only rent a house as a last resort." His heart leapt, but he didn't so much as twitch.

At the next complex, she looked around the tiny kitchen in dismay. "I'm afraid your kitchen has spoiled me forever. There certainly won't be much dancing in here!"

He came up and pulled her into a hug. "Oh, I don't know. We'd just have to dance extremely close!" He went to kiss her. The manager made a disgusted sound and Lexie slipped out of his embrace and wandered into the bedroom. Her expression there wasn't any happier and she turned back to him with a shake of her head.

They hadn't quite made it to his truck when he got a phone call from the superintendent of one of his projects back home. He was calling to tell Sean that the stucco crew had accidentally started a house that was all but complete, on fire that morning. Sean was sick about it. Now was not a good time for a crisis away from Flagstaff. "How badly was it burned?"

"The whole south wing is torched. The insurance people will be in to inspect it tomorrow. I told them you'd be here to meet with them around nine."

Sean glanced at Lexie and shook his head. "I can't come back right now Rick. You'll have to handle this one."

"Rockland, that's a seven hundred thousand dollar house! What do you mean you can't come back?"

"I know it's a seven hundred thousand dollar house, Rick. But I can't come back right now. Handle it as best you can and I'll be available by phone, but that's as good as it gets at the moment. You're okay. You can handle this. Stay in touch."

After he got off the phone, Sean helped her up into his truck without commenting on the phone call, but she was watching him with big eyes. They moved on to the next complex.

After another two full days of pounding the pavement to exhaustion they found a place that, although it wasn't ideal, he felt he could live with long enough to get a house built. They went back into the office and he started to fill out the application. He could feel Lexie pacing behind him. As he wrote he was praying hard, knowing she was struggling with something, and hoping with all of his heart that whatever it was, it would come down on his side. Finally, she tapped him on the shoulder and whispered, "Sean, could I talk to you for a moment? In private."

He searched her eyes as he nodded toward the door. To the manager he said, "Excuse us for a moment, would you?" Once outside, he turned to look at her again. What was he seeing in her eyes? "What? What's up?"

She was looking at him as if she was trying to see into his soul. "Sean, why are you renting this apartment?"

His hands almost involuntarily found their way into her hair. "So that I have a place to live here in Flagstaff, Lex. Isn't that obvious?"

"No. I mean why are you doing this? Why are you leaving your home and family and business to move here into a dinky little apartment in a town where you know no one? Why are you here?"

He took her by the shoulders. "Lexie, you know the answer to that. I want to be near you. I can't live away from you anymore. I can't do it. If it means that I need to leave everything and move into an apartment here, then that's what I'll do. I still want to marry you, Lexie. I'm still hoping to convince you to marry me and be with me forever. I'm not going to give up on that. Not until the day you either marry someone else or get a restraining order against me. Isn't this apartment one that if you someday finally agree to marry me, you could live with? It's bigger than the others and in a nice neighborhood and has a pretty view." He looked out over the city in front of them and then back at her.

Her head never turned toward the view. She was looking only at him. "Sean, how long have we known each other?"

"Four months and twenty six days."

"And how many days of that time have we actually been together?"

He had to stop and count for a minute. "Twelve.

Thirteen if you stretch it." He smiled his biggest smile.

"How can you know for sure that you want to marry me, when we've only had that much time together?"

"I've asked myself that same question about a thousand times. I couldn't understand why I couldn't get over you when you'd only been there such a short time. Finally it occurred to me that maybe you hit that elk for a reason. Maybe there was something bigger than both of us at work there. Can there be that many coincidences without us admitting that maybe they aren't coincidences at all?"

He gave her a sad smile and said positively, "When it's all questioned and analyzed and over and done, do you know why I know for sure that marrying you is the right thing to do? I asked, Lex. I needed some answers to the troubles I was having in my life and I asked. More fervently than I've ever asked for anything before. This was killing me. I asked and I got my answer and knowing that God thinks this is a good idea is all the reassurance I need. He doesn't make mistakes, Lexie. It's us imperfect mere mortals who screw everything up.

"I'm not naive enough to think that we won't have our struggles. Everyone does. The greatest marriage in the whole world still has some hard times and I know that. I'm okay with that. We'll handle whatever we have to. I'm willing to do whatever it takes to make this work with you. But I don't doubt for a minute that we can have a great marriage. You're an amazing lady and I know you have the important things down."

He squeezed her shoulder and said encouragingly, "Lexie, don't you realize that even if you weren't beautiful and smart and strong and fun and all of those good things you are, that I'd still love you and want to be with you? Don't you understand that this is something that has nothing to do with logic and deduction? You've fascinated me from the first night I met you. It's more than thinking it out and making a wise decision. It's more than pheromones and physical attraction. It's more than anything I've ever experienced in my life. It's like the need for air. Without you in my life, there is no life. There's no joy, no energy. No passion. I don't understand it either, but I asked. I asked and I know now that it's all going to be okay. Haven't you asked?"

Twisting her hands, she looked down at them. "Yeah, I have. Several, several times."

"And?" He held his breath.

She let out a sigh. "And I'm supposed to marry you." Reaching up, he turned her face up so he could see what she was thinking as he waited patiently for her to go on. She said, "I don't get answers as easily as you do." He almost rolled his eyes. "I didn't know the other night. Then, I truly did feel that agreeing to marry you would have been foolish. I still wasn't sure that you weren't going to change your mind again. That would have killed me. I'm such an emotional mess right now." He pulled her close in a hug. "You need to know that my parents' marriage was terrible."

"I'd already gathered that. We'll figure it out."

"What if this is just infatuation and that we're not really in love?"

He pulled back to look her in the face. "Do you honestly question that?" Shaking his head, he looked from her eyes to her mouth and brushed his thumb tenderly across her lip and then looked back into her eyes.

She shook her head and asked quietly, "What if

you fall out of love with me?"

That made him laugh softly. "You don't honestly question that either do you?"

"Well, no, but what if the way I squeeze the toothpaste drives you crazy?"

The manager of the apartment complex came out and said, "I don't mean to rush you, but I have to leave in fifteen minutes. Is there any way you could finish your talk later?"

Sean took Lexie's hand and headed for the parking lot, saying over his shoulder, "Uh, we'll come back in the morning. We have to finish this talk now."

As they hustled along, she pulled him to a stop. "I can't cook all that well. You do realize that, don't you?"

He chuckled and started to walk again and she asked, "What if one of us is a compulsive liar or something?"

He stopped and turned to her. "I'm not. Are you?"

"No, but…" They were almost to his truck. "I have to be honest. I have like eighteen pairs of shoes."

They reached the truck, but instead of getting in, he backed her up to it and put both hands on either side of her head and leaned in to kiss her and said, "If you're pulling out your worst skeletons then I'm in trouble 'cause I have way worse stuff than this to admit."

"What if one of us snores?"

He hesitated while he tried to talk himself out of saying it and then gave up and teased her, "Then we'll spend a lot of time awake in our bed."

She raised her eyebrows. "Sean! I can't believe you just said that!"

"Yes you can."

"What if I turn out to be a really bad wife?"

He began to kiss her neck. "No problem. I'll just

315

throw you in the nearest body of water again."

"I was afraid of that. I have to tell you. Every once in awhile, I swear at stupid drivers."

Now he was nuzzling her ear. "Every once in awhile I do the same thing at stupid cows."

"Sean, what if I got cancer and all my hair fell out?"

This one got his attention and he looked up. "Lexie, I hope that doesn't happen. Cancer would be horrible, but that's the kind of thing I was talking about when I said we'd do whatever it takes. I'm marrying you for forever, so while I hope I have you in this life for a good long time, in the eternities, cancer and no hair won't matter."

She still seemed unsure and he put both hands on her face and kissed her and then said, "Look, honey, there are a couple of things that truly would be a problem. But only a couple. If you were a serial killer or child molester or something. Or if you had no intention of being faithful or were an addict of some kind and weren't fessing up. Oh, or if you were a lesbian. That would be kind of awkward."

She elbowed him. "Sean!"

"Are we all clear on those few?" He leaned back to look at her.

"Yes."

"Excellent. Any interesting questions for me?"

"You're not going to be throwing me in bodies of water all that often are you?"

"Only when you shatter things in anger."

"Oh, good. I think we're relatively safe then."

"Can I come back in the morning and rent the apartment then? Are you okay with this place?"

"Actually." She looked down and couldn't meet his

Jaclyn M. Hawkes

eyes again, and he tipped her chin up with one finger and she continued, "Is there any way we could just go home to Wyoming to your house?"

His eyes searched hers. In an infinitely gentle voice he asked, "Does that mean you'll marry me?"

Her expression was absolutely earnest. "Are you sure you're not going to want to forget me in the next seventy million years?"

"Not a chance."

"Then yes, I'd love to marry you." He picked her up and spun her around in the parking lot, and then set her back down and kissed her.

When he finally loaded her in and got in to pull out, as he released the parking brake, he asked, "Are you sure you want to live in Wyoming? I'd live wherever you want to. We can go to Wichita if you want."

She was thoughtful for a minute. "No, home feels like your house. Your valley. Your family. Let's go back to Wyoming and see if we have any better luck finding me an apartment there than we've had here."

"Actually almost every one of us has an apartment of some kind in our house. Like a mother-in-law apartment or caretaker's quarters or something." This time he was thoughtful. Finally, he asked, "Lex? How big of a wedding do you want?"

"Eric and a few others from my side. Why?"

"Not your parents?"

"No." She shook her head vehemently. "That's all I'd need. My parents fighting at our wedding in front of your whole family! I don't think so. I'll tell them after the fact or something. Why do you ask?"

"Well, we can't be married in the temple until

you've been a member for a year, which is more than ten months away. And I don't care if we have a big wedding. Let's just get married here and we'll go on a honeymoon and then go home and surprise my family. We'll send out announcements, and then have a reception of some kind later, maybe when we're sealed in the temple. What would you think about that?"

"Won't your family be offended? What about your mother?"

"My brothers will all be eternally grateful I didn't make them dress up and wear tight shoes for the whole night, and they all know you. They'll understand why I want to make it official sooner rather than later. And my mom already knows I'm the rebel of the family. She's probably expecting it and anyway she'll be so happy to have us back home that she won't care what we did! I mean, she would have loved a temple wedding, but she's not a proponent of long engagements. I'm sure she wouldn't want us to wait to go through the temple. She says that once you know it's right, don't drag it out and give the adversary time to turn God-given attraction into too much temptation." He grinned and shrugged.

Lexie was thoughtful for a moment and then asked, "You really think we don't need to hold off for a little longer and spend more time with each other before we really do this?"

"Wouldn't that be tantamount to saying, yes, God answered my prayers, but I'm not going to trust him? If we know we're getting a yes, can't we spend the time with each other married instead of dating?"

She nodded. "You're right. And I'm sure."

"Perfect." He kissed her again and then went on. "I'll make a lightning flight home to see about a problem on a house, while you buy you a really gorgeous dress and lots of flowers. I'll wear a tux and we'll take some pictures and focus on kissing the bride instead of shaking a bunch of people's hands all night. What do you think?"

"I think it sounds far better than a stuffy party where I won't know anyone. Let's do it!"

Once Enchanted

Chapter 36

They did do it, and Eric laughed when Lexie had a hard time trying to get up into Sean's truck in her dress and heels afterward. Sean just smiled and picked her up and set her in. Eric and Josie offered to drive Lexie's Mountaineer up to Wyoming in a week or so and meet Sean's family.

Sean and Lexie didn't tell anyone but Rossen that they'd made plans to sneak into the little cabin for a few days before showing up at Sean's house. Rossen met them with horses and a brilliant smile and hug for his new sister-in-law. As he shook Sean's hand, he said, "I told you it'd all work out."

At the little cabin, Sean loaded the packs in, then took the horses to the corral, and unsaddled them. When he got back to the cabin, he'd lost Lexie already and called, "Lex, where are you now?"

"You always ask me that. I'm right here, by the pond. I'm just getting ready to climb into it, but look what I found. This one has twins, just like Eric and me. Black and red. Look at that!"

She was carrying three new little fairy figurines. He studied her expression. "You're sure you don't know who's sending these?" He truly didn't think she did.

"I have no idea. Honest." She looked around her, then came to him, and put her arms around his waist as she smiled at him and happily said, "Somehow, you're just enchanted."

Epilogue

Seven months later, they were headed into town to their third prenatal visit. Naomi had been thrilled when they'd announced they were expecting. There were now three new grandbabies on the way and she couldn't have been any happier.

When they got to the appointment, the doctor checked Lexie's vitals and listened for a heartbeat and then unexpectedly sent them into another room for an ultrasound. Sean was thrilled to get to see the baby as well as just hear its heartbeat.

As the doctor stood by watching, the tech proceeded to slide her transmitter over Lexie's tummy until she found the tiny, beating heart that she'd been looking for. It looked like a heart; at least it had a rhythmic beat. Sean asked the doctor, "What's that?"

"That's the baby's heart."

"Then what's that?" Sean pointed to a different part of the screen.

"That's the other one's heart."

The End

About the author

Jaclyn M. Hawkes grew up with 6 sisters, 4 brothers and any number of pets. (It was never boring!) She got a bachelor's degree, had a career as a cartographer for the federal government, and traveled extensively before settling down to her life's work of being the mother of four magnificent and sometimes challenging children. She loves shellfish and pizza, the out of doors, teenagers and hearing her children laugh. She and her husband, their last two children, and their happy dog live in a mountain valley in northern Utah, where it smells like heaven and kids still move sprinkler pipe.

To learn more about Jaclyn, visit **www.jaclynmhawkes.com**.

Author's Note

I loved writing Sean and Lexie's story. Because, who doesn't love a truly good guy who still has just a touch of the dickens in him? Sean is one of my favorite heroes. He was such a tease, and yet vital and powerful, and a gentleman at the same time. Not to mention such a romantic! I love dancing in the kitchen!

In addition, I could totally relate to Lexie and her struggle to find her place in a world that doesn't celebrate gentle women who truly want to be a mom more than they want a high powered career.

When I was a recently married, recently graduated from college young women, it was tough to balance the pulls of money and power, versus my soul deep desire to have a family. When I chose to have a child, one woman at work asked, in a very negative way, why I would choose to waste my intellect when I could be making a contribution to society. Duh. (Please don't tell my children I used that word.)

Another accused me of breaking "the sisterhood" and never spoke to me again after she found out I was expecting a baby.

Occasionally, when they cross my mind, I pity them. If they could only see what an incredible individual that sweet little baby has turned out to be, or how all four of my children have turned out, in spite of my short comings, they'd realize what fools they were.

In a way, I hope they never do. That would have to be a heartbreaking regret to realize what they've missed out on.

In the meantime, I'm thoroughly enjoying my husband and children, and now have even re-entered the career world. Being a romance novelist beats the heck out of being a cartographer, by the way! That's another no-brainer, huh?

The only thing that tops coming up with a dancing in the forest night wind scene, is dancing in the forest night wind with my own personal romantic hero.

My husband has been my best time for years and years now and he's still as much fun as ever! He truly does make me laugh. And hugs me when I cry. I can honestly say I have never regretted marrying him and having my family over choosing to stay in my career. Although motherhood has been more challenging, my marriage and children have been far more fulfilling.

I hope you liked this story. Joey's next! Who does she end up with? Bryan? Or Seth? Or a maybe a completely new guy we haven't met yet? Oh mercy! You'll find out next in the Rockland Ranch Series in a story called, And A Dog Named Blue.

Life is short, choose happy, Jaclyn